THE HYPERION LEGACY

By Ben Osborne

CHAPTER 1

Danny Rawlings crouched cat-like, poised. His blue, alert eyes stared out at a stretch of green beyond steel grilles caging him.

'Two to go,' the starter barked.

Danny's left hand reached down, fingers briefly pressing the lip of his finely polished riding boot before swiftly recapturing the reins. His grip tightened as if the tack sustained life and he puffed his flushed cheeks. Weeks of anticipation and meticulous planning had been for this career-defining moment, now just seconds away. Every muscle taut, yet primed for action, like a predator hovering.

'One to go,' came the starter, crystal clear at this loneliest point, away from the imposing grandstand, a shimmering strip of grey and blue off in the distance.

Like those dreaded moments before an exam, Danny's mind felt numb, blanked of all he knew – the race tactics and riding orders of trainer Michael Raynham, even his own name if it hadn't been sewn into his black and yellow quartered silks.

He fixed his gaze ahead, praying instinct would take over. A rush of adrenalin spiked his veins as the starter ordered with the authority of a sergeant major, 'Jockeys ready!'

And then, the grille disappeared. The loud mechanical clunk drowned by seventeen jockeys' growls and snorts as they jostled for a decent early pitch.

Danny knew his mount Wintersun was a powerful and progressive four-year-old colt, bred to be smart and he'd lived up to the pedigree on track under his previous guidance. The handsome chestnut was in peak condition and, as if able to feed off Danny's thoughts and wishes, found plenty and was soon tracking the prominent racers in fifth, two horse widths off the rail.

The cheers and hollers of the sixty-thousand thronging the grandstand were still well beyond earshot. Above the warm rush of air, Danny merely heard the rumble of hooves and rustling canopies of established oaks and cedars towering to his left. It would be a peaceful, almost serene setting if it hadn't been the most important race of Danny's burgeoning career – the King George VI and Queen Elizabeth Diamond Stakes.

On the morning gallops, Danny could clock a furlong to a fraction of a second and that instinctive gift of pacing a workout told him to sit off this frenetic mid-race tempo. Content to hold a handy midfield berth, he shadowed champion jockey Ryan Cross aboard the favourite Mary Rose. And then, without even a cursory glance, Cross edged out from the rails, forcing Wintersun further wide as they approached the first turn. Danny reined Wintersun back, narrowly evading collision. But Cross continued to angle wider and wider, making room away from the rails as they fanned out turning into the back straight at Swinley Bottom.

'Watch it!' Danny growled, holding his pitch. No way was he going to corner wide and forfeit valuable ground.

A loud click sent a wave of foreboding crashing over him. Had Wintersun gone wrong or merely lost his stride? Instinct told him something terrible had happened.

Momentum shunted his slight frame forward and his gloved hands let slip the reins. He reached out, yet merely grabbed thin air. He'd lost his main method of steering and, having felt the horse fall away from beneath him, his stomach turned over, an unworldly sensation.

Having walked the track that morning, Danny knew only too well the underfoot ground conditions, and he grimaced as the turf came rushing towards him. Among the final flashes of clarity Danny recalled a frantic struggle to free his left foot from the twisted stirrup. Survival impulses took over as he desperately scrambled for his life. His spine hit the ground with a crack, whipping his head back with a sickly thud. The horse crumpled to his side. Every jockey's worst nightmare, being dragged along the ground by a fired-up racehorse - a herd animal bred to race no

3

matter what – was averted. His last image was Wintersun's legs threshing the air as he slid along the ground to a stop.

Danny strained to reach out for the stricken horse but couldn't move. And soon, his leaden eyelids slowly drooped, body and mind shutting down from the pain. The final curtain, he feared. And then nothing.

'Aint got all day.'

Danny broke from his reverie, surprised by the existence of an outside world. He shifted his weight impatiently on a thick carpet of lush grass that was the historic Berkshire Downland, blood struggling to service his tired, numb limbs. The rich, ancient soil on which he stood - left untouched by farming for countless centuries - provided ideal underfoot conditions to work thoroughbreds.

Despite wearing a thick blue fleece, waterproof bottoms and Doc Martens, his arms and legs felt like gooseflesh and all sensation had long since left his feet.

'Well?'

Danny didn't turn; he knew who owned the voice and he wasn't worth turning for.

'Get your head out the fucking clouds and start doin' what I pay ya to do.'

'First off, which one of us has been freezing his arse off here, Gash?' Danny said.

'Yeah, right,' Gash said, shrugging dismissively.

'Just remember,' Danny said, turning to eye Gash. 'I'm the one running this show.'

'Couldn't give a flying fuck what you think,' Gash said.

Danny sighed and said, 'One of the Jenkins' Lot caught the eye earlier.'

'Name?' Gash asked. He removed a notepad and pen from his green padded jacket wrapped tightly against a barrel stomach.

'A three-year-old chestnut colt, Gold Marquee. Been watching it for a while, caught my eye in a Chepstow maiden not long ago, came fourth.'

'Confident?'

4

Danny never lacked confidence when it came to horses; he often wished it was mirrored in other areas of his life. Back in his days in the saddle, before the accident, he remembered vividly those pep talks his father used to give him after a bad ride. He used to say it all boiled down to confidence. If you felt it, so would the horse and things would go right, no matter what. Confidence is everything, he'd say.

'It's come on a ton, if the way he passed his elder stable-mates just now is something to go by.' He paused, hawk-like eyes tracking three horses working the gallop path made of Polytrack used when frost riddled the ground. Steam curled from their flared nostrils and silky coats as they rushed by, showering some of the surface over him. His Dad always scoffed at this new stuff – sand, wood chippings, rubber tubing all mangled up. Danny recalled him often saying, what's wrong with good old-fashioned grass, always meddling they are.

But Danny could see they were low grade inmates of little interest. His attentions returned to the paunchy man stood beside him. 'Time I clocked, reckon it was a serious piece of work, so gotta be on track soon.'

'We talking days?'

Danny dropped the binoculars to nestle next to a stopwatch on his chest. From his coat pocket, he withdrew a WAP mobile. He went straight to the online form database, and typed Gold Marquee. 'It's entered in a sprint maiden at Newbury tomorrow.'

'Is that a *yes*?'

'Dunno, I'll give Jenkins a bell, see if he plans to run. I'll give that Chepstow outing the once over again and, if he's among the final decs for the race, I'll let you know tomorrow morning.'

'And today?'

'Wait,' Danny said, his thumb bowed over the timer. He was transfixed by the next Lot – three colts growing larger. They were magnificent specimens, the thick winter coats long since shed. Powerful hindquarters propelling their half-ton of flesh, muscle and bones up the stiff incline of the exercise strip.

Danny was blessed with a good eye for spotting talent. He could sort the wheat from the chaff a mile off. He punched the timer and, having read the figure clocked, he thought aloud, 'Impressive.'

Danny smiled; he enjoyed his work. His mates thought he was a professional gambler, but he knew it was nothing so glamorous. He was a work-watcher.

If the job were to be advertised in a local rag, it would read: Want to make money from your passion? Love the outdoor life? Like to travel?

Reality, however, was hours of standing in the cold against sheeting rain, stuck in a jam on the motorway, or mixing with unsavoury types, like whining ticket touts loitering by turnstiles or drunken bookie-dwellers hankering for some inside info. Apart from a long-held desire to return to the saddle bubbling beneath the surface, he wouldn't do anything else right now. Beats a regular nine-to-five office job he'd say to those who expressed a curiosity in his livelihood, which happened to be most, given its unusual nature.

Long-term betting profits were the key to survival and if you didn't get results, there were no hiding places. If you weren't the real deal, the unforgiving game of the Sport of Kings would soon expose your limitations. Many of the guessers retired from the betting game drained of all cash and dignity within a matter of months. Danny had survived six years.

'What about today?' Gash repeated.

Danny scribbled the figure clocked by the latest Lot on one of many time-charts held together by a brass clip. He'd look over those times later, analyse them and, having been blessed with a photographic memory, would have no trouble in recalling them as and when needed.

'Nothing doing today,' Danny said.

'Great, so wasted my time coming down here.'

'Could've phoned.'

Sensing a growing presence, Danny glanced up at the wooded copse on the peak of Ewe Hill, alongside the distant

6

watchtower, standing like a black cut-out against the rusty edge of the iron-blue sky.

Suddenly, a panicked cry broke the morning stillness like a clap of thunder, startling a murder of crows from the copse. Through the static mists that hung low over the gallops, the silhouette of a diminutive figure emerged. His olive skin and sculpted features were etched with pain and fear. Danny knew something was very wrong. The young lad stopped bent double in front of Danny and Gash, who exchanged worried glances. He gasped, 'It's Deano.'

'What?' Danny asked, fearing the answer. 'Ross?'

'He's . . . he's dead.'

Danny replied, 'He can't . . . I just, I saw him just an hour ago.'

'He's dead, I tell you,' Ross cried. 'He's dead.'

'Where?' Gash asked.

'Up there.' He pointed. 'The tack room's where I found him.'

'You've called an ambulance, right?' Danny asked.

'No.'

'Why in the hell not?'

'Cos,' Ross paused. 'They'd be no use, he's hanging from one of the saddle pegs, a right mess.'

'This better not be some sick joke,' Danny barked, empty stomach tightening, though the look of blind terror in the young lad's eyes told him the answer. 'Where's Michael?'

'I dunno,' Ross replied, still short of breath. 'I came here thinking he's with you.'

'You tried the Lodge?'

'Didn't get no answer.'

Danny began pacing back up the gallops, towards Millhouse Lodge – home to former champion trainer Michael Raynham, who'd taken out a licence some twelve years ago. He turned and shouted, 'Gash, be of some use, call the police.'

Ross, grabbing the coattails of Danny, added, 'Don't, not yet.'

'Why in the hell not?'

'Mr. Raynham won't like it.'

'Stuff Michael, the police have to know,' Danny replied. 'We're all innocent here.'

He stopped and turned on his muddy heels. 'Ross, if there's something you're keeping from me? Cos if there is, now's the time to say.'

Ross paused.

'Well?'

'Mr Raynham had a massive barney with Deano last night, see. I heard 'em, shouting they were. Sounded like Mr Raynham was pissed.'

'Anything else?'

'No,' Ross said, his face drained of all colour. 'I'll take you to the door, but I'm not going back in there, no way.'

As the pair strode the short walk to the stable quarters, no more words were spoken. They turned the corner into a square courtyard of tan gravel framed by horse-boxes on all sides, over half vacant nowadays.

'Give,' Danny said, motioning for the torch. He then pushed the tack room door wide open and flashed light inside.

With a vice-like grip of the torch, he splashed light over his dead friend's face. 'Oh, fuck . . .no,' he cried. 'Deano! Deano!'

The scraggy corpse of stable lad Dean McCourt hung, like a sorry piece of meat, from one of the metal hooks normally reserved for saddles or loose tack. His gaunt, ghostly face scarred by ink-black eyes, open yet vacant. Panicked sweats during his final minutes alive had left a waxy residue coating his pallid skin, reflecting light like tinfoil. Fangs of blood dribbled from his blue lips; the droplets fell from his slack jaw, like a slowly leaking tap. From the black cove of his gawping mouth the spiked tip of the hook glistened in the stark artificial light - it had pierced the nape of his neck, sliced through the oesophagus and the carotid artery supplying blood to the lad's brain.

As a nauseous wave rose from within, Danny's hand moved quick to cover his mouth, but the acidic bile surfaced and, like a dam burst, sprayed from between his fingers. A mushy

8

squelch underfoot made his stomach cramp. With some reticence, he lowered the beam toward the slate floor. The sight made him violently retched forward again. The blood-soaked entrails of his friend were lying in a placenta-like mess beneath him, from which the intestinal tubes stretched like guide ropes all the way up to a heavily garrotted hole where Dean's stomach used to be. It smacked of something you'd see in an abattoir.

Danny stepped over the mess, torch remaining firmly fixed on Dean's face. He inched closer. And closer. Suddenly, Dean's eyelid twitched ever so slightly. Danny stumbled back and tripped over a stray saddle-cloth, letting slip the torch which smacked the floor before flickering out. He scrambled to his feet. *This ain't true, no, it ain't happening.*

CHAPTER 2

Danny's raw knuckles rapped the iron-studded oak door of The Lodge. Silence. 'Check the rear.'

Ross circled the large house. He emerged from the gloom, saying, 'Danny, he's in the kitchen, the light's on. Something ain't right. I shouted, but he didn't move.'

'Oh Christ, not another one,' Danny whispered under his breath.

From the rear garden, Danny could see the slouched silhouette of a man, head resting on the kitchen table. One of the windows was ajar. He returned the torch to Ross and slowly waded through the thick shrubbery framing the abode.

He braced himself before pushing his way through the gap in the leaden windows, grazing both elbows on his way. He then padded across the quarry tiled floor to the side door and turned the key. Gash and Ross rushed in from the cold.

'For fuck's sake, Michael, what's up with you?' Danny barked, picking up one of two empty whisky bottles resting on the marble worktop. Raynham remained slumped, face pressed hard against the rustic pine table in the centre of the kitchen. He lifted Raynham's head by his lank, unkempt hair. Red stains, like birthmarks, blemished his ashen face where he'd rested, passed out. He groaned and slowly blinked his dry eyes open. 'Get upstairs and freshen up, you stink of booze.'

Gash sighed, 'He's alive.'

'Thank you, doctor,' Danny replied.

Raynham's opaque eyes stared into a distance that wasn't there, heavy eyelids drooping. He didn't reply.

Danny knelt beside the trainer. 'Michael, hello!' There was the slightest of reactions, as Michael stirred from his drunken somnolence. 'We need you awake, tell us what the fuck is going on. The police are on their way, something horrific has happened. Do you understand?' he said slowly, as if talking to a small child.

Raynham croaked, 'From one nightmare to another.'

'Gash, make a strong coffee, quick.'

'How many sugars?'

'Not for me.' Danny said incredulously. 'Him.' He pointed at Michael, who continued to come around. 'Michael, do you realize what's happened? Dean is *dead.*'

A spark of recognition suddenly fired Raynham's eyes.

'Dean is dead,' Danny repeated, feeling progress was finally being made. 'What happened?'

Raynham dropped his jaw, his mouth frozen open like a fish, as if about to speak. 'Yeah?' Danny asked in anticipation. He moved in close. But without warning, vomit sprayed from Michael's mouth, fanning the table's breadth.

'Fucking marvellous,' Danny groaned, reeling back from the mess. 'Ross, kitchen roll. Gash, the fuzz said they'd be here when?'

Gash turned from trying to work the coffee percolator. 'I wouldn't know, you called them.'

Danny's fingertips pressed his furrowed brow. 'This just gets better. I told you on the . . . don't matter, I'll do it.'

He fished for a mobile in his fleece jacket and punched 999. 'Police and ambulance, there's been a . . . a murder.'

'A murder?' asked the call centre woman. 'Where are you calling from?'

'Millhouse Stables . . . Lambourn . . . Berkshire.'

'And your name?'

Danny paused, before reluctantly giving his details. He flicked the mobile shut. 'They'll be here in twenty. Now, Michael, one last time, what happened?'

Michael looked up with a fiery glare and slurred, 'Why you asking me? You're the one edgy, got something to hide have you?'

Danny paused to soak up what he'd just heard. 'Don't look at me, I've done fuck all. But, stop me if I'm wrong, I'm the one with bloody previous, and I'm sure as hell not going back inside. D'ya hear.' He tried to forget the nine months he'd served for break-ins having got in with a gang, attracted by the fast, risk-taking style of life they offered after leaving school.

Michael rubbed his head. 'Not my problem.'

11

Danny ignored the veiled accusation of guilt and asked, 'Michael, you with us now?'

'What?'

'I've just told you one of your best lads has been killed and you act like nothing's happened. You've asked no questions, you're not even surprised.' Danny rested his weight against the table. 'If you're hiding something, tell us now?'

'Don't care no more.'

'Great, yeah, now's the time for some self pity,' Danny said. There was a moment's stalemate, before Danny continued, voice softened, 'I'm trying to help you here. How long have we known each other, it does me in seeing you like this.'

'I've been here all night,' Michael barked, his gimlet eyes scanned the faces staring back. 'Alright!'

'I'm amazed you can remember a thing with that lot down your neck,' Danny said. He glanced over at the whisky bottles. 'Voices were heard last night, arguing - you and Dean.'

'Who said that?' Michael growled. He stood, using the table as a steadier. 'It was you, wasn't it.' He started to sway, like a pitching ship. Danny rushed forward. Raynham grabbed Danny tight, arms wrapped around his fleece. He whispered in Danny's ear, 'Forgive me.'

'What for?' Danny asked, gently placing Raynham back down, but he got no response.

Gash pointed at Ross, 'What about you?'

'What about me?' Ross replied.

'You've been quiet throughout all of this *and* you discovered the body.'

'He's always quiet,' Danny said. 'And he's a stable lad, for crying out loud, where d'ya expect him to be.'

Ross raised an accusing finger back at Gash, 'When did you last come down to the yard, funny how it's the one day we get a murder.' His young beady eyes welled.

The four began to argue, raised voices lost in a sea of noise.

'Shut it,' Danny shouted, hands cutting the air. The room fell silent. 'Paranoia's fucking with our minds. Just everyone tell the truth and we'll all be okay. No doubt, it's gonna be an outside job or someone else at the yard. Case closed.'

The distant blast of police sirens grew louder. A tension, like that of a dentist's waiting room, filled the air as the foursome waited for the knock on the door.

CHAPTER 3

Danny sat in interview room three. He shifted his weight awkwardly in the chair and scanned the windowless room. Grey panelled walls met with a black carpet-tiled floor. The silence was broken by the ambient whirr of the air conditioning clicking on.

A fresh-faced officer sat opposite, wearing a starched sky-blue shirt and tie with oversized knot.

'Will Taylor be long?' Danny asked, slowly strumming the dull veneered surface.

The officer didn't reply. He fleetingly made eye contact before averting his gaze, as if ordered not to say a word.

They're doing this on purpose, Danny thought, *prolong the agony.* His heart thumped like a battle-drum. *Slow, calm breaths.*

The door opened and a suited man entered. He cradled a bundle of brown files under one arm and steadied a brimming cup of coffee in his free hand. Taylor's craggy face was all too familiar to Danny.

Taylor said, 'I'd hoped I would never see your face again.' His manner was like that of a headmaster towards a mischievous pupil.

'Likewise,' Danny replied. 'Look, am I under arrest?'

'Why would you be under arrest? You've done nothing wrong, right?' His lips stretched into a smile, revealing jagged teeth stained by years of nicotine and caffeine abuse. He smacked the files on the table and dropped on to the chair opposite.

Danny remained silent. His blank expression belied the growing fears of going back inside. *Can't bring shame on my family again.*

'I understand that you've refused your right to be represented by a solicitor.'

'Fat lot of good it did me last time.'

With raised brow, Taylor said, 'Very well, your prerogative.' He then stretched his arms and cupped the back of his head with a satisfied look, as if anticipating a good meal.

'Interview conducted at Newbury Central Police Station, room three, with Mr. Daniel Rawlings, taking place at,' Taylor glanced up at a large white circular clock on the wall, '10.23 A.M. For the purposes of the tape, people present are myself, Detective Chief Inspector Jonathon Taylor, and Police Constable Sean Daly.' Taylor paused. 'Daniel, can you tell me where you were at 11.20 P.M. last evening.'

Danny's eyes narrowed. 'I'm here to make a statement, didn't know I was a suspect.'

'You're not, for now. I'm merely trying to eliminate you at these early stages of our enquiries.'

'I was at my flat in Cardiff.'

'All evening?'

'All evening, until leaving for Lambourn, before dawn.'

'Is that your girlfriend?' Daly piped up.

Danny looked at him quizzically. 'I meant before the break of dawn. Where did you get him from, rent-a-cop?'

Daly's face flushed.

Taylor asked, 'Are you still wasting your money on the gee-gees?'

'No.'

'How do you explain your presence on the gallops, and your close association with trainers and several stable lads, including the now deceased Dean McCourt?'

'I've given up betting. But I do make my money from the sport.'

There was a pause before Taylor said, 'Go on.'

'I collect info and make judgements for others. People with money, people I don't know and hopefully never will.'

'What kind of information?'

'I'm a work-watcher. I look out for the next big thing on the gallops, before anyone else cottons on. Like a talent scout, only for horses.'

'Is that what these people pay you for?'

'I do my homework and I'm out all hours, so I reckon I'm worth it. It's not easy, but a photographic memory helps. I know my business and, if you knew yours, you'd be after whoever killed Dean.'

'Who are these people?'

'Like I said, don't know 'em by name, though Gash once told me they weren't the types you'd expect. High-flyers they were. Lawyers, accountants, city traders, prison governors, even some of your mob are in on it.' Taylor's eyes narrowed. 'So it's totally legit.'

Taylor offered him a cigarette. Danny showed Taylor his palm. 'Given up.' He didn't want to reveal any weaknesses, make any friends. But Danny needed to calm the growing anxiety. 'Just one.'

Taylor dropped the pack on the table and continued to probe. 'And you make it pay?'

'It's no science and they're not machines, but if you know when to strike and how much to stake, long term profits are there for the taking, easy money.'

'So it pays well?'

'No comment.'

'I'm only interested in this murder enquiry, Danny, not your tax returns. Does it pay well?'

'Yeah, not bad. But I get results, see, and the financial backers do a good deal better than me.'

'So you're a tipster for these . . . third parties?'

'Kinda,' Danny replied. He never liked being called a tipster. While there were good ones out there, he didn't like being bundled in with some of the more clueless hacks. 'But that's like calling a dentist a tooth mechanic.'

'I don't understand, if you're as good as you say, why not back the winners yourself?'

'Look, having the inside info is only part of the package - patience and willpower are just as important, if not more. I don't have those, but others do.'

'I find that hard to believe.'

Danny blew smoke across the table. 'Tried quitting these three times this year alone.'

Taylor's eyes narrowed. 'And Dean McCourt was another informant?'

'Wasn't one of my main contacts,' Danny said, shaking his head, 'but he would fill me in if I'd missed something special at Raynham's yard, or one nearby. Apart from that, he was just a friend.'

'You were close?'

'Not really.'

'I understand that you were his best friend.'

'Where d'ya get that from?'

Taylor glanced down at a hand-written sheet in front of him, 'Ron Grainger.'

Danny craned his neck forward. 'What else has Gash said?'

Not intimidated, Taylor also moved in close, his broad shadow cast across the table. 'Were you Dean's best friend?'

'I was his only friend, there is a difference.'

'And your relationship with Grainger?'

'He relays the info to the financial backers, protecting both our identities. A middleman between me and this betting syndicate codenamed Phoenix,' Danny said, sitting back.

'So you're nothing without this Gash.'

'No, I'm nothing *because* of Gash, that's his job. And before you ask - no, we're not friends, far from it. So whatever bullshit he's spouted about me on that sheet, don't believe it for one second.'

Taylor pressed his back against the chair and said, 'I'm still intrigued by your connection with Dean. How often did you meet him?'

'What is this?' Danny protested. 'Bet you ain't giving the others this Spanish inquisition.'

'I can see why you've given up the betting,' Taylor said, his tone and brow lowered noticeably. 'We'll be questioning all those connected with the yard, no one is being picked on.'

'Look, I'm no killer. For Christ's sake, the last fight I had was with my older brother over who had the TV remote.'

'Come on Daniel, you're hardly squeaky clean.'

17

'Can't see how the odd break-in years ago has anything to do with this, I'm a changed man, kicked the betting habit, turned my life around. Was only a kid back then.'

Danny had left school with seven GCSEs, as his career as a jockey began to blossom. His dad, a hardened gambler himself, was all for the switch to racing, but Danny could sense his mum had her misgivings, despite never saying anything on the matter. When Danny's gambling became a problem, he consoled himself with the reasoning: *must be in the genes.* As he dug himself deeper in debt and with nowhere to turn, it wasn't long before he'd gotten involved with the wrong crowd.

'Come on, you've done time. Admit it, *Danny*, you're still an addicted gambler, results went bad, and you blamed Dean.'

'I'm no murderer,' Danny barked. 'Think about it, how could I possibly skewer a good friend on a hook before disembowelling him. I'm no psycho.'

'Somebody did, though.' Taylor laid a see-through evidence bag carefully on the table.

Danny picked it up, hands starting to tremble. Settled at the bottom of the bag was a key, freshly cut and tagged. 'Never seen it before in my life.'

'Well can you explain,' Taylor said smugly, 'why this was among your possessions handed over at the front desk?'

'I dunno,' Danny cried. 'Look, all I know is - Ross collared us on the gallops and we all waited for you lot to arrive.'

'This is a skeleton key for the yard, taken from Michael Raynham's office,' Taylor said. 'Do you admit to using this skeleton key?'

'No, never seen it before in my life and I swear I dunno why the hell it was on me.' Taylor jotted something down, like an examiner marking a wrong answer. He looked up. 'What time did Ross meet you?'

'Dunno, about seven . . . forty.'

'What time did you raise the alarm?'

'Soon after.'

'Our records say it was half an hour later, at 8.13. Why the delay?'

18

Danny paused. 'It was an innocent mix up. I thought Gash - sorry Ron Grainger – had called you, but it turned out he hadn't and he thought the same, that I'd called.'

Raynham slouched in his chair and breathed heavily in interview room one. Dark rings shadowed his bloodshot eyes. He tilted a polystyrene cup forward and croaked, 'Need a refill.'

DCI Sheppard signalled to a young officer with short cropped hair and glasses stood near the only door in the room. Sheppard's sallow face fixed back on Raynham. 'Tell me what you saw.'

'Danny was having a right go at Dean.'

'Where were you?'

'I was upstairs at the Lodge. I heard noises, so I went to the security monitors and saw the pair, shouting and bawling they were.'

'Dean McCourt and Daniel Rawlings?'

'Yeah.'

'Within the courtyard where the stables are?'

'Yeah, outside the tack-room.'

'What did you do next?'

'I did nothing, wasn't anything unusual about those two arguing, going at it hammer and tongs they were. As long as they weren't intruders hurting the horses, I left them to it.'

Sheppard gestured the young officer over and scribbled a note. The officer promptly left the room.

'Have you ever seen this?' Sheppard said. He placed a polythene bag containing folded paper, spattered with blood, onto the table. The young officer returned with a fresh cup of water. Raynham paused to gulp most of it down, and then leant forward. He picked up the evidence and held it at arm's length, as if it were contaminated. He stared blankly at a list handwritten in blue ink on the sheet.

'No, what is it?'

'It's a list of initials together with times and dates. Take a closer look.'

'I tell you, I don't know.'

19

'If I say to you, the paper has your watermark on it – Michael Raynham Stables underscored – and it was found in the coat pocket of Dean McCourt at the murder scene.'

Raynham shook his head in disbelief and raised his callused hands. His face turned an ashen pallor. 'All the lads use my paper, pens. I get them free, but I still remind them it's a perk of the job.' Raynham scowled and barked, 'For Christ's sake, the boy's fleece has that symbol on it, are you going to read anything into that?'

'We've got to be thorough, look at all angles in our enquiries. By the sound of it, the lad had few friends, keeping himself to himself, so we need to get as much info from those who knew him, get a clearer picture of his life.'

Raynham whispered something to his solicitor sat attentively to his side.

'My client would like to take a break,' the solicitor said firmly.

Sheppard checked his watch and said, 'Very well.'

A younger officer entered interview room three. He forced a scribbled note into Taylor's hand.

Taylor read the note, whispered something to the officer, who promptly left as swiftly as he'd arrived, and said, 'I'll give you another chance to tell me the truth about your whereabouts last evening.'

'I was in Cardiff,' Danny said. 'What word of that don't you understand?'

'I hear you,' Taylor remarked, stroking his poor excuse for a jaw-line, 'but sadly there are no witnesses or alibis to corroborate this.'

'What more can I say?' Danny protested.

'It's just, CCTV shows you arguing with Dean last night, just hours before he was found dead.'

Sweat now glazed Danny's furrowed brow. 'I dunno, can't explain that.' He cupped his face in sticky palms before emptying his lungs and rubbing his tired eyes, deep in thought. 'Have you seen those security monitors?' Taylor didn't respond. 'Well, I have and they barely work on a clear day. They certainly haven't got night vision and, anyway, if we were shouting and brawling, you'd think any self-respecting trainer would be down there like a shot, upsetting the horses and all.'

'What are you suggesting?'

'I'm suggesting you pay closer attention to Michael. He's a drunk, has been for years, ever since his wife left him,' Danny said. 'Don't get me wrong, he's a nice bloke and all, I stayed at his gaff several times years ago back in my riding days, he's just fallen on hard times.'

Taylor thumbed to a sheet in a file on the table and said, 'This is the former champion trainer we're talking about.'

'A lot has happened since those glory days. And I mean *a lot*.'

'What are you saying?'

Danny sighed. 'Look, racing's like politics, even a week's a long time. One minute you're up, riding the crest of a winning streak, next minute, half the string are coughing and soon, owners get the jitters, switching their horses to rival yards. We're talking over six years since Raynham was flavour of the month.'

'And you're suggesting he's not now.'

'You're clearly no racing man. Check Raynham's results for the past few seasons. Not only have the winners dried up, but runners have too. Half the boxes are empty, owners deserting like rats from a sinking ship and I for one don't blame 'em. From a betting angle, I wouldn't touch one of his runners with someone else's bargepole, not any more.'

The young officer who was assisting interview room one entered and placed another evidence bag on the table. Taylor acknowledged him, before continuing. 'He doesn't appear hard up. I mean, the estate must be worth a million or two.'

'He pays rent along with three other trainers to use those gallops and when drunk at a party once, he told me the yard is mortgaged to the hilt. Negative equity he said.'

'Couldn't he sell up? Start afresh.'

'Like most in the racing game, it's his life,' Danny said. 'Look, when Michael retired as a jockey, with the help of some

21

financial backer, he took out a trainer's licence straight away. He left school at 14 and there's no chance of him getting a proper job thirty years on, no experience in the real world.'

'You seem to know a lot about him.'

'Used to ride for him way back when. Anyway, it's my business to know who to trust and who to avoid. I make friends with those I trust.'

'And you trust Michael.'

'Yeah, at least I did.'

Taylor pushed the evidence to rest in front of Danny.

'What's this?' Danny asked.

'You tell me.'

'A sheet of paper.'

'Don't get clever, Daniel.'

'I'm not, you just make me nervous.'

'It was found in Dean's jacket at the murder scene. Have you seen it before?'

Danny picked up the bag. There were columns of numbers and letters handwritten in blue ink. 'Nope.'

'Do you recognize any of the initials or figures in the list?'

'No.'

'What do you make of it?'

Danny looked again. This time his eyes scoured the sheet, as if studying the small print of a contract, absorbing every detail. He was more than curious where this was all going and it took little effort in memorising the contents. Being a slacker at school, his teachers viewed his passing end-of-year exams with great suspicion, to an extent that he was wrongly accused of cheating when he was thirteen. As a consequence, he still had trouble obeying authority figures to this day. 'The figures look like race times and dates, the letters . . . maybe initials of connections or horses, just a guess like.'

'Could Dean have been involved in one of these betting syndicates?'

'Who knows? He never talked about it, certainly never asked me for any tips.'

22

'This symbol was painted on the wall beside the victim.' Taylor handed Danny a Polaroid taken from the crime scene. The picture showed dripping letters GH painted in red within conjoined circles, resembling a Venn diagram. Taylor added, 'The killer used the victim's blood.'

'I dunno no one with those initials.' Danny felt his stomach tighten once more, as the horrific scene flashed before him. He slid the photo back to rest next to Taylor's file. 'Might be the killer's signature, but that's your job to find out, ain't it.'

Taylor returned a look of indignation, broken by the young officer entering again. He whispered something else in Taylor's ear. Despite straining to hear, Danny couldn't decipher the message.

'Forensics have found your prints on the doorframe of the tack-room and on this sheet of paper.' Taylor lifted the bag containing the bloody sheet.

Danny swallowed hard. 'I may have left prints when Ross took me to see Deano,' he croaked. 'Can't explain the sheet.'

'This isn't looking good for you, Daniel. It will be a lot easier on you and for the rest of us if you start telling us the truth.'

'I dunno any more than you.'

Taylor's beeper went. He read the message and wrapped the interview up.

'So am I a suspect?'

'Put it this way,' Taylor said. 'Don't go disappearing, I have a feeling we'll be talking again soon.'

Danny was ferried in a squad car back to Millhouse Lodge to collect his car, a bottle green Toyota MR2 - smart enough to create an impression, yet inexpensive enough not to raise an eyebrow with the taxman. Much of Danny's work was paid cash in hand and, although the majority was declared, he couldn't help but store some aside for a rainy day.

A uniformed officer guided him, keeping a wide berth from the murder scene now swarming with forensics wearing plastic overalls and facemasks, to the Toyota parked in the grounds of the Lodge. Danny was handed the key to his car and once out of view, pushed the pedal to the metal.

23

'What a fucking day!' he shouted above the engine's roar as he snaked the country lanes before joining the heavy traffic heading west on the M4. The sight of the monolithic supports of the new Severn suspension bridge towering above sea mist and the blue motorway sign Croeso i Gymru - Welcome to Wales - never felt as welcoming as it did at that moment.

CHAPTER 4

Cardiff was grey and cold by the time Danny arrived back at his apartment; a third floor, two-bedroom flat on a new development in the Bay area that had thrived ever since the regeneration. The place had a dank, unwelcoming air, like when returning from a holiday, though it had been just a day since he'd last visited. During the summer, he'd split his time between Cardiff and London. He rarely left the Welsh capital, however, during winter months, as National Hunt racing wasn't Danny's area of expertise. It was no great loss to him socially, in any case, as he didn't fit in with the jumping set, *all teeth and tweeds they are.* During those bleak months, his attentions turned to the All-Weather tracks of Lingfield, Kempton, Wolverhampton and Southwell. Using contacts within the specialist All-Weather yards - those that kept a large proportion of the string on the boil for the artificial surfaces of Polytrack and Fibresand - he provided the syndicate with a steady all-year-round profit.

His stomach groaned, yet Danny had lost his appetite. Stress had left a hollow, sickly feeling inside. However, he was low on energy and thought it best to refuel. He made a beeline for the stainless steel kitchen. The fridge was about as empty as his stomach. There looked like some blue cheese on the bottom shelf, though Danny suspected it used to be Cheddar. A milk bottle stood in the door looked more like yoghurt. He tried the cupboards, hoping they would yield a more pleasant surprise. Closing the last of them he thought, *pizza it is then.* His own cooking rarely left beyond the realms of beans on toast or pasta with readymade sauce.

He stretched and kneaded his knuckles between stiff, cold shoulder blades and cracked his spine into shape. His tired eyes widened when he saw a three-quarter full bottle of vodka on the work surface next to the draining board, a way to empty himself of the world around him. He slugged back a generous measure, before braving the answerphone. Having feared yet more bad news, a sales call asking if he was interested in a showroom conservatory came, for once, as a light relief. The next two messages were from his mother, who lived in a small village just outside Ludlow.

A bleep sounded. 'Hello, love,' she said. 'Oh, I do hate these things. Could you call me, it's just I've seen the news, that young stable lad. Could you call, let me know you're safe. Bye.'

She must've heard me talk of Dean before, he thought.

A shiver shot down his spine. He filled the glass again, and ordered a Mixed Grill pizza. He ate what he liked, when he liked - a possible reaction to the years of being denied such luxuries as an apprentice jockey in his youth. He flicked on the wall-mounted plasma screen and turned to BBC News 24 to find out any more details on the case and whether his name would be mentioned. He pressed the red button on the remote and keyed in the News Multi-screen covering the day's big events. His mother was right, screen 4 was underscored by the headline RACING: STABLE LAD FOUND MURDERED.

The reporter said, 'The horseracing community in the quiet valley at Lambourn was left in shock after the badly mutilated body of stable lad Dean McCourt was discovered. Police are treating the death as murder and have revealed details of a marking left on the wall by the killer. Chief Inspector Jonathon Taylor, who is leading the case, stated that the letters GH were written at the scene and appeals for anyone connected to the yard, or who knew him, with those initials to come forward.'

Danny turned off the TV; he'd seen and heard enough. He ambled across the polished laminate wood flooring, littered with the odd empty takeaway box picked up from one of the many late-night eateries along the infamous Caroline Street, known by locals as chip alley, after a heavy night's boozing with the lads, plus McDonald's cartons bought from the nearby drive-thru after a long day on the track and the road.

Must get a cleaner, Danny thought, picking them up and dropping them in a bin liner. The current state of the apartment reflected the disarrayed mess his life had slowly become. He caught glimpse of the only spot in his flat that didn't resemble his present way of life. In one corner, resting in orderly fashion on a bookshelf, were a set of files and photo-albums, kept in pristine condition, untouched. An uncomfortable wave of sadness washed over Danny, catching him with defences down. For a brief moment, he recalled the extraordinary time and effort his father had taken in compiling those records of his riding career. With the exuberance - bordering on arrogance - of youth, Danny paid no attention to the care and pride his father had shown within those pages. They contained a montage of clippings and photos, all of Danny's successes and triumphs in the saddle some years back.

His father would rather stick a fork in his eye than express his emotions verbally, Danny recalled, the result of a chastening upbringing in the small mining community in the Rhymney valley. Now, Danny knew that was his father's way of showing his love, though at the time it simply didn't occur to him and now it was too late. To know his father cared for him gave him some solace at his darkest hours. To this day, he still dreamt of landing a big race, aspirations he later found out through his mother that were shared by his father. No one, absolutely no one, was allowed to even lay a finger on those books but him.

He opened the Parisian balcony doors and dreamily gazed out at the streetlights of the flyover splashing a flickering barcode of white and yellow on the still water of the bay. The copper shimmer from the armadillo shell of the Welsh Millennium Centre, the St David's Hotel – futuristically designed to resemble a ship, though Danny couldn't see the likeness - silhouetted against dying rays of the setting sun. He allowed his mind to drift back to happier times, when he was with his long-term partner Sara Monk. Those rosy memories blanched when Sara once again packed her bags after handing Danny an ultimatum – it was the racing or her. She'd grown fed up of the daily stress associated with the unpredictable and unsociable hours, and, once Danny made the impossible decision to pick his job over her, she carried out the threat, leaving him in pieces. Danny was consoled by Sara's promise that they'd get back together one day if his priorities changed.

Once a gambler, always a gambler she always used to say, so Danny suspected it was a hollow gesture to soften the parting, but it was one he clung to after they'd separated and he'd realized his mistake. His older, more sensible brother Rick always said the betting would end in tears. You never see a poor bookie, he used to say. Just cos the bookies finish on top, don't mean all punters have to lose, Danny would snap. Though deep down, given his wild and random punting habits in those early days, he knew there was a grain of truth in his brother's words. Perhaps that's why it riled Danny so much; the realization he'd become your typical bog-standard mug punter that he'd so despised.

His reverie was broken by the tinny tune of his mobile. 'Danny speaking.'

'Hello love.'

'Hi mum.'

'I tried your flat but got no answer.'

'I know, just got the messages, been a bit . . . waylaid recently.'

'Did you hear about that poor stable lad? Terrible news wasn't it.'

'Yeah, I know,' Danny replied. He briefly thought about reliving the day's events, but knew it would only serve as yet another thing for her to worry about. *What good would it do?* His mother was a professional worrier, a family trait he'd successfully managed to suppress over the years.

'You go to that neck of the woods, did you know the poor lad?'

'Knew of him.'

'No more than a boy, such a shame. You look after yourself. I've told you before racing's full of unsavoury types.'

'Thanks,' Danny said wryly. 'I think he just got in with the wrong crowd, mum.'

He signed off and closed the balcony doors. He pushed back on his leather recliner, shutting his eyes but keeping his ears open for the buzz of the pizza delivery.

The following day, Danny took a hot shower and shaved. Helped by a tall glass of water, he washed down two rounds of toast made from stale bread he'd previously missed at the back of a cupboard. He had the option of staying at home to watch the

28

Newbury race involving Gold Marquee on one of two channels dedicated to horseracing. However, the events of the previous day left a sour taste in his mouth and he felt the need to keep on the move.

The fresh afternoon air helped blow away the mild hangover left from last night's vodka as he strolled the twenty minute walk to St Mary's Street, stretching to the drawbridge of the famous Cardiff Castle, situated alongside Bute Park. Having visited the castle as a kid, he knew its lavish and opulent interiors restored by the third Marquess - once the richest man in the world - attracted swarms of tourists year round.

Danny carved a path through the busy mix of shoppers and workers, zigzagging to avoid the predatory clipboard carriers, dressed in brightly coloured uniforms and clutching their arduous questionnaires, determined to stall you for 'just a moment of your time.'

Why they don't get a proper job, Danny thought wryly, as he pushed past the frosted-glass door of the bookies. A wave of cool air brushed over him as he entered the establishment, decked out in blue. The grey low-maintenance carpet was scarred by streaky ash stains, and littered with cheap pens, cigarette butts and discarded betting slips.

One of the counter staff was sweeping the floor. She made small talk with an elderly regular hunched over a circular table with a tabloid open at the back pages.

Danny acknowledged the frumpy middle-aged woman dressed in company uniform matching the décor. He ventured deeper into the bookies, climbing two steps to a mezzanine level where a twelve-screen bank of inset monitors provided the focal point for the several punters present. The screens were alive with activity, some relaying the latest market shows - prices from the various horse and greyhound tracks - leaving the others to show live racing feeds from up and down the country. The screens were constantly changing, even during lulls between races, helping to create a lively atmosphere and grab the attention of those on the shop floor.

Danny glanced at screen 12 showing a virtual horse race, computer generated and predetermined by a random selection process according to each of the runner's odds. No skill or judgement involved, little more than a lottery. He shook his head in dismay and turned. His eye was caught by a familiar tweed cap with matching jacket of a regular called Stony, a nickname that stuck after years of his whinging about being constantly broke. The former jockey and longstanding friend was sat scouring the Betting Shop edition of the *Racing Post* pinned to the walls, providing horse-by-horse form of the feature meeting at Newbury. None of the regulars knew for sure whether indeed Stony was broke, but, if his record at betting was anything to go by, he wasn't bluffing. *They do say jockeys make the worst tipsters.* Danny crept up from behind.

Stony turned and grunted, 'Oh, it's you.'

'Good to see you too, Stony. What's wrong – luck's out?'

'Could say that.'

The pair went way back. Danny looked up to Stony - successful in the saddle and on the verge of retirement at the time they'd first met - as a role model when he set out on a career as a jockey himself. They kept in regular contact after Stony called it a day and saw more of each other since Danny had also packed in the riding game due to losing his nerve after the crashing fall he'd suffered in the King George. He couldn't even face returning to the saddle after that confidence-sapping day at Ascot, still haunting his dreams.

Having deciphered Stony's scribbles on the betting slip, Danny said, 'Good luck with that project.'

Stony flicked his cigarette at a foil ashtray and rasped, 'What? Got no chance has it?'

Stony's career was cruelly cut short by a back injury incurred in a horrendous pile up in a selling race on a rainy Monday at Catterick. In many ways, it was a damp and dreary end to a career that had, initially at least, promised so much.

Racing had been Stony's whole life until that fateful day and being robbed of his livelihood plus the main reason for getting up each morning had eaten away at him ever since. He was a shadow of his former self, the one that Danny recalled like it was yesterday. He would never forget the first time he'd seen Stony after the accident. He found it hard to contain his emotions, not at seeing his good friend strapped in a body and neck brace, but it was seeing the dark rings of sadness framing eyes that seemed dead, lacking any of the old spark.

One of only a handful of jockeys based in Wales, Stony, being very much the senior presence, acted as a mentor and kept Danny, who was always prone to go off the rails, in check. Much of their contact since the accident had been making small talk in the bookies now and then, Danny passing on the odd 'good thing', as a thank you.

Stony was about to back Jubilee Honour, running in the third race against Gold Marquee - the colt Danny had given the green light to Gash yesterday.

'Well?' Stony asked again. Danny now had his full attention.

'Myself, I wouldn't back it with counterfeit euros.'

'Why's that?'

'Got something a bit special up against it.'

'What?' Stony asked. Eagerness now fuelled his voice, as if about to find the meaning of life.

'It's all a bit hush-hush.'

'Yeah, yeah, but what is it?' Stony asked. 'Won't go any further, promise.'

The voice of a presenter at Satellite Information Services (SIS) blared through the speakers. 'They're going down at Newbury for our 2.50 race. The opening show is as follows. Shakee is our 9/4 favourite, followed by Gold Marquee 4/1, Return To Sender 11/2, Jubilee Honour opened at 7/1 and immediately out to eights and it's 12/1 bar the rest.'

Danny looked up and studied the structure of the market. As with most opening shows, particularly in races full of unexposed types that precious few knew precious little about, the bookies were as wary as the punters and nearly always erred on the side of caution when forming a betting market. This being a maiden for inexperienced types, the on-course bookies, those who

31

created and formed the market, were taking no chances. Danny quickly added the equivalent percentage of the odds for each runner and could see that the bookies were betting to a 38 per-cent profit on the race, also known as the over-round.

Plenty of scope for them to push some of those odds out, Danny thought, *best delay the call.*

Part of his remit was to tell Gash, who was sat attentively at his computer in London with three betting exchange websites open, when to strike. Placing the bet to gain the best odds available was a critical part of beating the betting markets in the long term. Danny strived to get the best deal, like stock-traders aiming to buy low and sell high, or shoppers seeking out a bargain.

'Which one is it, Danny?' Stony asked, patience now wearing thin.

Danny moved in close, hovering over his friend, who was perched on a stool, resting his elbows on a wooden ledge running the length of wall. 'I'll tell you, but I need a favour.'

Stony paused and asked, 'What kind of favour?' He'd lived in Cardiff nearly all his life, and knew plenty of people in the area.

'Something's cropped up and I may need a safe place to stay if it hits the fan.'

'What have you done now?'

'Nothing, just need a fallback place to kip for a few days, no questions asked, like.'

Stony wavered before greed won the day. 'Only if this nag of yours does the business.'

'Deal,' Danny said.

'Deal.'

Danny rolled a betting slip from a dispenser on the wall and wrote the name of the horse he expected to win the 2.50 at Newbury – Gold Marquee.

'It's a certainty?' Stony asked.

'On a par with death and taxes.'

Stony scuttled off to the betting counter as fast as his prematurely arthritic legs would allow him. The condition was brought on by a lack of calcium during his twenty-five years as a journeyman jockey. 'I'll take the price, I'll take the 4/1. There you are, love.'

Danny flicked his mobile open; it was now time for the serious business to start. 'Gash, it's Danny. You ready?'

'What kept you?'

'Never mind, just letting you know there's nothing doing at the moment. They're only going to post, enough time for the odds to drift. What's it now?'

'Hovering just above 4/1,' Gash said. 'We need to talk about yesterday. What the fuck did you tell 'em?'

'Nothing, I was questioned by the same bastard that sent me down for housebreaks as a kid. Sure he's got a vendetta against me, reckon I'm a suspect.'

'Shit, well don't go opening your trap anymore for that lot.'

'Cheers for looking out for me, Gash,' Danny said, surprised by the apparent concern.

'It's not that, I need your arse on the outside. Otherwise, I'm out of a job.'

'You're all heart,' Danny said, 'I'm wellin' up.'

Danny's eyes remained fixed on screen four, showing the latest market moves for the upcoming race. He could see the odds remain steady at 4/1.

Clearly no one else was party to the recent gallop reports, Danny surmised.

'What's the price doing now?' he asked, keen to steer the topic back to business.

'Hovering around 4.8/1.'

'Put up £15,000 at fives, see if anyone bites.'

Gash's fingers skimmed the keyboard, entering the amount the syndicate wished to place on Gold Marquee and the odds at which they wanted to back. Almost immediately, the amount had been nibbled, small amounts at first, increasing to bigger chunks of hundreds and then thousands of pounds, as a growing band were willing to take him on.

33

Danny liked to keep close tabs on the latest news and goings on in the racing world. He was fully aware that the British Horseracing Authority (BHA) – the governing body of the sport - was working ever closer with betting exchanges to tackle corruption in the game. Their investigations primarily focused upon the laying of horses, where punters were predicting a particular horse would lose a race, and therefore leave it open to less scrupulous punters or trainers or jockeys to make sure that horse didn't win by drugging, or riding the horse with such restraint that it couldn't win, or in a jumps race, simply falling off. Danny was familiar with a whole manner of ways connections could lose a race, and with massive negative public exposure that such scandals brought, tarnishing the credibility of the sport, the rulers of racing were ever vigilant in tracking down those culprits.

'They're going behind at Newbury,' called the SIS commentator, signalling to punters that runners were preparing to enter the stalls, leaving only a minute or two before the 'off' of the race.

He could see Gold Marquee circling behind the stalls, perfectly calm and not sweating up. His jockey was Robert Shaw, an experienced pilot who'd ridden over 500 winners at the Northern tracks, but was signed to Jenkins's Lambourn string for the Flat season ahead. Danny was confident in Shaw's strength and tactical know-how to get the job done. Danny considered the jockey as an integral part of the selection process and often determined the outcome of a race; after all, it's no coincidence Ferrari teamed up with Michael Schumacher.

'Have they lapped it up?' Danny asked, with just five horses still to load.

'Every last drop,' came down the line.

Stony had returned from the counter and stood by Danny's side, out of the way at the back of the mezzanine level. He muttered, 'You'd better be right.'

The adrenalin began to pump through Danny's veins, an instinctive reaction harking back to his betting days.

'They're all in,' the commentator said. 'Under starter's orders and they're off!'

Danny crossed his arms and fixed his unblinking eyes on the screen, a peculiar trait that could be construed as a superstitious ritual, though it was more the body language of someone telling fellow bookie dwellers not to approach during an important race.

'And it's a fairly level break to the Berkshire Gazette Maiden Stakes run over the straight seven furlongs. As they sort themselves out, one of the outsiders, Johnny Be Good sets the early pace, tracked by the favourite Shakee and to the stands side Jubilee Honour also takes a prominent pitch.'

Danny's eyes tracked the movements of Gold Marquee, who was pulling in behind the runners due to greenness. Shaw wisely tried to keep his mount covered up in an attempt to settle him and therefore save some energy for the business end of the race, but it wasn't working. Danny raised the mobile to his ear, aware that he may be forced, if the horse continued with such antics, to lay off some of the bet as a damage limitation exercise.

The commentator continued, 'As they pass the three-furlong marker, Shakee now hits the front, Don Riley is wise to the move and goes second on Return To Sender, as Johnny Be Good begins to come under pressure and fades. Gold Marquee has been given a quiet ride out the back and starts to make a forward move into fourth on the rails and another one picking up from the back is Diamond Digger.'

Danny could see Shaw steer Gold Marquee a daring route up the rails, but was met with the backside of leader Shakee. To his left, he was penned in by Riley, who used perfectly legal tactical race-riding on Return To Sender to keep his rival boxed against the rail.

Danny grimaced as he saw his horse stuck in a pocket and muttered, 'Edge out, edge out.'

Passing the furlong marker, Danny knew Shaw had less than ten seconds to make his move, or else, with the finish line in sight, he'd run out of real estate to catch the favourite.

The commentator narrated the unfolding drama, 'Shakee is working hard to hold on to this slender lead, Return To Sender's beginning to tire, with Gold Marquee still stuck on the rails.'

35

'Push out!' Danny shouted. His pleas were lost in the dozens of cries from punters urging on their own selections.

Shaw edged Gold Marquee into the side of Return To Sender, causing Riley to stop riding for a couple of strides. The gap was now big enough for Gold Marquee to slip through, and the keen and willing youngster didn't needed to be asked twice, quickening up for a vigorous shake of the reins. With just 150 yards to go, Gold Marquee had just over a length to make up, but was eating up the ground on Shakee, who had been out in front long enough and, as with many juveniles, didn't know what was required of him and began to idle with no rivals to pass. Just 50 yards to go and Gold Marquee had drawn alongside Shakee's quarters, 20 yards left and the pair was level. Danny knew this was going to be a head bobbing finish and the anxiety was etched all over his face.

'Photo! Photo!' sounded the racecourse speakers.

Danny swallowed hard. Initial instinct told him that Gold Marquee had got up. He dialled the memory button for Gash. 'What's the betting for the photo?'

'It's 10s-on Gold Marquee has won, you jammy bastard.'

'Lay just the initial stake of £15,000 off at that price, I'm not taking any chances on this. Anyway, there's gonna be a Steward's Enquiry, I just know it.'

'Can't see it getting chucked out for that minor bump,' Gash assured.

'I know, but I don't trust the stewards as far as I can throw 'em,' Danny said. 'Done laying it off?'

'Done.'

Danny went to the drinks dispenser and grabbed a piping cup of dark coffee. He'd just split the sugar sachet when the result came through.

'First, number seven, Gold Marquee 4/1, second, number 11 Shakee, the 9/4 favourite, and third, number nine Jubilee Honour 10/1,' the announcer stated clearly. 'And they're weighed in.' Hearing those words meant the result was official, allowing the bookies to start settling up on the successful bets and, more importantly, pay out the winnings.

With the best part of £60,000 added to the syndicate betting fund, a warm feeling came over Danny like a wave. *Job well done.* Controlling emotional responses to the outcome of a particular race were the key to long term success, with many punters coming unstuck when letting their hearts rule their heads. But the events of the previous day still cast a shadow over his mood.

I've done nothing wrong, a thought that kept running through his mind like a broken record, *they only want me back for further questioning, and they've nothing but circumstantial evidence.* However, his reasoning failed to temper the anxiety building within.

Danny's opaque gaze was broken by Stony shoving a crumpled betting slip in his hand. 'He owes me a favour, big time.'

'Cheers, Stony,' Danny said. He glanced at the telephone number scrawled on the back of a crumpled betting slip and swiftly placed it in his wallet.

That evening, back at the apartment, Danny called Raynham.

'Michael speaking, hello?'

'It's Danny.' Silence. 'Michael?'

'Don't ever call me on this line again.' The line went dead.

Bemused, Danny barely had time to flick his mobile shut when it sounded in his hand. He looked at the caller's number; it was from Raynham's mobile. 'Hello?'

'The police are monitoring incoming calls to the yard, last thing I need is your number cropping up. What the hell do you want?'

'I need to know when and where Dean's funeral is.'

'Tomorrow, 11.30 at . . . St Martin's Chapel in Barnstaple. I guess you're going then?'

'Yeah, poor lad didn't have much of a family, or many friends for that matter. Do my bit. Are you?'

'Can't deal with it right now,' Raynham said. 'Anyway, keeping a low profile, there's bound to be some press lurking about.'

'St. Martin's Chapel, Barnstaple,' Danny confirmed, but Raynham had abruptly hung up.

He'd just settled himself on the sofa when he received a call from Gash. 'What's the goods for tomorrow?'

'No rest for the wicked,' Danny sighed. 'Hold on a minute.' He picked up a copy of the *Racing Post* lying on the glass coffee table and ran his finger down tomorrow's declared runners, a significant day on the Flat calendar, with a couple of Classic trials scheduled on the Craven meeting at Newmarket. Many of the top yards had representatives, with the aim to assess their classic potential and to see how they'd wintered. The trials also helped to sharpen them up for a possible tilt at the opening two Classics – the 1000 and 2000 Guineas – at Newmarket, the headquarters of British Flat racing, the following month. Three weeks back, he'd relayed to Gash a possible runner worthy of a bet, called Sapphire. A leggy filly that'd caught his eye in recent pieces of work at a Newmarket yard, and boasted a pedigree and form to match. He'd also had good word for the filly from one of his most trusted contacts, Seamus O'Malley. She'd won her juvenile maiden well and, from what Danny had seen of her stretching out on the gallops, she'd strengthened both physically and mentally during the winter months. However, on the flipside, the competition facing her tomorrow was fierce, with four similarly unexposed types yet to be beaten in the line-up, two of which Danny knew little about.

'You still there?' Gash asked.

'Just thinking,' Danny said distantly. 'I'll ring you first thing in the morning.'

'Make sure you do.'

'The lad's funeral's tomorrow afternoon, thought you'd want to know,' Danny said, changing the subject.

'Why should I? Didn't know him. And if there's work to be done, you're not going either.'

38

'Well you're gonna be disappointed on that score,' Danny replied curtly.

'You're not going,' Gash barked.

'He was a good friend, I wanna pay my last respects. Got a problem with that?'

'Yeah,' Gash said.

'You can't stop me going. Just cos you're gonna miss out on a possible winner and a cut of the profits. More important things in life,' Danny reflected.

'I'm the one who deals with the syndicate, I'm sure they'd love to know where the fifty big ones went yesterday, questions will be asked.'

'And where would that leave you?' Danny asked. The following silence told its own story. 'Look, the horse's name is Sapphire. I'll check again first thing tomorrow and give you a target price, if she meets that price, back her, if she doesn't, no bet. There's no way I'm missing Deano's funeral, can't imagine many will be going. I wanna show my face.'

'Keep your mobile on at all times,' Gash said. 'I want to know of any changes of plan right away.'

Danny flicked the mobile shut before muttering, 'Shut the fuck up.'

CHAPTER 5

Danny woke well before his alarm went off; his body-clock still tuned to being an early bird, a throwback from working the first Lots on the gallops years back. He now lay there stewing in the gloom for a good hour, regularly glancing at his black-and-white Swatch, a twenty-first birthday present from his older brother Rick. In many ways, that simple gift summed his brother up, he reckoned - dependable with a touch of style. Danny looked up to Rick. As a kid, he remembered crashing and burning in fights and arguments with his cooler brother, much to his annoyance. *Guess that need to succeed later spurred me on as a jockey*, he thought distantly, as he caught himself staring at the second-hand as it slowly skimmed the watch face, willing it to go even slower. *It's no use, gotta get up*, he thought, nerves now frayed.

He sunk his arms deep into the closet for his best, albeit only suit. Below, he could see his riding boots lying in one corner, kept as a memento of his days in the saddle, though secretly he still harboured the desire to get back in the plate. Danny noticed a scuffed patch on the lip of his left boot where he'd glued a photo of Sara on the inside as a good luck charm. He would touch that photo religiously moments before every race. It had proved a winning ritual until that fateful day at Ascot. He fished the suit out and, having smelt the worsted wool fabric, he left it to air from a coat hanger over his balcony. Having never had a nine-to-five job, he rarely needed the use of a suit. He found wearing a tie prohibiting, so he rarely did. His mother believed it was linked to reincarnation, something about being hanged in a past life; she was a great believer in that sort of thing. Danny, being more pragmatic, was less convinced.

He downed some soothing orange juice, savouring the cooling sensation on his dry, tingly throat. He showered, shaved and dressed. Facing the vertical mirror in his bedroom, he looked at the jaded 29-year-old staring back at him, the suit had looked better on the coat hanger. He slumped back on the bed, catching a glimpse of the framed photo of Sara. Alongside was a picture of himself as a kid standing proud next to his father, Paul, on a fishing trip, cradling a 9lb carp. Danny recalled the harrowing moment he'd learnt of his father's death in a car crash on his way to meet him. Paul was told to travel down a day later than previously arranged because, at the last minute, Danny had been invited to a poker session with the lads that night; he hadn't picked up a pack of playing cards since. He adjusted the lapels on his funeral attire and sighed, 'Death seems to follow me.'

Also on the bedside cabinet was a trophy, engraved with the inscription *Daniel Rawlings – Runner-up Apprentice Riders' Championship*, now collecting dust.

He rode the lift down to his car and made stealthy progress down the M5 to Barnstaple, North Devon. With the help of directions from a couple of friendly locals, he was there an hour early. The small stone church nestled among oaks and elms, with a well kept graveyard to the front. There was one open grave, presumably for Dean's coffin.

From a discreet distance, DCI Taylor sheltered under the lichgate. Danny occasionally glanced in the detective's direction, wondering why he was there. Was it to pay his respects for the victim of his enquiries, or was it to see who'd turn up for the funeral?

With no sign of the vicar, Danny poked his head around the heavy oak doors leading to the nave of the church. Dust danced ethereally in the shafts of tinted light, filtered through stained-glass windows, slicing through the gloom. Rows of wooden pews led to a pulpit made of carved stone and framed tapestries hung from the wood-panelled walls. Danny's footsteps on the cold slate floor echoed. With no sign of life, he left and continued to wait awkwardly outside in the spring sunshine.

Emerging from the shadows, a white-haired lady appeared. Her face shimmered in all its fine wrinkles as the sunlight stroked her skin. She was closely followed by the vicar, whose long cassock flapped in the spring breeze. She glanced over at Danny. Dark rings of sadness framed her eyes.

She approached and said, 'You must be Daniel.'

41

Taken aback, Danny replied, 'Yes, Danny Rawlings.' He found himself talking with a posh accent, like he did when talking to parents of friends as a kid. Whether it sounded softer, less threatening, he didn't know; it just felt right, more appropriate.

'Elena,' she said, offering her hand. 'Dean's grandma.'

Danny gently squeezed her hand. 'I'm so sorry.'

'Dean described you well. He talked a lot about you.'

'Nothing bad I hope,' escaped Danny's lips. Such a throwaway comment would pass at an office party, he thought, but the words seemed awkward, disrespectful at this time. His face flushed.

'I was hoping you'd turn up.'

'I had to come, Dean was a good pal. When are the others arriving?'

The elderly woman's smile was betrayed by her eyes. 'Looks like this is it,' she said. 'I hoped there would have been someone from the yard, didn't even have to know him. He lived for his work, said so in his letters.'

'They're very busy this time of year,' Danny said. *Why defend Raynham?* 'You're right though, it's out of order.'

The vicar coughed; a signal to get the ceremony underway. The service was brief and respectful. Elena had a short speech prepared, saying what a sweet and good- natured boy Dean had been and how he'd kept the rich family tradition in horseracing on his father's side of the family.

'His father - my son - is buried there,' she said and pointed to the adjacent plot. 'We've lived in the village for over forty years and have first refusal on these plots. Hardly something to live for is it? This one was meant for me.' She glanced down at the six foot hole. Resting at the bottom was an oak casket, a small floral wreath lying beneath the brass nameplate.

The nests of skin beneath her yellowing eyes began to twitch. Her eyes welled and tears began to roll down her high cheekbones. Danny moved forward to comfort her. He held her tight as she sobbed incessantly. 'Dean was a special kid. They'll catch who did this to him.'

He glanced over at the lychgate. Taylor's face remained fixed firmly in their direction, talking on his mobile; he'd clearly not come to pay his last respects.

The vicar shook their hands. Danny turned. Taylor had gone.

'Well, I suppose this is it,' Danny said.

'Not quite,' Elena replied. Her eyes widened as if remembering something. 'Come. There's something I need to show you.'

She led him to a small thatched chocolate box cottage - with creepers and roses climbing up the red-bricked walls - in the grounds of manicured lawns and borders, and located on the outskirts of the village.

Inside, it was a treasure trove of art and antiques, with a slate fireplace dominating the far wall. A musty smell of wood polish and cats filled the air. Danny caught sight of old illustrations of jockeys in silks on racehorses above the fireplace, at least half a dozen of them, framed behind glass. Although on the short side himself, Danny was forced to stoop beneath the low, beamed ceiling.

'Would you like a cup of tea, coffee . . . or something stronger?'

'Yes, tea's fine, thanks,' Danny said distantly, eyes tracing over the pictures.

'Cake?'

'No thanks, watching my weight.'

'Nonsense, you're a growing lad.'

Danny smiled. 'Outwards perhaps.'

'It's homemade,' she said. 'I'll bring the tin in.'

He didn't mind being mothered, the week he was having.

She scuttled off to the kitchen. He rested his weight carefully on the arm of a leather fireside chair and waited, occasionally glancing at his watch. He'd yet to check the latest news on the fillies' classic trial the Nell Gwyn Stakes – run at Newmarket in less than an hour's time and he knew Gash would be straining at the leash waiting for an update. But he felt sorry

43

for the old lady, she seemed to be glad of the company; Danny seemingly the only living link she had left with Dean.

'My ex-husband introduced him to racing,' Elena said, balancing a tray of tea and fruitcake. 'Dean knew as soon as he set foot on the race-track, he wanted to be a jockey. He had such a bright future.'

'What happened to his mother?'

'She moved to America, just months after my dear Steven left us.' Danny needn't have asked how Elena felt about Dean's mother; the look of scorn said it all.

'Tell me, Daniel, have you any idea who would do such a terrible, evil thing?'

'I wish I did, I really do.'

'I just don't understand it. I mean, why? Tell me why?' Elena asked, momentarily losing her composure.

The tick of the grandfather clock cut the subsequent awkward silence. She began to nibble on a slice of fruitcake and then sipped her tea, still piping hot.

'You said Dean left something for me.'

Elena swallowed what she'd been chewing and said, 'Last week, Dean gave me an envelope addressed to you. He said that I should give this to you if he had to go away for some reason. I asked if he was in trouble, but he said 'no'.' She paused. A film glazed her eyes, as if a wave of guilt broke over her. 'I should have called the police then, if I'd only called, perhaps he would still be alive.'

Elena rocked herself out of the leather chair opposite and, gently lifting the wooden mantelpiece clock, retrieved a small white envelope from beneath.

'This is it.'

Danny took the envelope with his name written in child-like capitals on the front. He ran his finger across, tearing it open.

'Don't,' she said. 'Not here.'

Danny stopped. 'Aren't you curious?'

'It's none of my business, I don't think I want to know. I mean, some things are best left alone. I cannot turn back the clock.'

Danny paused, head bowed. 'Speaking of which,' his eyes returned to his wristwatch, 'I really must be off.'

'Yes, of course, my dear.'

'This has my mobile number, if you need a chat or anything.' He placed a card on the table next to the cake tin. 'Thanks for the tea.'

'It was nothing,' she said. 'And any time you're in the area, don't hesitate to pop in.'

'Okay, thanks.'

Danny waved goodbye and returned to his car parked by the churchyard. He flicked his mobile on. As he'd feared, his inbox was flooded with unanswered messages, all from Gash.

'Hello?'

'It's Danny, clocking on.'

'About fucking time.'

'What price is the filly Sapphire?'

'Don't you know?'

'No, got held up.'

'Let me guess, the funeral?'

Danny yanked the tie from his neck. 'No.'

Gash audibly sighed. 'It's hovering around 5/2, the morning tissue was twos.'

Danny was well aware that the tissue prices for each race were created by on-course bookies in the morning, a forecast to what they believed each runner would start at come the afternoon's action. The morning tissue often provided a good indicator but, since the advent of betting exchanges, they were becoming increasingly obsolete.

Markets these days were controlled primarily by the dominant internet betting exchanges as they best reflected public opinion in the morning. If the price suddenly shrinks on the exchanges, the bookies merely followed suit by shortening their own odds.

'Have you even looked at the race?' came down the line.

Danny paused, 'I'll get back to you.'

He connected to the internet via his WAP phone and scanned through the form of the race. Much of the runners' past

45

performances involved backend juvenile maidens at some of the top tracks. Danny had learned the hard way that these were often used by trainers to get a run into green two-year-olds, accruing some valuable racecourse experience before being put away for the winter. Often well contested, these races were a hotbed for finding future winners. Danny swiftly assessed their merits, many he could recall in his mind's eye, and, although he rated Sapphire a very bright prospect, he reckoned there were too many unknown quantities in the field to merit a bet given such short odds. *Tomorrow's another day*, he reasoned, something every astute gambler had to learn, often as result of fingers being burnt. Patience was one of the most important traits in the professional gambler's armoury. If you couldn't resist waiting for the right time to strike and start chasing losses, you're fodder for the bookies and would soon be knocking the door of the poorhouse.

Danny returned Gash's call and told him no bets were planned for the rest of the day. He gave a hollow apology and told Gash to keep in touch as there was a potential runner that caught his eye in the Greenham Stakes at Newbury on Saturday.

He reclined in his car seat and slowly ran his hands through his hair. He removed the envelope from an inside pocket sewn in the silk lining of his jacket and finished opening it. From within, he removed a piece of paper, plain and neatly folded. It was a letter, written in the hand of Dean. Danny slowly worked through the letter. It read:

Danny,

If you read this I am dead. Please look after something. It is in that watchtower on Ewe Hill. Behind a stone in the wall on step nine. It is worth everything. Please keep safe. Promise me.

Good luck mate

Dean.

Danny's heart felt leaden. More than ever, he'd wanted a simple life and this sounded trouble. *Was it the reason Dean was murdered?* He'd just about settled in his mind to leave it well alone and hand the letter over to the police when a potent mix of curiosity and pangs of guilt swayed him the other way. After all, what on earth could be worth that much? *I can't let the lad down*, he thought.

He replaced the letter, fired up the engine and left for home in Cardiff.

CHAPTER 6

The following morning saw Danny drive to Upper Lambourn and park as close as he could to the peak of Ewe Hill. He climbed the rest on foot. He blew hard, making a mental note to pay a second visit to the gym he'd joined nine months previously.

As a couple of walkers passed by on the descent, he paused to admire the view, but was merely catching his breath. Once reaching the peak, his attentions then turned to the weatherworn stone monolith stood before him. He'd seen the tower so often as a small black nodule on a silhouetted hill at daybreak from the gallops in the valley below. Although time had taken its toll on the ancient lookout point, the main tower was still intact, albeit propped by scaffolding on the south-facing wall.

Danny dipped under the metal safety railing cordoning off the watchtower. He recalled Raynham warning the stable lads not to go there, given the unsafe structure.

Perhaps that's why Dean disappeared up here so often, he thought, *get some peace and quiet.*

Piles of rubble lay around the circular base of the tower. Danny clambered over the debris and stepped into the main chamber of the edifice. Inside, a staircase was cut into the wall, spiralling to a point where the lookout used to be; there were only the remnants of what had been a roof, letting in jagged dim light from the sky above. Bruised clouds were gathering and dark spots began to appear on Danny's fleece. Not wanting to hang around, he cautiously put his weight on the first step, then the second. Steadily, with no railing to assist, he continued to climb the narrow, decaying staircase.

He counted to the ninth step and placing his hand on the tenth, he turned and sat. Just as Dean had suggested in the letter, one of the stones was a lighter shade to the rest, as if it had little place being there. There was a slight gap either side of the brick. He placed his fingers in the gaps and slowly dragged it away from the wall. He had no idea what he'd find, but he knew it must have been precious, enough to die for. He stooped his neck to see into the dark cavity, but to no avail. Cautiously, he spread his fingers, like a spider, and pushed them in. Deeper and deeper they searched. He began to wonder whether this was the right stone, or the right step, or whether Dean had, in fact, sent him on some wild goose chase. And then his doubts vanished. His fingers touched what felt like cold metal. He ran them around the object to gain a firm grip and carefully pulled it from the crevice. The object he'd been led to was slowly revealed. Danny raised it to bask in the natural light from above. He held at arm's length a small oval-shaped box, with silver walls and a lid made of what looked to be enamel, sporting a miniature oil painting of a horseracing scene, printed or painted, it was hard to tell.

Danny's dusty fingertips traced over the lid and then skimmed the smooth, shiny surface of the walls. At first glance, the item he cradled in his palms didn't look all that valuable. He was no antiques expert, but even his untrained eye could see it wasn't worth a fortune. *Perhaps it was merely sentimental value*, he thought, *a family heirloom*. His shoulders sank. But he had yet to look inside.

Perhaps that's where the real value lay, he thought.

The rain began to beat hard as the storm clouds above shed their load. Heavy drops stung the back of his neck. Fleece absorbing the rain, his sharp blue eyes remained fixed on the object in hand. Although, at first glance, nothing in its appearance appeared unusual, it had a certain alluring quality; Danny felt like Gollum holding the precious ring. Half expecting the box to be locked, he applied growing pressure to the lid. Much to his surprise, it glided open with ease. He adjusted his weight and leant forward. Rainwater now dripping from the tip of his nose, he peered into the box. But it was empty, just the sheen of the inner walls and what looked like a base made of ruby. He raised the box close to eye level.

There must be something in there, he thought.

He turned it upside down and started to shake, but nothing fell from within. Disappointed and somewhat perplexed, he flipped the lid shut, pushed the box deep into his fleece's pocket and left the watchtower. He glanced over both shoulders to make sure no one had seen him. After all, he was now the owner of an object that may have led to its previous owner being garrotted.

Hardly a good luck charm, he thought.

He sped back to the comparative safety of his apartment in Cardiff, still wondering whether he'd done the right thing. The rain continued to sheet down as he fumbled for the key to open the communal front door of his tan-bricked apartment block. He shut the door to his flat and quickly changed into dry clothes. He flicked on a night lamp on his bedside table, splashing light over the silver box.

A closer look helped him see the intricately painted racing scene, the unnatural configuration of the horses, with small front and hind legs - in relation to their elongated bodies – stretched out in anatomically impossible fashion, suggesting it was an old picture and, therefore, an old box. He slowly revolved the silver box in his hands. He could make out a small engraving on its side. He traced his fingers over the writing. It read: *by Gainsborough*. Although Danny's knowledge of paintings was sketchy at best, he knew Gainsborough was widely regarded as one of the great masters. His pulse began to race.

Could this be an original, he thought. *If so, should I flog it and would my conscience be clear?* He downed a large whisky for a nightcap before placing the box on the table, leaning back on the bed and flaking out.

His mobile sounded. Awoken from his slumber, he blinked his sleepy eyes open. It was still dark outside and he checked his watch. 2.23 A.M. *It's never good news when someone rings at this hour.* His hand skated over the bedside table from where the sound came. His fingers touched the smooth lid of the box, sparking flashes of the previous day's events. He sat up, now fully awake. He stretched for his mobile. The number was unfamiliar. He glanced again at the box, this time with fear in his eyes. *Should I answer*, he thought, *if it's important, they'll leave a message.*

On the fourth and final ring before the answerphone kicked in, he opened the mobile. A sense of foreboding filled every sinew and fibre of his being.

'Yeah?'

'Hello?' cried the voice of an old lady. 'Hello, is that you?'

'It's Danny, who's this?' Nothing. 'Is that you, Elena?' The silence was broken by a quiet whimpering. *It had to be Elena,* reasoned Danny, *though it sounded more like one of her cats.* 'You okay?'

'Yes . . . yes, of course. I . . . I need to see you.'

'Why?' No reply. 'I'll meet you, course I will. What's wrong?'

'I can't say,' she croaked. 'Meet me . . . please meet me,' she paused, 'at the old mental hospital . . . it's not safe here. And bring Dean's gift with you.'

'Where's that?'

'West of Barnstaple,' she said, 'turn off at Fremington, head for the marshland, it's on your right. And bring it.'

'What? Bring what? Elena?'

'You know.'

'Now?' Danny asked, a sense of urgency fired his voice. But the line was dead. 'Hello? Elena?'

Danny returned the call, but got no answer. *Gonna regret this,* he thought, as he grabbed his coat and flicked a torch found in the hallway chest of drawers; the beam shone bright. He placed the box carefully in the cavity beneath the spare tyre in the boot of his Toyota.

He turned the car's heater and lights on, typed Fremington, Devon into the GPS system and pulled away from the car park. He pressed his iPod on. Coldplay's *Trouble* was playing on repeat. Danny hoped it wasn't an omen of what he'd find at his journey's end.

CHAPTER 7

Within three hours, the in-car navigator had successfully directed Danny to Fremington, beyond Barnstaple, North Devon. Turning off the B3233, he drove the poorly lit, winding road and, as Elena had stated, he soon met, to his right, the overgrown gates fronting thick vegetation.

Not knowing who or what he might find, Danny dipped the headlights and crept forward in first gear. He turned the engine off and softly opened the driver's door. All he could hear was the crackle of rain on tarmac and gusts of wind rustling the trees over this exposed part of headland, above the mudflats of the River Taw to the north.

He checked the time but couldn't see his own arm, let alone those on the watch's face. He flicked the torch on and approached what appeared to be the front gates. Brushing aside the creepers and ivy masking the brass plaque on one of the crumbling pillars, he read: Wordsworth Mental Hospital; a past left to fade away by locals who'd rather forget. He swallowed hard. A sickly taste stung his dry mouth.

Why would she want to meet me here, in an ex-nuthouse?

The dilapidated wrought iron gates were opened invitingly; probably vandalised by teenagers on a dare or drug pushers, seeing if there were any medication left over from when the asylum was full. Danny clasped the torch as he stepped onto hospital grounds. *This don't feel right.*

A long sweeping drive was sheltered completely by the canopies of tall trees either side, like walking through a tunnel. The path widened to the expanse of a courtyard. *Must've been where the doctors and visitors parked,* he guessed.

He swept the torch along the ground. Weeds had surfaced through great cracks in concrete, overgrown in parts. He tracked the curb and was met with the front porch. He climbed the concrete ramp and stood over the windows of what he'd guessed had been the main entrance. He raised the torch through the window frame - the reinforced glass had clearly been taken years ago - but the bright beam was swallowed by the impossibly black foyer. For a beat, he thought about turning and getting as far away as possible. *Must've misheard her*, he thought, *she was distraught*. And then he recalled the fear, desperation in her voice, unlike anything he'd heard before. *What if her life was being threatened? She'd have little chance against the twisted fuck that killed Deano*, he thought. He felt he had no choice but to carry on.

Dripping wet, he pushed the door frame open. A fetid smell of damp and animal faeces pricked his nostrils; a stench that took him straight back to when he played in the backyard of his parent's terraced house as a kid. One of the neighbours used to hoard animals, cats, dogs, even a goat, until the council took them away after complaints were made. Tying a rope to a drainpipe, Danny and Rick used to spend hours skipping. Sucking in the stench that drifted over the neighbour's wall didn't seem to matter at the time, just made it that much more challenging as the ever competitive brothers strived to break the record of successful jumps in a row.

Feet now crunching on broken glass, he crept deeper into what he figured used to be the main reception area. He could hear persistent dripping water from the ceiling somewhere. The torch-beam swept the room like a searchlight. He could see three grilled windows to his right. Ahead, institutional green wallpaper hung loose from the wall. *The rectangular black holes must be corridors leading further into the hospital*, Danny guessed.

He edged forward and shone the torch down one of the corridors. The damp riddled walls and wet floors reflected light down a hall that appeared to have no end. A startled rat scurried across his path. Danny jumped back, losing his footing on the slippery floor. He fell to the ground like a dead weight, letting slip the torch which flickered out. Despite cracking both elbows on the slate floor, he scrambled desperately for the torch, pawing in the dark like a blind man searching for his white stick, until he finally grasped its metal shaft. Above the smack of rain on the flat asphalt roof, like distant applause, Danny could hear what sounded like the clap of footsteps growing louder and louder. *Or was it the trees smacking the outside walls*, he hoped.

53

He stalled switching the torch back on for fear of exposing his position to whoever or whatever was there. The footsteps had stopped. Had he imagined them?

He remained kneeling on the ground, torch held in front of him in the pitch black. Cold, wet and lame.

He braced himself, finger resting on the torch's button. And then he pressed. Confronted by a tall silhouette, he flinched instinctively. *This can't be happening.*

The figure stepped forward into the guttering light of the torch. His cheekbones, grey and chipped, like they'd been sculpted from granite, were partially hid by a scarf wrapped tightly over his mouth. A black panama hat cast a shadow over his eyes and trench coat hid a slender frame.

Danny struggled to his feet and asked the formidable figure, 'Where's Elena?'

From the shadows emerged the broad shape of two heavies carrying torches, flanking the trench coat man. Danny squinted, not sure if he was hallucinating.

'What took you, Daniel?' the lead man said.

'Who are you? What've you done with Elena?'

'Her wellbeing is none of your concern,' the figure said, muffled. The man stepped forward and began to peel the scarf from his face. Standing at about six-foot, the man's sloe eyes looked down on Danny. 'I'm not here to hurt you, if you cooperate.' He spoke well with a Home Counties accent.

'Did ya kill Dean?' Danny asked, failing to disguise the tremor in his broken voice.

'None of us can turn back the clock,' the man replied in a firm, business-like manner.

'Why? What d'ya want?' Danny asked, wagging the torch threateningly, knowing deep down, though, he had no real weapon to defend himself. He thought about fleeing. *But did they have guns?*

'I'm looking for something,' the man said, now just a few yards away, his henchmen stood either side. 'And I think you may have it, or know of its whereabouts.'

'I . . . dunno what ya mean.'

54

'Come on, Daniel, you have to do better than that.'

'Perhaps he's swallowed it,' the man on the left rasped.

'I do hope you haven't, it got terribly messy when that poor lad lied to us.'

The sickly scene of Dean's remains spread across the tack-room flashed through Danny's mind, as vivid as when he first set eyes on the horrific setting. His legs nearly buckled.

'Well, have you?'

'No,' Danny said. 'No way,' he underlined, just in case they hadn't heard.

'Where is it?' the man took another step forward.

'What?' Danny cried. 'I don't know.'

'Dean left it to you, didn't he,' he barked. 'Where is it?'

Can't give in, Danny thought, envisaging Dean mouthing the words: 'Please keep it safe. Promise me.' It would be so easy for him to reveal where he'd hidden the box - under the spare wheel in the boot of his car - but Dean had entrusted it to him and he wouldn't let his dead friend down.

'I've never seen it,' Danny said. He flicked the torch off, scrambled to his feet and sprinted as fast his sore legs could carry him, it felt like he was running through treacle.

'Get him,' boomed from behind Danny, echoing down the maze of corridors leading off the reception. He could hear the henchmen close, their heavy breathing and growls, like a pack of dogs. Suddenly, he felt heavy arms lock around his waist in a rugby tackle. Anchored, he was dragged to the floor in a heap, banging his head with a dull thud on the blanket of broken glass. A sickly groan escaped his lips.

'And that would be your first mistake,' the man said, looking down at the wet floor where Danny lay. He wriggled and writhed to cut loose from the henchman's vice-like grip, but it was pointless; his movements becoming weaker and weaker, like a fish slowly starved of oxygen. He then blacked out.

CHAPTER 8

Danny shook his head, trying to rid himself of the throbbing pain behind his eyes, worse than any hangover he could remember. 'Oh fuckin' hell,' he croaked.

A sickly metallic taste in his mouth told him he'd been cut. As his tongue touched his lower lip, he'd discovered the source of the blood.

Where am I?

He tried desperately to recall the previous night. His blurry eyes scanned the surroundings, as the shower-screen haze began to lift. He lay slumped in a square room with padded walls, though most of the foam had been torn away. Bright daylight flooded into the room from a row of clerestory windows high above. His gaze, now focused, ran along the windows, all shut tight with glass still intact. He'd awoken legs crossed awkwardly and tried moving them, but they felt heavy and numb. For one horrific moment, he thought he was paralysed, only to feel sensation slowly flow back into his limbs as circulation improved. He tried moving his hands from behind his back, but they wouldn't budge. He struggled upright, using the wall as a steadier.

Distant voices could be heard beyond the one and only way out. It was a heavy iron door painted acid green with a metal shutter at eye level. A sinking feeling hit him as he realised where he was and how he'd come to be there. He got to his knees and with an almighty heave, lifted himself to his feet. He felt groggy and started to sway, the room spinning. Staggering, he fell against the far wall adjacent to the door. He paused to recapture his bearings before edging in front of the door, hands still pinned behind his back with what felt like wire.

The keyhole was blocked. He swiftly backed away from the door and considered his next move. He circled the room disturbing the dust, peeling paint and pieces of foam with his feet. Scanning the floor intently, he soon came across a spoon, probably left behind by a junkie who'd cooked up some crack. Normally, Danny wouldn't go near it with bare hands, but the thought didn't even cross his mind. He sat back down and felt for the spoon behind his back. Pushing down on its stem, he started to lever apart the metal ties binding his hands together. With each lurch, the spoon parted the wires ever so slightly. Minutes passed and he felt progress had been made, but needed a moment's rest as he felt the nauseous rumblings return. *Mustn't hurl*, he thought. The sound would have blown his cover in such a tall room with no carpet.

He resumed the repetitive, almost feverish rocking motion, the spoon rammed against the crevice where floor met with wall. 'Come on,' he kept whispering.

The wires that had been cutting into his wrist throughout the night had now slackened sufficiently to prise them away from his red-raw skin. He pulled again and again. Hands released, he looked down fearful of what damage had been done. Although his wrists were sore to the touch, the wires hadn't broken the skin. He pushed his ear to the door, but could hear nothing. *Had they left?* He prayed they'd given up.

Resting his hand on the door handle, he steadily applied pressure downwards. His face grimaced, waiting for a loud clunk that'd give the game away. The handle glided down smoothly and quietly, and the door swung open with only a gentle pull. The door's bolt and lock mechanism had clearly been removed, presumably when the place was stripped bare on closure. Danny poked his head around the door. There was a long corridor with rows of iron doors, similar to the police cells Danny had been detained in during his wayward youth.

At the end of the corridor, a man - shaved head and as broad as he was tall - sat facing away. Danny carefully placed the spoon as a stopper to wedge the door open, took his Doc Martins off and placed one either side of the door. As quietly as he could, like when he returned home plastered from a lad's night out, trying valiantly to clamber into bed whilst not waking Sara, he lifted one foot upon the metal handle on the outside of the door. One last glance toward the guard in the distance and he was ready. Fully focused and centred, he hoisted his weight onto the apex of the handle. He moved quietly, his well honed skills as a cat-burglar coming to the fore. Both hands held the top of the door tightly as he adjusted his weight to gain the best possible angle of ascent. He then lifted his right leg so his foot rested on top of the door and then pushed himself up. He now straddled the top of the door which started to swing close, his Doc Martin pushed aside. He reached out to the wall, preventing the door closing further.

Now the difficult bit, he thought.

He pushed the wall, the door gently swung open until again meeting resistance against the spoon handle on the floor. He grimaced at the clunk of metal on metal. *Had the guard heard?* He wasn't prepared to find out, hoisting himself up to balance on the top of the door, which was now anchored against the metal on the floor. His feet traversed the thick width of the door's top, like a gymnast on the long beam. Feeling his balance go and the spoon begin to dislodge, he leant forward, clawing the wall, arms fully extended towards the sill of the window.

Starting to wobble, he caught the finger-hole of the window latch, and pulled. The window opened inwards. He leapt for the frame of the open window. He yelped from the searing pain of gripping the sharp metal rail lining the window frame. He knew his cover was blown and could hear the guard approach, bellowing for help.

Danny's feet danced in desperation, trying to regain a foothold on the door. With all his strength he started to lift his ten-stone frame. With sweaty palms, he felt his grip starting to loosen. The guard below reached up, but Danny's nimble legs kicked him off. His bare feet finally found some traction against a tear in the padded wall and he soon managed to hoist himself through the slender gap in the window. He looked back, but didn't taunt the man below, face flushed with rage, as he knew he hadn't cleared the hospital's grounds. He looked around, standing on the asphalt roof, level with the clerestory window and just one floor from the ground. He splashed through the puddles and reached the edge. Peering over the guttering, he could see no sign of life, just overgrown lawns and a gravelled path, but he knew that would soon change once the henchman had raised the alarm.

He stepped back and took a running jump, clearing the path and landing with a roll, partially cushioned by the weeds. His days as a jockey taught him how to shape his body to minimize the impact on landing. He stood erect above the tall grass and glanced in all directions, like a meerkat.

Turned out he was trapped in a narrow strip running alongside the main building. To his left, there was fifty yards of long grass beyond which was the driveway he'd walked the night before. To his right was the rear of the building. He didn't know what lay beyond. *Way too risky*, he thought.

He started to hobble towards the front exit. Knowing he was against the clock, he broke into full stride, biting back the pain. If they were to appear now, he would be trapped. He reached the front of the building and, back to the wall, poked his head around to see if the coast was clear; it was. He made a beeline for a gap where the meandering driveway was swallowed by the dense tree-line. Despite pain slicing through his left ankle which had taken the brunt of the fall, he continued to descend the twists and turns of the driveway, still not sure whether his car would still be there.

He heard shouting from behind, but didn't turn. The frantic calls grew louder and a distant engine could be heard revving.

'Shit!' Danny gasped as he swept around the final turn. Seeing the front of his Toyota parked by the gates, his pace quickened. He unzipped a pocket in his khaki trousers where he'd kept his keys and jumped into the car. With one swift movement, he turned the key, shifted into gear and slammed the accelerator pedal. Mud sprayed like fountains as the wheels gripped the rain-sodden earth. He spun the car round and began the descent towards comparative safety of the B-road skirting Fremington.

Glancing in his wing mirror, he just caught sight of a 4x4 passing the rusted gates, until swallowed by the curvature of the road, hedges and barbed wire fences either side. He snaked the wet, meandering country road, expecting to skid off at each blind corner. He afforded another brief glance in his rear-view mirror and could see the roof of what appeared to be a Range Rover some fifty yards behind and closing. 'Fuck off!'

He noticed the road's breadth could barely hold two car widths and knew he would crash if meeting oncoming traffic, or a farmer moving cattle. He pushed those thoughts to the back of his mind, distracted by lights flashing in the rear-view mirror. He glanced up, the Range Rover's headlights repeatedly dazzled whilst veering threateningly just yards off the Toyota's tail bumper.

'Fucking nutters,' Danny shouted. *Should've stayed at the funny farm*, he thought.

He banked another turn, momentum throwing him wide. The wheels touched the muddy verge, sloping to a deep ditch running parallel to the road. A straight stretch lay ahead providing Danny with a moment's relief, broken when the 4X4 pulled out and accelerated alongside, forcing him to race with two wheels on the verge. Danny glanced over, but the windows were blacked out.

They must want me alive, he reasoned, but it didn't appear that way.

The Range Rover started to bully the Toyota, barging its side with a jolting crunch. Danny steered into the threat. Holding his ground, the vehicles came together like dodgems. He knew his car couldn't hold the larger, more powerful off-roader. The Toyota began to edge further and further off the road, towards the ditch. A quick jink left on the wheel, and the vehicles had separated. Although another blind corner fast approached, he knew he had little option but to floor the pedal. The car's two-litre engine roared and found plenty, speeding clear of the pursuing vehicle.

Once a few car lengths ahead and just yards from the sharp turn, he rammed the brakes skidding into the corner and only just holding traction. The manoeuvre cost him momentum, sending the Rover careering into the back of him. That didn't matter to Danny, who'd regained the lead and, more importantly, was still on the road. His eyes widened, as he saw a fork in the road ahead grow larger. 'No!'

Glancing across to his right, he could see the Rover draw level again, its blackened window lowering to reveal a shotgun held by the henchman he'd escaped from. He sported shades, despite a thick brooding cloud cover.

Danny sank in his seat, bracing himself for the shot. With the split in the road now yards away, he yanked the steering wheel sharply to his right, the Toyota crashing into the side of the 4x4, forcing it onto dirt. Danny then spun the wheel to the left, just missing the wooden post on the apex of the split in the road. With the Rover forced right and the Toyota left, Danny was clear.

He whooped in delight as the adrenalin pumped through his veins. He glanced over his right shoulder and could see the Rover's roof above the hedgerow become smaller and smaller, as the roads fanned away from each other.

The distant crack of gunfire could be heard, but Danny knew he was safely out of range and clear of the vermin. The brief feeling of elation was soon replaced by one of anger. *Who was this Elena? And why had she led him into a potentially fatal trap?*

He needed to find out. With his freehand, he fished for his mobile in the passenger compartment and dialled Elena's number. After three rings, the answerphone kicked in: 'This is Elena McCourt, I'm afraid I'm busy at the moment, do please leave a message after the tone.'

Danny wasn't fooled by her polite, frail old-lady routine. 'Elena, if that is your name,' he barked, 'I dunno what the bloody hell you're playing at and what this is all about, but I'm sure as hell not going to let this one lie. I'm coming around, don't you dare move.'

He dropped the phone on the passenger seat and continued the ascent to Fremington before progressing further west along the North Devon coast to Barnstaple. He pulled up outside the now familiar cottage owned by Elena. *If she really was who she claimed to be.*

He rushed to the white front door and knocked firmly. The door rocked on its hinges and there was no response. Slowly, he pushed it open. The hallway was empty and its contents were undisturbed, handstand and pine dresser left untouched.

'Elena?' Silence. 'Elena?' Danny edged deeper into the hallway and, turning the corner to the living room, he felt his legs give way. He saw the old lady who he'd met the day before, sat slumped in the seat, her white blouse and knee-length tweed skirt saturated with blood. Her chin rested on her chest and a thin red line circled the loose skin around her neck.

'Oh Christ no,' Danny cried and started punching 999, but then thought better of it. *Nothing they could do*, he reasoned.

He searched the room. No signs of a struggle and the fire still smouldered. The ghostly quiet and eerie stillness of the scene were broken by a deafening shrill from beneath the kitchen table. A black cat shot across his path, making him jump. *Perhaps it would bring a change in luck*, he thought, though he didn't believe in old wives' tales.

He crouched down and peered beneath the dining room table where it had taken cover. The black cat sat perfectly still, staring unflinchingly. The feline's piercing green eyes fixed firmly on Danny. His every move covered. Danny slowly stepped towards him, but was warned back by a long, menacing hiss, suggesting the petrified cat had just witnessed the attack on his defenceless owner.

He glanced around, desperately searching for a clue as to why she could be murdered in cold blood; the likely suspects now after his. Painfully aware that this was now a murder scene, he tugged his jacket sleeve over his hand and carefully slid open one of the top drawers in the Welsh dresser dominating the wall opposing the fireplace. Within, Danny sifted through the hoarded knick-knacks. He carefully opened a phonebook, decorated with a floral pattern. He flicked through the pages, but only the first had been written on. Dean's number was there, among others, but the one that caught Danny's furtive eyes was written in bold red ink at the bottom. Neither a name nor initials to its side, but the sentence *Father of the sun!*

Danny's eyebrows arched. He made a mental note and slowly closed the book and drawer. A firm knock sounded at the front door. Danny turned sharply. He held his breath and slowly backed away, retreating out of view from the front bay window. He knew the front door was open. *Would they enter?*

He couldn't take the risk and scanned the room, *need some cover*. He thought about joining the cat, but then caught sight of a small, painted door beneath the stairs, possibly an alcove. The imminent danger was brought home when a shadowy uniformed figure approach the net-curtains draped over the rear window, pushing his face to the glass, hand acting as a visor. *The police!*

He froze, back to the wall, knowing any shadowy movement could be seen through the lace drapes. He heard the front door creak open; trapped both ways. He quickly unlatched the alcove door and forced his way in, body pressed tight against a cache of household items. Crouching as still as he could, with the handle of the vacuum cleaner digging into his back and the leg of the ironing board intertwined with his own. *They're never gonna leave once they see her.* Indeed, Danny reckoned the room was minutes from being flooded by police and forensics.

Danny drew breath and flung the door open. He turned and made for the hallway. A policeman blocked his way. Momentum helped him barge past the officer, forcing him to the ground. Without daring to look back, he jumped the garden gate and with key in hand, remotely unlocked the Toyota. He leapt in and slammed the lock down from the inside. The officer, who'd been swept aside in the hallway, thumped the window, shouting. Danny prodded the key into the ignition and fired the engine. The officer stood back, flicked the telescopic truncheon and smashed the driver's side window, showering Danny with shards of glass. Danny slammed the accelerator pedal and skidded away. Glancing over his shoulder, he could see the officer mouth something into a radio attached to the breast of his navy jumper.

'Oh this just gets better and better,' he shouted, wondering how on earth he could explain himself out of this one. He left the country roads as soon as possible, fully aware of the heavy police presence already on their way from Barnstaple. He joined the main A-road en route to the M5, glancing up suspiciously at the countless cameras looking down like Big Brother on the motorway, *monitoring every move.*

The motorway was no place to be with a smashed window attracting unwanted attention. He flicked his mobile open and, from within his wallet, he unfolded the number Stony had scribbled on a betting slip two days previously.

'Answer, fucking answer,' Danny whispered, still shaken.

'Hello?' a faint male voice answered.

'Is this Mick?' Silence. 'Don't hang up,' Danny continued, above the roar of the engine. 'It's Danny Rawlings. I'm a good friend of Stony. Nigel Watts.'

'What you want?' came down the line, stronger this time.

'Stony said that I could stay at your place, payment for a favour.' Danny clenched his teeth waiting for an answer that didn't come. 'You still there?'

'Yeah,' Mick replied, again distantly. 'What's this about?'

'Nothing,' Danny replied. 'Just need somewhere to stay, where can I find you?'

'What you called?'

'Danny.'

'This ain't nothing dodgy, cos I'm on a suspended sentence, know what I mean.'

'Nothing dodgy,' Danny confirmed.

Danny arrived and removed the box from beneath the spare wheel cavity. Parking a flash sports car in a rundown estate outside Bristol where most vehicles were jacked up on bricks or burnt-out shells left by vandals would normally be asking for trouble, particularly as the open invitation of a smashed window would save them half the bother. But Danny didn't care. If anything, he wanted rid. After all, the police knew his number plate, had no doubt run it through some database and would now be on high alert. Given what he'd been through to keep the box safe, there was no way he was letting it out of his sight now. He knocked on the front door of a stone-clad semi with bay windows, one of which had been boarded. He was let in by a short, squat man, who grunted, 'Mick.'

Mick glanced down the street both ways, as if he were the one running from the law. Danny began to wonder if a simple B&B would have been a better idea. Mick's face bore several days growth and was slightly pitted. He reeked of fags. His pot belly strained the weave of his stained vest, and garish Bermuda shorts clashed with the drab surroundings.

'You're not staying long,' Mick said. Danny shook his head, though it was clearly more a statement than question.

'I'm off out.'

'In those,' Danny pointed. Big mistake.

Mick approached, humming with the stale odour of beer, smoke and sweat. 'You do wanna stay here, right?'

'Sorry, mate,' Danny said, showing his palm. 'Just been a bad day, that's all.'

'There's no electricity or gas,' Mick said. 'Got cut off last week. Bastards.'

'Don't matter,' Danny said.

'And there's a takeaway round the corner, Chinese. Your treat tonight, yeah?' Mick asked, tugging his denim jacket from the banister. He moved in close. His intense, beady eyes narrowed. 'Here,' he said, as if about to share a secret. 'You ain't a druggie.'

'Don't look that bad, do I?' Danny smiled. Mick continued to stare. 'No,' Danny said, not wanting to offend his host before he'd had chance to sit and rest his aching feet.

'Shame,' Mick said. 'Be back about three. If the social call, I'm looking for work.'

The door slammed shut.

For a moment, Danny stood in the middle of the cold hallway, pondering his next move. Even for someone who made his living from predicting future events, he couldn't have foreseen the mess he was in right at that sobering moment.

He thought briefly about turning himself in, but the police wouldn't even listen to him. He needed to talk to someone, a person he could trust. His brother, Rick, was his only chance. He pushed memory button three and prayed Rick hadn't changed his phone since the last time they'd spoken, last Christmas.

'Hello?'

'Rick, it's Danny.'

'Danny, what the hell is going on. Police just called, asking if I'd seen you, they'd tried your flat.'

'And what did you say?'

'I said no. Well, I hadn't, had I.'

'I need to meet you.'

'For fuck sakes, Danny, you promised mum to keep your fingers clean. What on earth have you done?'

'Nothing! I've done nothing.' Danny paused, overcome by the situation. 'I need to meet, you're my only hope.'

There was a painful silence. 'Where?'

'On the track at Sandown this afternoon. I need to watch a horse that's been working well.'

'Still married to the job.'

'Please, Rick.'

'I'm working.'

'Take a day off,' Danny said. Rick was in the antiques trade, and was quite a shrewd dealer by all accounts. On leaving school at sixteen, Rick had worked for a time as an auctioneer's assistant.

After a particularly fruitful week for the betting syndicate two years ago, Danny used his bonus to gift Rick the set-up funds to go it alone. Rick worked the auctions in the South East and reaped the rewards, specialising in antique furniture. Danny knew full well his brother could pull a sickie at the drop of a hat. 'It's vital I see you.'

'Why the track? It's risky.'

'Like I said, there's a good thing running, need to check the ground conditions first hand and see the filly in the flesh, parading. She's tended to sweat up in the prelims as a youngster, I need to be sure. Anyway, racetrack's busy. We'll be lost in the crowd. And bring some spare shoes.'

'Why?'

'It's a long story.' Having borrowed football boots for a preseason jockeys' charity match in his riding days, Danny was fully aware that they shared the same size and, with his DMs left at the hospital, this was a good opportunity to avoid a potentially conspicuous visit to the shops.

66

Danny knew he was now prime suspect and time was running out, but there was a chance Rick would know the true value of the box and, more importantly, who would be after it.

CHAPTER 9

The spring sunshine blinded Danny as he left the council house for his car. Much to his surprise, it was still there.

He drove as near as he could to the town centre and parked in a shady, quiet backstreet. He walked the rest, shades and fleece hood helping to conceal his face.

He caught a train from Bristol and, once arriving, joined the flurry of race-goers funnelling out of the small Esher train station. Most were from London out on a day at the races. He met Rick outside the gates. The lean thirty-three-year-old ran his free hand over his thick hair before forcing a copy of *The Times* he'd pretended to read beneath his arm and casting a scornful eye towards his younger brother. Rick dropped a pair of leather shoes he'd been carrying in a bag onto the tarmac and, without a word, Danny slipped them on. The pair bought tickets for the grandstand enclosure and joined the growing crowd mingling between the paddock area and the shelter of the main stand.

The Cranbourne Classic Trial was the feature on the seven-race card. Danny had one lined up for the race. He'd forewarned Gash nearly a month ago that Sally's Gal had wintered well and connections were laying her out for this race. Subsequent spins on the gallops had done nothing to temper his enthusiasm for the three-year-old filly's chance in this influential prep race. Whilst queuing for drinks at the bustling Bendigo bar on the first floor of the grandstand, Danny, who still had his hood up, sent a text to Gash. It read: 'Sally's Gal 3.40 Sand, max. bet 12000, min. price 5/2. Wipe once read.'

Although his appetite for the game had waned since Dean's discovery, he was a creature of habit and needed to inform Gash, even if it put his own freedom on the line. He knew it was important to keep his job secure, it was the one constant keeping him sane.

The pair found a small table free, discreetly positioned away in one corner. Danny bought two pints of lager and then wasted little time cutting to the chase. From within his pocket, he

68

handed Rick the box under the table. Without looking, Rick asked, 'What's this?'

'It was left to me by a friend, Dean McCourt,' Danny said. 'He was murdered, it was on the news.'

Rick nodded. 'They think you did it?'

'I dunno,' Danny said defensively. 'I reckon so. But I didn't, you must realise that. I'd nothing to do with it. Nothing whatsoever.'

'Is it worth anything?' Rick asked.

'That's what I need to know. What the hell it's worth for people to die?'

Rick closely examined the oval box.

'It's got by Gainsborough engraved on the side, could it be an original?'

Rick gave a hollow laugh. 'You really don't know much about art. Gainsborough didn't do miniatures.'

Danny wasn't laughing. 'No chance it's a small copy of an original then?'

'Doubt it very much. He did paint scenes of horses, but this one doesn't ring any bells, it's not his style.'

'Who painted it then?' Danny asked.

'Just looks like a generic racing scene in the eighteenth century or early nineteenth, you'd know more about that than me.'

'So it's old,' Danny asked.

Rick casually pulled a small eye-glass from his pocket, as if it were a regular thing to do. 'I didn't say that.' He continued to examine the object, face pressed close to its silver walls. 'There's a date letter. It was made-' Rick looked up, eye-glass still held tight in his right eye. 'Early nineteenth century, 1810-ish. The maker's mark, GH, I'm not sure about.'

'GH you say,' Danny said, his mind already rewound to the news report two days previously. The same initials had stained the tack-room wall. *So it wasn't the killer's signature*, Danny thought, *but why write the letters in blood at the murder scene?* Perhaps it was to warn the box's new owner that they were closing the net and willing to kill. *They knew the chilling sight would attract media coverage like flies to shit.*

Rick raised the object. His burnished brown hair swept back away from his face. 'And you say people have died for this?' Rick sighed as if he was about to say something he'd regret. 'My old boss may know. He's given up the auctioneering game, but has an antiques shop just outside Guildford. Deals in this sort of thing, small items like trinkets and silverware. I've got his number.' He pulled an electronic personal organiser from his leather jacket and dictated the contact number to Danny, who scribbled it down on a stray betting slip.

Rick pushed the organizer deep into his jacket pocket. 'If you've done nothing wrong, just give yourself up.'

Danny gulped down the rest of his pint. 'Another?'

'You'll be over the limit.'

'I think my car will be gone. In any case, it's marked by the police, too dangerous for me to go back there. Taxis and buses for me now on, I guess.'

'You can't live like this, Danny. I know you're a stubborn sod, but come on, just go to the police and sort this out.'

Danny leant over the table, casting a shadow across his brother. 'I don't need this brotherly lecture. I'm not handing myself in, it's too late for that.' A few drinkers nearby looked over. Danny's voice lowered. 'I was found at the scene of two murders, fingerprints probably everywhere and I've got form. Banged to rights in my eyes, let alone theirs.'

'So what'll you do?'

'Whoever's after this,' Danny rested his hand on the box, 'were willing to kill for it and while I'm still a free man, I'm gonna track 'em down and clear my name. Couldn't do that banged up waiting for a court date.'

'Wouldn't you get bail?' Rick asked.

'Not with previous form,' Danny said. 'They won't give me another chance, no way.'

Danny headed for the bar and the brothers sank another pint each, like old times. Although the alcohol had kicked in by the post-time of the feature race, Danny's steely professionalism took over. He'd clocked the times recorded in the first four races and surmised, with the help of the track's standard times, the ground was on the soft side of good. *Yesterday's scattered showers had clearly gotten into the track.*

Sally's Gal had won with a bit of cut in the ground on her debut at Ripon and, with strong stamina influences in the female bloodlines of her pedigree, Danny knew the stiff configuration of the track wouldn't be a problem. The spring breeze cooled his face flushed by drink and cleared his mind as he strode to a quiet spot just around from the Tote screens. He checked his phone. Gash had returned the text and also left a message on his answerphone: 'Danny, the police called an hour ago.' The message was quiet, so Danny pressed the phone hard against his ear. 'Scared the shit outta me. Call them and sort this out. You're innocent 'til proven guilty.'

Another pearl of wisdom, Danny thought wryly, though he knew he had few options. He returned the call.

'Hello?'

'Gash, I'll make this short, everything's fine for Sally's Gal. What's the best price you've got?'

'A shade under 3s'

'Mop it up with twenty big ones.'

'You're having a laugh.'

'I'm serious.'

'You thinking straight?'

'Trust me, Gash. Have I ever let you down?'

There was a pause. Gash replied, 'Job done.'

'They're going behind the stalls,' echoed the course commentator's voice over the sound system, sparking a palpable buzz of anticipation from the sizable crowd.

Danny hung up.

'There he is,' a man's voice shouted.

Danny's heart missed a beat as he ducked instinctively. He quickly pulled his hood up and glanced furtively over his shoulder and, much to his relief, from where he'd heard the booming call, he saw a group of half-cut lads stagger about and play fight. Paranoia had struck and Danny didn't like the feel of it.

He climbed the concrete steps, head bowed to avoid eye contact with the other race-goers, and joined up with Rick near

71

the back of the tiered viewing gallery of the grandstand. The horses loaded swiftly and the commentator said, 'They're away to a fairly level break'. To which, the well-wrapped crowd cheered. The ten-furlong start at Sandown couldn't be seen well from the main grandstand, onlookers mostly relying on the commentator for the early skirmishes. The nine-strong field were still tightly packed cornering into the straight.

The commentator continued, 'The Good Lord still holds a fractional lead, pressed strongly by the favourite Danepower, Sally's Gal third and comes under pressure with no immediate response.'

Danny could see his filly was in trouble, clearly not primed for her return. He immediately blamed himself for making a stupid error of judgement – basing his selection on impressive homework over a month ago. *A week is a long time in racing.*

Perhaps she'll rally, he hoped. But she didn't, fading into a tired fifth.

Danny sunk his face into his hands, as a cocktail of emotions coursed through his veins. He rarely felt any emotional reaction to the outcome of an individual race. But this time a peculiar sensation - one of disappointment and guilt – overcame him.

It wasn't the fact that Sally's Gal got beaten that riled him – every pro gambler had to take losing on the chin, it was part and parcel of the job - but it was more his lack of preparation in assessing her chances thoroughly.

Deep down, he felt his judgement may have been clouded by his current troubles off track. Such an inexperienced filly wouldn't normally merit a five-figure bet, particularly given the lack of race-fitness on her seasonal return.

'I shouldn't have done it,' he said. A film glazed his flat, saddened eyes.

Rick's cheeks suddenly drained of blood, like a chameleon, as he feared an admission of guilt was on its way. 'Is there something you haven't told me?'

Danny turned to his brother and said, 'No.'

'Don't do anything stupid,' Rick said, holding Danny's forearm with a vice-like grip, like he did when he was small. 'Mum couldn't take it.'

Danny nodded, though he didn't know what was stupid anymore. 'I'll ring her.'

'I don't think that's wise, not right now,' Rick said. 'Police might be tapping her phone.'

Danny looked up in frustration, swallowing back the tears, 'Tell her I'm fine and well. Send her my love, will you.'

The pair left the track before the final race was run, avoiding the inevitable crush of the crowd spilling from the popular track. They stopped in a rough town pub called The Antelope, full of aging men with a décor to match. A glimpse of a forgotten time, dusty shafts of light filtered through the frosted glass windows, and the stale smell of smoke and beer hung heavy in the air. It was a place where Danny felt he could blend in at this present time. Danny placed his pint on a damp, torn beer mat and sighed.

'You'll be alright?' Rick asked, forcing a bundle of notes in Danny's hand under the table.

'I can't take this,' Danny said, handing the money back. 'I'll be fine, results have been kind to me recently, my account's looking healthy.'

'You plank, they might've frozen it,' Rick said, pushing the wad into Danny's jacket pocket. 'You'll need this for food and somewhere to stay.'

'I won't call you, but that doesn't mean I'm in trouble . . . any more trouble, I mean,' Danny said. 'Just lying low until I can sort myself out.'

'Won't you think again,' Rick pleaded. 'The police will look into all angles. Just tell them the truth, exactly what happened. They'll find the right man in the end. The longer you stay on the run, the worse it'll look.'

'It already looks bad,' Danny said.

An old man, who was slouched at the bar reading a tabloid, looked daggers at Danny. *Had the newspaper printed a mug shot?*

73

Time to leave, Danny thought.

He stood and rested a hand on his brother's shoulder. He scanned the dimly-lit pub before saying, 'I've gotta go and cheers for these.' Danny glanced down at his shoes.

'Call me.'

'I will and Rick, thanks again,' Danny said.

'Gotta look after my kid brother.'

Danny left the pub, pushing the swing doors into the cool dusk air of an Esher side street, the alcohol warming him while he got his bearings. Off to his right, he could see the busy high street, the silhouetted shoppers scurrying in the distance. He felt sure his Toyota, with its smashed driver's window, would be long gone and even if it was there, it would either be clamped or set as a police trap. He thought it best to scour the backstreets for a hotel or B&B; give him some precious time and space to plan his next move.

As it grew visibly darker by the minute, he knew it was imperative that he found someplace soon. As he walked the meandering streets, he noted an antiques shop. Above, the sign read: Cartwright's Antique Emporium; its windows crammed with ornaments, plates and small pieces of furniture. He felt the reassuring bulge of the box still safely concealed within his fleece pocket and made a mental note of the shop's location.

After a good hour, he stumbled across a small privately run hotel set back from the road in a secluded spot. Trying to hide the nerves within, he paid for a single room. It was a cosy place, peach wallpaper and red plush carpet. With Rick's words of caution still ringing in his ears, he kept his debit and credit cards in his pocket and ate into the £300 his brother had lent him earlier in the day. The hotel's receptionist was a pleasant man sporting a blue cardigan and a wide grin. He was handed the keys to room 12 from a rack with 23 hooks.

'Do you have a safe?' Danny asked, fearing the killers would track him down during the night.

'Yes, of course we do, sir.' The receptionist smiled obligingly and, with sticky palms, Danny slid the box into a Jiffy bag and grudgingly handed it over to the porter. After all he'd been through to honour Dean's dying wish, he felt a strange connection with the inanimate object.

'It'll be safe, right?' Danny said, like a concerned parent looking after the welfare of a child.

'Of course.'

Once safely locked in his room on the second floor, he slumped on the single bed, cheeks burning and mind racing. His clothes stank of sweat and smoke, but he lacked the energy to shower and freshen up.

Sort myself out tomorrow, he thought.

Within minutes, the alcohol had helped him drift off to sleep.

CHAPTER 10

After a restless night, Danny awoke rubbing his bloodshot eyes and sore head. For a brief moment, he'd forgotten where he was and how he'd got there. As reality struck home, a sickly feeling turned the pit of his stomach. He showered and changed into the same clothes. He glanced at his watch. 9.20 A.M. Not bearing to be parted from the box a minute longer, he ventured down to reception and retrieved it from the hotel's safe. Returning to his empty room, he held it beneath the harsh artificial glare of the bedside lamp. *Time to get this baby valued*, he thought.

Skipping breakfast, he walked the long drive leading to the main road cutting through Esher. The area looked different to him in daylight. Heavy clouds threatened rain as Danny retraced his steps. Two lefts and then a right, directions he repeated over and over. *Couldn't dare ask for help*, he feared. And there it was.

As Danny pushed the door, a bell rang. An eager shop assistant appeared from a backroom, like one of Pavlov's dogs, almost salivating at the chance of a sale. He was tall and lanky. His shirt draped loosely over his wiry frame like a smock. He walked with a pronounced limp, aided by a brass rimmed stick. *Mid-forties would be generous,* Danny guessed.

A strong scent of beeswax fused with a hint of cigar smoke in the musty air. The man bowed his head, allowing his reading glasses to slide down the bridge of his prominent nose. His enquiring eyes looked Danny up and down. 'Can I help you?'

Danny coaxed the prized possession from his pocket. It was the reason why he was in this mess and, as a consequence, he felt anxious about knowing its value. *Had it been worth it?*

Hung from his neck, the man raised a pair of spectacles with a magnifying glass attached and slowly turned the object in his saucer-like hands, like a pig on a spit. 'It's silver, 1810, George III. Most probably a skippet box.'

'A skippet box?' Danny asked.

'It was used for keeping seals for letters and documents back in the day.' Danny nodded. 'I think it's a Chester maker's mark, GH, Giles Hamner. Excuse me for one moment, will you?' The man disappeared through a curtain to a backroom before returning. 'Sorry about that,' he continued, 'where was I? Yes, they used them for keeping documents or seals safe back then.'

'But what's it worth?'

The man frowned at Danny's abruptness, but his attentions soon return to the box in hand. 'Nice decorative item . . . I would be prepared to pay, no more than £800 for such a piece.'

'You sure?' Danny's shoulders dropped. 'Totally sure.'

'Perfectly,' the man replied curtly, seemingly insulted. His hazel eyes fixed intently on Danny. 'I hope you don't mind, but I've returned a call to a gentleman that left a message expressing a strong interest in such an item just last night.'

Danny leant forward and prised the silverware from the man's clutches, 'Did he leave a name?'

'No,' the man said, taken aback.

'Sorry,' Danny said. 'But you should've warned me.'

'Why? He sounded perfectly harmless and seemed genuine enough. I'll tell you what I'll do, I'll make you a very generous offer to you of £1000.' His lips stretched to a smug smile, as if waiting for Danny to jump at the increased offer.

'No chance,' Danny snapped. 'I've been through too much to let this go for a grand. And you haven't seen me. Tell 'em you were mistaken. Don't have anything to do with 'em, they're trouble.'

'I don't understand.'

'Believe me, you will,' Danny replied. 'I need their number.'

'And miss out on my cut.'

'Number?'

The shopkeeper said, 'No. What's in it for me?'

'Then you give me no choice.' Danny said and then brushed his way passed the man and the curtain.

'What the hell do you think you're doing?' the man cried. 'I'd kindly ask you to leave or I'll call the police.'

The phone was on a desk in a room packed with a cache of stored antiquities. 'I'm sorry, but this is a matter of life and death,' Danny called back. He keyed in 1471, but the last caller had blocked the number. 'Shit.' He returned to the front of the shop. The shopkeeper waved his walking stick threateningly, its brass point sliced through the still air. 'Don't you dare come any closer,' he cried, his free hand visibly shaking. 'I've called the police.'

'I'm not gonna-' Danny said. 'I'll leave the back way. I'd lock up. If you're scared by me, there's worse to come.'

The man didn't respond. He just held his ground.

Danny pushed the skippet box back into his fleece pocket and strode down the corridor to the rear of the shop building. He unlatched the wooden door and stepped out on to a rear yard. He rattled the gate set into the far wall, but it was padlocked shut. The weathered red bricks were chipped in places, leaving Danny with a foothold. With what little grip he'd gained with the caps of his leather shoes borrowed from Rick the day before, he hoisted his weight up and desperately scrambled over, falling in a heap on the cobbled backstreet to the other side.

He picked himself up, brushed himself down and sprinted to an opening some forty yards to his left. The back alley spilled onto the busy main road. Despite the greater chance of being spotted, Danny felt safer out in the open. *They wouldn't dare pounce in broad daylight with people around*, he reasoned.

He paced back to the hotel, mouth dry. Most of the residents had eaten breakfast and left the building by the time Danny arrived back. He went straight to his room on the second floor. He slowly turned the key and opened the door, enough to poke his head around, fearful that a hotel worker or guest had shopped him to the police, or even worse, the enemy after the box had tracked him down. His fears were unfounded - the room was as quiet as he'd left it under an hour ago. He grabbed a handful of soap sachets and fruit from a glass bowl next to the TV. *What now?*

Sat hunched on the corner on his unmade bed, head in hands, he sifted through the mental list of people he could turn to.

Those he could trust and those that the police weren't aware knew him. *Sara Monk!*

Even thinking the name lifted Danny's waning spirits. He'd split with his ex on relatively good terms and he'd left her number on his mobile, just in case. They'd made an agreement that if neither had married by the wrong side of forty, they would settle for each other. How romantic, she would say, but it was the biggest commitment Danny was prepared to make at the time.

CHAPTER 11

Hood pulled up, Danny rode a train and then a bus close to the address that Sara had, after some persuading, told him earlier the same day. She hadn't appeared glad to hear Danny's voice, so there was a chance she'd given him the wrong address; or was paranoia taking over? Danny checked the address he'd scribbled down, Denver Road, Ilford, Essex.

From the bus stop, he walked the rest of the journey. It was 4.20 P.M. by the time he'd arrived at his destination. He stood and looked up at the yellow-bricked three-storey block of flats. He couldn't help notice a prying flick of the curtains of one on the ground floor as he pushed the buzzer for her flat. Moments later, the door swung open. Sara wore a black t-shirt, draped over denims, and a scowl on her face. Without a word spoken, she ushered Danny into the building.

'I can't stay long, got to pick up the kids.' Danny eyes widened. 'Don't worry, they're not yours. My sister's had another baby boy with John, you remember him.'

Danny nodded. He thought the less said the better. Like when he was a kid watching TV with his parents, the best way to stay up past bedtime was to sit still and keep quiet. After all, he needed a safe haven and this was perfect.

'You've put me in an impossible situation, Danny. I saw Crimewatch last night.'

'Oh fuck, I wasn't –'

Sara forced a smile.

'Don't do that,' Danny sighed, holding his chest.

'It's not far from the truth, your picture's been in the papers, wanted for questioning over two murders, do not approach him,' Sara replied, the smile now gone.

'Don't worry, the police won't be round,' Danny assured. 'No one's going to mention your name; you're a very old flame.' The scowl returned. 'Not very old, just old. Sorry.'

'Stop digging and tell me what you want.'

'Need a place to stay for the night. And your name was the first that came into my head. I'll pay.'

'You mean I'll pay. Harbouring a suspected murderer, that's serious stuff.'

'I'm no murderer,' Danny said. 'And I need to be on the outside to prove it.'

Sara gave an enquiring stare that drilled into Danny's tired eyes, as if trying to seek out the truth and whether he was telling it. 'One night, that's all. I want you gone in the morning and I don't want to see your face for a long time.'

Danny took his weight off aching feet and his leaden eyelids began to droop.

Sara settled with a tray on her lap holding a pasta dish and a large glass of red wine. She took the remote resting on the arm of the chair and flicked the TV off; an annoying habit that harked back to the days they were together. Danny opened his mouth to protest, but quickly realised the different circumstances; he wasn't about to rock the boat.

'Why do they suspect you?'

'Easier to say why they don't,' Danny muttered. 'Got previous form, I knew Dean, the young lad that was killed, and I was one of the first to discover the body. A sheet of paper found on Dean at the scene had my fingerprints on and he left me a letter saying I should look after this.' Danny produced the skippet box and placed it carefully on the coffee table. 'He told me, in the letter, to guard it with my life. To make matters worse-' he stopped himself, 'it's a long story, let's just say, I was in the wrong place at the wrong time.'

'What was on it?'

'What?'

'The paper found on Dean.'

'Initials and numbers, handwritten by Dean.'

'Perhaps Dean wasn't killed for the box. Perhaps Dean said that in the letter to steer you off the real problem, like a smokescreen. Was he in any trouble?'

'Not that I know of. He'd been quiet, withdrawn, last two times I saw him, but he'd often be like that. He struggled to do the hours see, while keeping his weight down for the riding. Up at six, no breakfast and next to no lunch for sod all pay. Enough to get the best of us down.'

'Can you remember exactly what was written on this sheet found on the lad?'

Danny had little trouble recalling the list of letters and numbers, partially soiled by spattered blood. 'Have you got a pen and paper?'

Sara swallowed a mouthful of pasta. 'In the drawer over there, the top one.'

'Thanks,' Danny said, uncurling himself from the sofa. He crossed the laminate floor of the living room and opened the drawer. On seeing an old photo of the pair of them together on holiday in Cyprus, he momentarily stopped rummaging and, pretending he hadn't come across it, continued to delve deeper until finding the notepad. 'Got it.'

He sat back down and started copying the letters and times onto the sheet as he'd remembered them. He'd found another use for his photographic memory, other than his daily form analysis.

FH 220 L 26/2, DB 330 N 4/3, L 120 H 3/2 . . .

Can't see a connection or sequence, he thought.

But when he skated over the series of figures again, their significance soon became transparent. He felt for his mobile, and went online to the *Racing Post* results database. Firstly, he checked the abc – a list of runners on a particular day – for February 26. Scrolling down the pop-up window, he stopped at those horses whose name began with F. The two that stood out were Frosty Heath and Firebird Horizon. The former was an unraced three-year-old trained by John Sampson. The latter was more familiar, it was a mare he'd watched many a time on the Raynham gallops. He clicked on her form and could see she'd trailed home a one-paced fifth in a claiming race - one which the runners can be bought for a set amount in the ring after the contest is run - at 2.20 on the Leicester card.

Nothing too out of the ordinary there, Danny thought. But when he looked at the betting patterns for the race, he could see Firebird Horizon had drifted alarmingly in the market during the final minutes before the 'off'. Having routed the opposition by three lengths the previous week, the bookies had priced the mare up as 2/1 on the opening show, but she was allowed to start at over double those odds at 9/2.

Sifting through the cuttings library within the website, housing all articles written for the newspaper in recent years, Firebird Horizon came up with 12 matches. Within the one dated February 27, Danny found the mare was listed as one of three referred to Portman Square, the headquarters of the Jockey Club, in central London. An excerpt of the article was of particular interest to Danny, it read: 'Given the suspicious betting patterns and the apparent underperformance of the mare Firebird Horizon, the stipendiary steward at Leicester has referred the case under Rule 151 concerning non-triers to the Jockey Club and has ordered a routine dope test.'

Had Dean been involved in an illegal betting ring or scam?

Danny clicked on a more recent article, hoping to find the result of the dope test. There were none relating to the topic. Therefore, Danny assumed it came back negative and no further action was taken. *Only bad news sells newspapers.*

He moved on to the next initial on the paper. Double Breaker matched the third on the list DB and had alarming similarities with Firebird Horizon, who was also trained in the Upper Lambourn area, having been weak in the market for a Newmarket maiden on the date shown on the sheet and duly struggled home in a remote sixth.

Had these runners been got at?

There was something highly suspicious about the betting patterns together with the underperformance of these runners and it looked as though Dean was connected with both. *Was he doping them?* His furtive eyes returned to the runners on the list; this time noting the tracks each horse had run at, along with the other main features of their form, the trainers, owners and jockeys booked.

After noting the connections of each horse in question, a sudden realisation hit home, they were all under the same ownership – Definca Partnership. Was this a company, or a syndicate? Danny had to find out; it was too much of a coincidence that every horse, without exception, was owned by them. Most trained by Raynham and ridden by retained stable jockey Sam Johnson. There appeared to be growing evidence that Dean had become embroiled in an illegal betting ring that had gone wrong, horribly wrong.

Danny disconnected his mobile from the internet. He knew the most likely person to know the truth and he quickly punched their number.

'Come on Michael,' Danny whispered, 'answer.' He let the line ring several times, but to no avail. *Was Raynham's line still being tapped?*

Michael was Danny's only hope of unravelling the connection between Dean and this mysterious owner. This time he punched the number of Raynham's mobile.

'Hello, this is Michael Raynham-'

'Michael, it's me, Danny.'

'-I can't make it to the phone right now, but if you'd like to leave a message, please do so after the tone.'

Leave a message or not. He had a split-second to decide. *What've I got to lose?* 'Michael. It's Danny Rawlings. I need to ask you about one of your owners. It's urgent. As soon as you get this, call me.'

Danny paused before hanging up for fear of the call being traced somehow. *Was it a trap? Would Raynham shop him?*

Danny's fresh face winced, revealing the worry lines of an old man. He sighed, 'What now?'

He continued along the list of eight horses he could recall on the sheet. Six of them were ridden by Sam Johnson. Perhaps he knew what was going on. Was he being ordered to throw the races by tactically riding with restraint? He looked closer at the riding of horses on the corresponding dates and compared them to how they'd been ridden on previous sightings. The race comments were written by professional analysts to assist punters and were generally viewed as consistent and reliable.

Firebird Horizon had tended to hold a midfield position with a view to conjuring a strong finish and that appeared to be the plan on February 26. Except on that day, her customary late surge never materialised. It was the same for Double Breaker, who'd tended to race prominently in his three previous races and duly took front rank throughout before finding precious little at the business end of the race on the date in question. From what Danny could see, the finger of suspicion didn't point towards Johnson - a well respected jockey whose form had suffered along with the Raynham yard he was retained by. Recent years had seen Johnson spread his wings and get rides from outside yards. Perhaps his loyalty to Raynham and the owners connected with the yard had waned. He was still worth giving a bell.

Raynham's Christmas bash was the last time Danny had spoken to Johnson. His number was in his diary, but that was back at his flat in Cardiff, a definite no-go area now the police were involved.

He knew the only way to meet Johnson was to track him down. By now Sara had returned from the kitchen with a bowl full of Black Forest Gateau topped with cream. 'I'm sorry, did you want some?' she asked, knowing full well Danny hated desserts of any description.

'Don't mind me,' Danny said. Recent events had left a bitter taste in his mouth and, although his stomach groaned to be filled, it was an empty, uncomfortable kind of hunger that left him off his food. 'Do you still bother with an evening paper?'

'On the kitchen table,' she said. 'Don't know why, nothing but adverts and murders.'

Danny sighed, 'Please don't mention the m-word.' He stood and left the room. The *Ilford Gazette* was left open on a pine table in the kitchen. Danny briefly glanced out of the netted windows. It was now black outside and, even on the second floor, the bright kitchen inset spotlights made Danny feel conspicuous, as if the dark hid unknown dangers.

Turning to the sports pages, Danny stopped at the horseracing section, where the Press Association provides the overnight declarations for tomorrow's racing. Tuesday's menu comprised Flat meetings at Windsor and Ripon, plus a minor national hunt card at Fakenham. Danny's eyes were drawn to

Windsor, as he knew Johnson rarely ventured much north of Watford. Only a big prize would tempt Johnson to Ripon and that Yorkshire track rarely hosted such an event.

His search stopped at the opener on the Windsor track. Johnson was booked a ride on a juvenile filly in the first race, a six-furlong maiden. The jockey had a quartet of rides set for the Royal venue. Danny had seen enough. *Windsor here we come*, he thought.

He returned to the lounge. Sara had drifted to sleep, the bowl beside her scraped clean. He got a thick travel rug from the airing cupboard and placed it carefully over her. She twitched ever so slightly as he gently patted the blanket down. She hadn't changed a bit since she'd left him.

After a restless night in the tiny spare room, he awoke with a start. His mind took a moment to click into gear. For a second, he thought he was cooped up in a cell, a fear that dispelled when he turned to see the hazy morning sunlight filter through a gap in the curtains. He stretched, got dressed into his already soiled clothing and went into the living room, expecting to see Sara still coiled on the sofa. There was no sign of her and the blanket was neatly folded on one arm of the chair. Danny picked up a note left on the coffee table. It read: 'Gone to work, back about 7. Love, Sara.'

He looked out on to the busy litter-ridden street of this drab suburb on the outskirts of London. There was a row of small shops the opposite side of the road, including one selling fruit and veg, a butchers, and a newsagents. A line of cars queued by a set of traffic lights below, exhaust fumes curling into ghostly swirls evaporating in the cold morning air. Danny felt he was on the inside looking out on a busy world; one which he was no longer part of. He momentarily shot back to his time at Cardiff prison. A four-month stay at Her Majesty's pleasure in a cell that tantalizingly overlooked a side street bustling with activity. It was done on purpose to antagonise the prisoners by showing them what they were missing.

Danny turned to the fridge and downed a glass of cool milk, trying to sooth the heartburn he felt after the previous night's tossing and turning. He nearly brought it back up, retching forward, his stomach still unsettled.

He checked his watch. 9.15. His wallet still contained over £200. With his bank account likely to be frozen, it was all he had to survive and he knew it would soon be used up on public transport and food.

Danny showered, grabbed his fleece and left for Royal Windsor racecourse. With the risk of pick-pockets on course, he left the box under some towels in the airing cupboard.

He caught the train and then rode the rest of the journey via a riverboat on the picturesque Thames. The idyllic stretch of water, with budding willows drooping over the riverbanks, beyond which lay grand houses of the rich and famous, was all lost on Danny.

They docked outside the track an hour before the first race scheduled for 2.00. Although the Royal track wasn't one of Danny's regular haunts, he quickly located the weighing room and jockeys' changing room. No sign of Sam Johnson yet.

Danny kept a low profile as his face was familiar to some in racing circles, avoiding crowded areas, like around the bar area and in front of the grandstand where the lines of bookie pitches manned by an assortment of larger-than-life characters barking out the latest odds while waiting patiently for the circling punters to fill their satchels.

The horses contesting the opener had by now left the paddock and were spilling into the parade ring. Their pilots began to leave the jockeys' room and make their way to meet the connections of the runners and receive riding orders. Their richly coloured silks dazzled in the harsh spring sunlight. And there he was, Sam Johnson, last out as usual, in pink body, white sleeves and red epaulettes. He casually glanced in Danny's direction and looked again, but hadn't clocked who it was. Danny moved forward to collar the jockey. He held out a racecard for him to sign, pretending to be a harmless race-goer. Sam looked him up and down; it still appeared he didn't recognize him with shades and a hood, seemingly just curious as to why Danny was so well covered up.

'Name?' Sam asked, pen in hand and eyes fixed toward the racecard.

'Danny . . . Danny Rawlings.'

Sam stepped back and handed the booklet at arm's length. 'What the fuck are you doing here?'

'We need to talk.'

'I've nothing to say,' Sam said, his eyes shifted towards the trainer, John Sampson, and owner left waiting in the centre of the parade ring.

'I need to know who was after Dean and why.'

'Why should I help you? Should turn you in, get what's coming to you.'

'I know you're involved, that's why,' Danny said, feigning confidence. Bluffing came easy after years of playing competitive poker during a misspent youth. 'The killer's after a certain object, a box.'

'Not now, the racing press are about, you do know your face is in today's *Racing Post*,' Sam said shiftily. He continued reluctantly, 'Meet me after the fifth race, by the main exit.'

Danny hid his surprise. *Sam had actually taken the bait.* He left the scene with racecard still unsigned.

He chose the mobile food stall next to the stewards' room as a good spot to wait. On a midweek afternoon meeting, the place was relatively quiet and Danny could remain anonymous with comparative ease. He knew Sam was his last available link with Raynham's yard and the wait felt like it would never end. *Would he even show up?*

CHAPTER 12

A chilled breeze stroked Danny's cheeks as he waited patiently near the main gates, lurking in the shadows of the toilet block. A security guard for the track eyed him suspiciously, but kept his distance.

With two races still to go on the card, there were only a few punters leaving the track in dribs and drabs, mostly those who hadn't paced themselves and run out of betting funds.

Sam emerged from behind the gates at the back of the grandstand, mobile pressed against his head. He soon caught sight of Danny and ended the call. He approached with a kit bag hanging loose from his shoulder and still wearing a blue padded bodyguard covering his slender torso. At 5'6", he was quite tall for a Flat jockey and had trouble keeping his weight down. A problem Danny knew only too well from his days in the saddle himself.

They acknowledged each other with brief nods.

'Tell me more about this box Dean passed on to you,' Sam said, a renewed enthusiasm fired his voice.

He seemed overly keen to see the box, Danny thought, *perhaps he was one of them.*

'First, tell me about the betting scam Dean was caught up in.'

Sam paused. 'I don't understand.'

'There was a list of horses found on Dean's dead body. All had been beaten. Did they tell you?'

'Who're *they*?'

'That's what I'm trying to find out. My fingerprints were found on the sheet. I think I was framed for the murder. Raynham pointed the finger at me, I think he may know.'

Sam paused and then said, 'Ask him then.'

'He's a drunk, I couldn't trust a word he says right now. But you worked with him daily. Did he have a moment of clarity

89

and tell you anything? The smallest thing might help, anything,' Danny urged.

'Look, I don't feel safe talking to you here. The boat won't arrive until well after the last race, you can catch a train. It's not far, twenty minutes or so, I'm going that way.'

They walked on and Danny asked, 'What do you make of all this?'

'I was sorry as you when I heard the news about Dean,' Sam said.

'I know,' Danny replied. 'Just didn't see it coming.'

'I said I was sorry,' Sam said pointedly, 'not surprised.'

'What d'ya mean? Were you caught up in it at all?'

'No,' Sam barked. 'I took my orders and took the riding fees, the ones they finally managed to pay me, that is.'

'Things got that bad at Millhouse Lodge?'

'You wouldn't believe.'

The pair followed the pavement to the side of the main road, sheltered from the spring sun by the swaying cedar canopies above.

'The list found on Dean, from what I can suss out, suggests he had something to do with getting them beat.'

'Why are you telling me this?'

'Six of those eight horses were ridden by you.'

'Whoa, I had nothing to do with any of 'em losing. I was just a small cog in the wheel at Millhouse.' Sam paused. 'Here's a tip, focus on who keeps the wheel turning.'

'Raynham?'

'I'm not saying any more. I've got a retainer from John Sampson now, made a clean break while I could. I'm sorry you've got mixed up in this whole mess.'

'But did you have any clue from Dean or Raynham that something fishy was going on? What were your riding orders?'

Sam stopped. Lost in deep concentration, his angular face contorted as if trying to work out a long division. 'Seem to recall him saying that they had next to no chance, so don't bust a gut on them. Yeah, that's right, bust a gut, that's what he said. But he was like that, ever the pessimist.'

'So he never told you to take a tug on any of them. Get them beat.'

'Never!' Sam barked. 'I wouldn't follow an order like that. Always trying, that's me. Punter's friend.'

'What do you know about the Definca Partnership? Who's behind it?'

Sam scratched his head, as if trying to remember, or was it a nervous twitch. 'Never heard of it.'

'Don't give me that,' Danny snapped. 'The partnership owned most of those you rode.'

Sam's subsequent silence spoke volumes.

'Enough lies, Sam.' Danny stopped and anchored Sam back with a firm grip round his slender arm. 'Lives are at stake!'

Sam snarled and shook himself free. He pointed towards the underpass. 'It's that way, straight on for another 200 yards, the station's on your right.'

'If the police ask about me, what will you say?'

Sam spun to face Danny, 'Can't promise anything.'

Danny replied, 'If it hits the fan, will you be a character witness?'

'No way. But I know you're innocent. Perhaps the safest place for you is prison.'

'Wait. If you know I'm innocent, you must know who's guilty.'

'You have to see it from my angle. You don't scare me, they do. I'm just protecting myself.'

'Who? Who are *they*?'

'You'll find out.'

'I don't understand,' Danny asked. 'When?'

'Sooner rather than later,' Sam replied, his gaze dropped to the pavement. 'I'm sorry.'

'No need to be,' Danny said under his breath, slightly perplexed by Sam's response. He knew it was vital for him to get back to the comparative safety of Sara's flat before nightfall.

He shook his head, clearing his mind while he swept down the concrete chute leading to the underpass. Strip lights behind frosted glass - where the walls met the ceiling - splashed light on the ceramic tiled walls, plastered with iridescent graffiti of pink, orange and blue. Suspicious stains and discarded chewing gum marked the concrete on which Danny strode purposefully, each footfall echoing down the tunnel.

Halfway along the pass Danny saw a man with hood pulled down huddled under a tartan blanket. A board lay on the ground beside him, it read: 'CHANGE PLEASE.'

Danny tossed him a £2 coin. The man mumbled something incomprehensibly but didn't make eye contact. *Things could be worse*, Danny thought, until looking ahead.

Stood not twenty yards from him was the tall silhouette of a man wearing the same trench coat as the stranger who'd imprisoned him in the mental hospital. *How the fuck did he know I was here?* He turned and shouted back for Sam, but got no response; the jockey had long gone.

Danny started to retreat, slowly at first. Seeing the mysterious figure close, coat flapping in the breeze that whistled through the tunnel, Danny turned and broke into a sprint. As Danny rushed by, the homeless man mustered the energy to lift his head. Then a broad menacing figure emerged to block the opposite exit.

Danny stopped in his tracks. 'Oh fucking hell.' He looked over his shoulder. 'What d'ya want from me?' he asked with a mix of fear and desperation shaking his voice.

The tall stranger drew closer, now just a few yards away. Danny could hear the man's muffled breath against a silk scarf tightly wrapped around his lower face. 'I would have thought that was obvious.'

'I ain't got it,' Danny croaked, 'not no more.'

'I've lost all trust in you Daniel,' the stranger said. Beneath the shade of his hat, Danny could see the man's eyes, black as soot. 'I've no time for games.'

The homeless man stirred uncomfortably in his blanket, as if trying to get to his feet.

With one swift action, the henchman to Danny's side pulled a gun from his jacket, like a professional hit-man. Its long silencer, glistening in the cold light, pointed at the tramp.

'No!' The trench coat man pulled the scarf away from his face. 'He's not worth it, last thing we need is the police following our trail. That wouldn't be very pleasant, would it Danny?'

Danny turned and said, 'You did kill Deano!'

'I cannot tell you,' the man's cold wet lips stretched into a broad unsightly smile. 'If I did, I'd have to kill you too.'

The henchman buried the gun deep within his jacket and, with a nod from his boss, thrust Danny against the wall with a jolting thud, the back of his skull smacking the ceramic tiles with such force he felt his nostrils fill with blood.

In a slow mannered voice, the trench coat man said, 'Your troubles will be over, just tell us where it is.'

'No,' Danny replied. 'I've been entrusted with it and I've been through too much shit to let him down.' These thugs were after the box and while he was the only one aware of its whereabouts, he knew they wouldn't kill him, right?

The homeless man had managed to clamber to his feet and started to stagger from the scene, blanket left in a heap. The trench coat man turned and the henchman again withdrew the gun, aiming at the meandering target just a few yards away. He released the safety catch.

'I said no!' The trench coat man barked, patience worn thin. 'Let him go, the police wouldn't believe a word he says.'

The tramp afforded the occasional anxious look over his shoulder before disappearing up the walkway the other side, safely out of view. Danny hoped he'd go straight to the police, report what he'd witnessed and bring the real killers to justice, but, somehow, he knew it was just a pipedream. *The law was the last place a homeless man would turn to*, he reasoned.

'Now, down to serious business.' The man's attentions, along with the gun, fixed firmly back on Danny's face.

'Why are you doing this? What is so special about this goddamned box?'

The man's unsightly smile returned. 'Its true value diminishes the more who know. Look what happened to your friend.'

'Why did you kill him?'

93

'Perhaps the victim made three ultimately fatal errors. One, he told of its existence, and then, two, foolishly, refused to hand it over.'

'And the third? You said he made three errors.'

'Three, he pointed the killer in the wrong direction,' the man said. 'I do hope you will not suffer the same fate, Daniel.'

Despite Danny's best efforts, his bottom lip began to shake.

The stranger continued, 'He was the only person alive that knew of its true value and, unfortunately, his fate was sealed. Sometimes, knowing too much can be a curse.'

'Why leave him in such a mess?'

'I never said we were the ones who killed him. Perhaps Dean made the mistake of telling the killer it was there.' The man's gloved hand pressed against Danny's belly.

'So you gutted him on the chance that he was telling the truth,' Danny said, making a mental note to cross his stomach off the list of possible places for the box's whereabouts. *They hadn't seen the box*, Danny reasoned, given its size, it would be impossible to swallow. *They'd clearly learnt of it through word of mouth, but whose mouth?*

'The killer trusted him and it had gone on too long. The killer gave him every chance to tell all and escape with his life, but the lad was willing to die for the cause. Fool.'

Dean must've written the letter whilst being threatened. 'He could've been lying,' Danny protested. 'You should've given him more time.'

'There was no reason not to trust him. He was stalling for time, like you are now.' His rasping voice echoed through the tunnel.

Part of Danny had hoped that a member of the public would stumble across them and save the day, though the wish was tempered by fear that the killers would not be as generous as they were by sparing the tramp.

'One final time, where is it?'

'You won't get away with this. You kill me, and not only will you never know where the box is, but you'll kill the prime suspect for the murders of Dean and Elena. Police will start look elsewhere and they won't be long in tracking you down.'

At this precise moment, he didn't panic. Far from it, his mind was sharp as a tack. Perhaps, a form of self-preservation had kicked in. He feared there was a need to keep track of these people if he was to find out what actually happened and to clear his name. 'But I will make a deal with you. I'll tell you where to go, but I need some assurance you'll spare me.'

'You have my word.'

'And what's that worth?'

'You'll have to wait and find out.' The single barrel silencer was placed against his clammy forehead.

Deep down, Danny knew he had little option now. 'It's at a friend's house, in the country.'

'Go on,' the stranger said. His sallow eyes widened. His skin was the colour of pencil shadings.

'Gloucestershire, at a farmhouse in the Cotswolds miles from anywhere.' Danny knew it would be hard to find, nestled away in remote Cotswold countryside. The house was owned by an ex-jockey called Seamus O'Malley. The pair had remained in regular contact. O'Malley was the purveyor of quality information and Danny had grown to implicitly trust him.

'I'm always true to my word,' O'Malley said whenever Danny ever questioned the inside info. Danny knew he would be away on his annual spring holiday in the Caribbean for the next week or two. *An empty house would at least spare any third party getting harmed*, he thought.

'How can we trust you?'

'My life's on the line, would I risk that for the sake of some crappy box?'

'Very well,' the man said, 'but we'll take no chances this time. Tie his hands, we'll take him with us.'

He was pulled away from the wall by his collar and pushed towards the far opening of the tunnel. The feel of metal pressed against the nape of his neck sent chills down Danny's spine and not because it felt cold to the touch. He was led to a black Mercedes, with windows to match, parked just yards from

95

the underpass in a secluded spot behind a thick covering of trees and bushes. How did they know Danny was there? Had they tracked him all this time before pouncing at his most vulnerable walking the underpass? And then it occurred to him - Sam Johnson. He had ample time to make the call between Danny approaching him and then meeting up again after the fifth race. And then there was the call he'd made when they met at the racecourse gates. After all, he was adamant that Danny took the route via the underpass. *Lying bastard.*

At gunpoint, Danny's hands were bound with the stranger's scarf. So tight, his fingertips began to tingle. And then he was bundled into the boot of the car, huddled into the cavity in the foetal position. As the boot door was slammed shut, Danny's ears popped from the sudden change in pressure. The tight space started to rumble as the ignition was fired and momentum pushed Danny to its rear as the car rolled away. He immediately got to work on loosening the knot of the scarf. Rubbing his wrists together repeatedly helped gain some leverage.

Danny reckoned it would take little more than an hour to reach the Gloucester border. Several minutes into the journey, he had broken free from the scarf and lay there perfectly still as the car drove at pace towards its location. *Must've surely reached the M4 westbound,* Danny thought, hearing the engine cruise in fifth gear. Like a blind man, his fingers traced over the lock on the inside. From his pocket, he produced a brass paper clip he'd used to hold time charts and gallop reports together. He uncoiled the spindly wire and fashioned a peculiarly shaped hook on its end. With what little room he could afford, he positioned himself at the best possible angle to attack the lock. Slowly, with almost imperceptible movements, he twisted the wire in the pinhole. After a few minutes of painstaking adjustments, twisting a fraction left and then right, he withdrew the paperclip. He felt its misshapen end and sculpted it into a hook once again. He continued to twist the wire, fired on by the thought of what would happen to him once they arrived at the house and realized he'd been lying.

Clunk.

The lock mechanism gave way and the boot door lifted ever so slightly. From the roar of the engine and the lack of movement side to side, Danny guessed that they'd yet to leave the motorway. Jumping clear would be out of the question. He waited, lying perfectly still not to raise suspicion from both driver and passenger. After what seemed like an age, the engine softened. Danny could sense the car shifting down the gears, with momentum forcing him hard against the back of the boot cavity. He knew now was the time to think about making a leap for freedom. After all, from past visits, it only took ten or so minutes from the M4 to reach O'Malley's house. It had already been around that time since they'd left the motorway and they would soon be there.

Carefully, he slowly applied pressure to the boot door above. It was now dark outside and the road on which the car snaked wasn't lit. Through a fine gap, he could make out the hedges lining both sides of the winding country road, illuminated by the soft light of the full moon. *When to jump? Timing was everything,* Danny thought. Jumping ship on a bend would not only ensure the car had braked to corner but momentum would hopefully send him flying off the road, into the relatively soft bank of the ditch.

He again felt the force pulling him back into the trunk. They were slowing. With what little energy he had left, he pushed himself up and out, lifting the lid by as little as possible. He fell to the tarmac surface of the road like a lead weight. His hands and knees smacked the ground. He tumbled and turned, grimacing and groaning. Almighty bolts of pain shot though his whole body as he rolled to a standstill, his legs strewn over the edge of the road, resting on the downward slope of the ditch. He was left slightly concussed and not knowing whether he'd broken any bones on impact. He shook his head, but the moon and stars kept spinning above like a kaleidoscope as he lay there now perfectly still. Although his thought patterns were muddled and he'd lost his bearings in the crashing fall, he was painfully aware that the enemy would soon realize they were a passenger light. The rattle of the boot door would surely give the game away.

He lifted his head. Breaking through the pain barrier, he hoisted his sore frame to sit upright, biting his lip until tasting blood. There was still no sign of the Mercedes; all he could hear was a ringing noise. Not sure his bruised legs would bear his weight, Danny slowly left the road in jerky movements on his rear, like a caterpillar. Every inch covered was a monumental effort as he raced against time.

He felt the warm trickle of blood down both forearms, leaking from open wounds on both elbows. Far in the distance, through the gaps in the hedgerows, he could see the dazzling headlights of a car slowly approach. It appeared to be moving at walking pace, clearly scanning the road for Danny's stricken body.

He was sure as hell they wouldn't find it. Now sitting on the road's verge, he rocked himself forward and fell on to the far side of the ditch, feet sunk into the mud. Using a thick branch of the hedge facing him, he hoisted his weight up and through a gap. He scrambled through, gasping for air, and collapsed to the safe side of the hedge, still dazed and confused. He continued to breathe hard, swallowing back the pain.

The purr of the Mercedes slowly grew louder. Danny lifted his hand to mask the bright light which splashed the road. On seeing a spattering of blood where he'd hit the ground, his heart began to thump. Just yards from where Danny cowered behind the thin veil of the hedgerow, the car ground to a halt. He held his breath, heart about to explode. The passenger door opened and out stepped the man with the trench coat. He walked slowly to the front of the car and knelt to the ground. He touched where Danny could see the red pools from where he'd struck the road, and raised his stained fingers to his nose. Danny looked over his shoulder, nothing but rolling gradients of farmland. He was finished if he was discovered right then.

Danny's eyes returned to the road where the stranger was now prowling. He peered into ditches on both sides of the road. *Move on*, Danny pleaded, *please move on*. For what seemed like an eternity, the man sniffed the air, as if able to smell fear. If he could, there would be no hope for Danny. And then, without warning, the silhouette of the man, his coat trailing like a cape, climbed back in the black car which drove off into the still, dark night. Danny exhaled loudly.

He lay there for a while as he recharged his batteries and assessed the damage. A peaceful moment to collect his thoughts. Although battered and bruised, he could rest his weight on both feet. *Nothing broken.* The same, however, couldn't be said for his mobile which took the brunt of the force on impact.

The starry sky was cloudless and the temperature continued to fall. He had to keep moving, or he'd freeze. With hedgerows traversing the land at regular intervals, he knew following the country road was his only hope of making significant progress. He clambered clumsily back through the gap in the undergrowth and climbed the ditch wall.

After brushing himself down, he set out to find help. Each step sent a jolting pain up his bruised spine. But he knew keeping still would be an even bigger mistake and so he kept going the way he'd come. Eyes glued ahead, just in case the enemy was close by. He could just make out the edge of the country road on which he followed; the glacier-blue luminosity of the moon his only guiding light.

After a good half an hour of slow, meandering progress, a faint light shining from between a small clump of trees in the distance distracted Danny. His limp became more pronounced as his pace quickened a stride. Where there was light, there would most probably be life, and most importantly, a telephone line. Who he'd ring was another matter, certainly not the police.

From a break in the trees, a sweeping driveway led from the main road. Without hesitation he left the road and followed the driveway. Turning the corner, he could see a tall double fronted Edwardian detached house, with a façade dominated by long sash windows. The light he'd seen from afar turned out to be on a security box on the side of the house. The curtains were drawn and the lights were out. The ceramic sign next to the front door read Dawson's Keep. Danny recognized the name, taking him instantly back to the weekend he'd spent there with O'Malley in the lead up to Christmas two years ago. With so many jockeys and trainers invited both past and present, Danny reckoned it was potentially a good chance for some networking and gaining some new contacts, though it deteriorated into a drunken mess, with the more hardy types doing a conga, led by Danny, around the garden gone three in the morning.

The place was a good deal quieter, stiller on this return visit. *Looks like O'Malley had again been 'true to his word', and was now sunning himself in the Caribbean.* With no one at home, Danny could break in and use the phone without danger. To make totally sure, he rapped his knuckles on the front door. There was no sign of life initially and Danny prepared to break in. But his blood ran cold when the porch light flicked on. *Had Seamus skipped the holiday this year?* With both legs lame, he had no time to find cover. The hall light then came on. The door swung open.

'Danny, how the devil are you?' O'Malley asked, though his eyes betrayed the seemingly warm welcome. Danny's suspicions were immediately raised by his deep breathing and flustered appearance, it didn't appear natural for this normally happy-go-lucky Irishman. Furthermore, an uninvited guest at this ungodly hour would normally raise some questions, but O'Malley welcomed as if half expecting Danny to turn up.

'Fine,' Danny whispered. 'Are you on your own?'

Seamus looked awkwardly back at him, his hunched shoulders frozen with tension. 'Yes, why shouldn't I be?'

'Something doesn't seem right,' Danny said. 'Are you sure nobody's called by?'

'For Christ's sake, Danny,' O'Malley said. 'I think I'd know, at this hour.'

Danny made a shell with his hands and blew hot air into it. 'Can I come in then?'

'I suppose you'd better had,' O'Malley sighed, a hint of regret tainted his voice.

Danny stepped edgily onto the navy thick-pile carpet lining the hallway. Wall lamps splashed a warm glow over the oak panelled walls. Pacing further into the hall, with guard now lowered, Danny asked, 'Can I use your phone?'

O'Malley glanced back over Danny's shoulder, towards the door. 'Sure.'

Instinct led Danny to turn on his heels, and his heart and stomach fell to the ground. The trench coat man stood before him, like a very bad dream. Through the dim light of the hallway, Danny saw a long graphite shaft of the silencer pointed at his chest.

'You can't escape us that easily,' the man barked, his go-to-hell eyes narrowed. He briefly glanced at Seamus and said, 'Thank you for your hospitality.'

'Danny, believe me, they just turned up, I have nothing to do with this,' O'Malley said, 'They threatened to kill my family if I didn't, you understand.'

'Doesn't matter,' Danny said with a degree of resignation. He felt they could well be the last words he'd speak. The trench coat man moved near, plunging the silencer deep into Danny's mouth. 'One last time, where is it?'

'Kill me,' Danny said, his voice muffled, like being examined on a dentist chair. 'Go on, you'll never find what you're after.'

'You're right,' the man said, slowly withdrawing the gun, striking Danny's chattering teeth.

'So you'll let me go,' Danny said, hope renewed.

'No,' the man said. 'Let's not be too hasty, there is another way.'

Danny couldn't make out what fate could be worse than your own death. *Would they torture me?*

With imagination running wild, he was led at gunpoint out to the Mercedes parked to the side of the house and was bundled onto the soft leather of the rear seat, the henchman sliding in beside him. All the time, the gun was trained firmly on Danny, its safety catch still off. The scarf was again tied around Danny, this time to cover his eyes.

They accelerated away. The windows blacked out, Danny knew his chances of being sighted and rescued were negligible, even the police seemed an appealing option right now.

101

The journey seemed to take forever, no words were spoken. Danny listened intently for any extraneous noises above the purr of the engine, partly to take his racing mind off what awaited him on arrival. At least an hour into the journey, the car's pace slowed dramatically. Danny swayed from side to side as the car took a left and then a right. The faint sound of church bells could be heard and a few minutes later, the grating rumble of what sounded like the wheels running over a grille, possibly a cattle grid. The car then stopped and, above the ambient sound of the engine ticking over in neutral, he could hear a whirring noise. Danny guessed it was electric gates parting. The car shifted into gear and there was a moving sensation again. From behind, there came a loud clunk. *Had the gates closed?*

For a couple of minutes, the car slowly followed what felt like a winding tarmac drive. Where had he been taken? His heart was fit to burst; the not knowing was the worst part. The engine cut off and Danny was dragged from the car, falling on the gravel surface with a crunch. He was manhandled to his feet and dragged with such force, his tired limbs felt like they'd be ripped off. He had no energy to fight and, knowing a gun was likely to be covering his every move, he daren't rip off the blindfold. He passed through what sounded like electric doors and was met by a clinical smell, one that reminded Danny of the last time he'd visited hospital, for a broken arm from a fall he'd taken out of a first floor window in a botched burglary job. Somehow, he knew his violent captors were not being as considerate as to nurse his wounds.

There were no sounds of other patients or doctors that you'd find in a bustling accident and emergency ward. *This was no hospital.* He fought the increasing urge to see where he was. He was dragged by the arm along a hard floor, each footfall echoing down what Danny presumed to be a corridor. There was now a slight gap from where the scarf had ridden up his face from his ungainly exit from the car. Danny looked down at his feet, pacing what looked like grey polished stone, reflecting light from the bright inset spotlights on the ceiling.

'In here,' a voice growled. He was bullied through a door to his left, one of many he'd passed since entering the building.

He was pushed deep into the room and, once his arms and legs were strapped down, the scarf was tugged away from his face. Danny blinked his eyes open as they grew accustomed to the harsh white of the walls and the ceiling. To his right, he saw rows of large glass examination chambers, next to which stood a couple of computers and what looked like a printer; it felt like a scene from a sci-fi movie, straight lines and pristine surfaces. A door directly ahead began to open. Danny looked on and saw four men dressed in white coats stream in.

'What is this?'

To his side, a tall man appeared into eyeshot. A familiar waft of unpleasant aftershave brushed over Danny. He knew instantly who he was - the trench coat man. He'd now disposed of his sinister hat and coat, revealing a slender frame and gaunt, almost macabre features. *Pushing mid-forties*, Danny guessed. He had a full head of jet-black hair, swept back and flecked with grey. He wore glasses with thick rims framing thick lenses, magnifying eyes as dark as his hair and cold as the room they stood in.

'We must stop meeting like this,' the man broke the silence.

'Who are you?' Danny asked, voice trembling. 'And why am I here?'

'I don't think you're in a position to start asking questions.'

'You can torture me all day long, I'll never give in. Not now, not ever.'

The man laughed; a harsh sound like the peel of a cracked bell. 'I won't torture you. I now know your resilience. No, I thought this may help to change your mind.' The man raised his arm toward what looked like a bank of two-way mirrors lining the far wall. When spotlights flooded the room adjacent, Danny's eyes widened in horror at seeing Rick, pinned down on what looked like an operating table.

'No!' Danny shouted. 'What the -'

103

'I though that would get your attention, now for some answers.'

'Why've you got Rick involved?' Danny strained at the straps that pinned him down. 'This is between us, he's got nothing to do with this, nothing! Let him go!'

'Not after we've taken the time and effort to bring him here. Now that would be a waste.'

'Let him go!'

'That will depend on you,' the man stood over Danny, who continued to writhe, panicking. 'Simple equation,' he said in a matter of fact tone. 'Tell us where the box is equals you and your brother are free to go. Silence equals a death sentence for you both.'

Danny had no option. 'It's at a friend's flat in Ilford, Dawson Street, Flat 6A. Just take the box and leave us alone. You'll find it behind the towels in the airing cupboard. If you lay a finger on the owner, there'll be hell to pay, right!' Danny snapped, hands pulling against the metal clamps holding him down.

'Good,' the man said softly. 'That's more like it.'

'How do we know he's telling the truth?' the henchman asked.

'Oh, the monkey talks does he?' Danny said.

'Quiet!' the man barked. 'I've wasted enough time on lowlifes like you. I'm normally a man of my word,' the man added, still angered. 'But, seeing as you've messed us around, I feel some payback is in order.'

Sweat channelled Danny's furrowed brow and he lifted his head off the hard surface on which he was fastened to. Rick looked pale, but was awake and conscious.

'Kill him anyway.' The man raised a thumb, a signal to the assistants beyond the wall of glass.

'No!' Danny screamed. 'No!'

He saw three men step forward and further clamp Rick's hysterical limbs to the steel worktop, while another squeezed the syringe held pointing upwards, a clear liquid shot from the needle point. He then proceeded to plunge the needle deep into Rick's neck. His brother's erratic movements gradually lessened and soon, he just lay there, perfectly still. The lights then went out. Now, all Danny could see was his own horrified expression reflected back at him.

The man approached, looming over him like a sceptre, and, barely containing a smug grin, whispered, 'Don't be distressed, Daniel, you must understand, we're all merely empty vessels whose sole purpose is to carry the gene pool forward. Life isn't that precious.' Lockhart paused to savour the look of anguish on Danny's face and then proceeded to leave, closely followed by the others.

Rage fuelled him as he pulled at the clamps with such force that they cut into his red-raw wrists. He lay there looking over at the bank of mirrored windows, hoping he'd just imagined the nightmare sequence or perhaps this was all merely a sick reality show and the cast would all come out laughing and saying, 'Got you!'

But, deep down, Danny knew this was all too real and the enormity of what he'd just been forced to see - the needless killing of his brother - would never leave him.

He lay there for what seemed like an age, but was probably just an hour or so, as if they left him there to simmer over what his actions had caused.

He felt strangely numb. Whether it was his nervous system shutting down from an overload, he didn't know.

One of the assistants returned on his own, and started to unfasten the metal clamps holding Danny's arms and legs in position.

'What you doing? My brother, Rick, where is he? I wanna see him.'

'There's nothing you can do. If I were you, I'd get out of here while you still can,' the man said, nervy. 'I just couldn't stand by and let this happen. This isn't what I joined for. Just don't say a word.'

'I won't,' Danny sighed, still in shock, as if hit by a stun-gun. 'Why are they doing this? What could possibly be that effing valuable?'

'I can't say,' the man said. 'I value my own life too much.'

'Can I see my brother one last time? Please.'

'Don't push your luck.'

Danny groaned as he sat up, wiping the blood on his already soiled fleece.

Knees buckling under his weight, he made for the door. He glanced over his shoulder with concern etched over his face.

'Follow the corridor to your left and you're out,' the assistant said. 'And, do me a favour, don't get caught, will you.'

Danny forced the ghost of a smile past welling eyes. With that one act of heroism, the assistant had restored some of Danny's diminishing faith in the human race. He pushed the button on the sliding doors and looking both ways, began to pace down the corridor in the direction he'd been told.

His limbs felt numb and fingers pricked by pins and needles; his broken heart struggling to contain frayed nerves.

On his way out, he passed a windowless door marked Toxic Waste – Restricted Area. *Was this part of the scam?* Had they been dumping toxic waste illegally? Danny needed something to call the police with, get a search warrant on the building. The state he was left in, his own health was the least of his concerns. He masked his mouth with a sleeve and cautiously pushed down on the lever. The air cushioned door glided open.

The room facing Danny was long and narrow with grey breezeblock walls and stained floor, lacking the pristine splendour of the rest of the building. Towards the end were three bins. He edged deeper into the dimly lit room, and prised the lid off one of the stainless steel bins. Peering into the container marked hazardous waste, he instantly recoiled at the putrid stench, a mix of disinfectant and rotting flesh. Was it human flesh? Although decayed to black mulch, the compost emitted a smell of death. An unmistakable stench Danny had last inhaled when a rat had died under the floorboards of his bedsit during the early days as a jockey.

'Oh Jesus!' he chocked. *What the fuck is this place? Why are they on a killing spree?* Not wishing to find out first hand, he

106

replaced the lid and applied pressure to the push bar on a door marked exit to the far side of the room. It led to a loading bay for a heavy goods vehicle to the secluded and shady rear of the building. *Must be a docking bay*, he thought, *get rid of the bodies discreetly by the back entrance*. Would his brother go the same way? He swallowed back the tears and pushed any feelings of grief to the rear of his mind. Clear thoughts were needed if he was to get help and raise the alarm.

With no mobile, finding a payphone was his only option. First, he had to get passed the security cordon. He knew his escape would be time-sensitive; they'd soon discover that he'd been let free and they're sure to have armed security guards paired with dogs baying for his blood. He sucked in a lungful of fresh morning air. The mottled clouds cast shadows racing across the concrete forecourt, beyond which lay lawns and a thick wooded area. Without daring to look back, Danny dashed for the cover of the darkening woods. His progress was halted by a tall wire fence, eight foot of mesh crowned by razor barbs.

Danny followed the impenetrable fence until he came to a clearing and the security checkpoint; the same one, at a guess, he'd passed through just hours before. It was a small hut with broad glass windows dominating each wall, allowing the security guard to keep a good look out. However, it also allowed Danny to see the coast was clear. He ran for the hut and, inside the checkpoint, pressed the release button. The gates began to slide open, the sound of whistling and then a flushing noise from the adjacent room signalled it was time for Danny to leave, pronto. The uniformed security guard opened the toilet door and, seeing Danny scramble past, he lunged forward, hat flying off whilst fumbling the radio on his lapel for back-up. Danny slammed the door shut, almost shattering the glass, and sprinted until his legs felt heavy.

CHAPTER 13

After two hours of trampling over farmland, he'd made it to a country lane. He continued to follow the road. He could make more progress on the tarmac, unlike the earthy undulations of the furrowed fields. Although he felt vulnerable in the open, he needed to flag down a passer-by to contact Sara, time was running out. Furthermore, the enemy may have lost interest in Danny. After all, they'd got what they were after. *Why should they needlessly kill again?* And then he thought of what had happened to his brother. Even against the cool early morning air, he began to sweat.

Up ahead, the country road was swallowed by a wooded area. Soon, he was submerged by the darkening trees, their thick canopies reaching out over the narrow winding tarmac strip, barely two car widths. Through the haunting gloom, the dazzling headlamps of a Ford pickup came into view, approaching fast. Danny shielded his eyes with one arm and, with the other, waved the van driver down.

The driver, late twenties and somewhat bemused, was dressed in orange overalls. A tattoo of an eagle marked his thick neck. The cabin smelt of oil and a Big Mac carton was on the dashboard.

Danny pleaded with the driver and, much to his relief, the driver obliged; turned out he was on his way to the nearest town, Ludlow, anyway.

The drive took no more than fifteen minutes, giving Danny an approximate bearing as to where he'd been held captive. He was dropped off near the town square where a payphone was situated. His fingers trembled, nervous circuitry shot from a destructive mix of shock and tension.

'Answer,' Danny whispered as Sara's mobile rang the other end. 'Answer.'

'Hello?'

'Sara, it's me, Danny. Where are you?'

'I'm at work.'

Danny emptied his lungs with relief.

'Why?'

'No reason, just don't go back to the flat today.'

'You're worrying me now. What's happened? You haven't burnt the place down, I know your cooking.'

'Listen!' Danny cut her short. 'I haven't got time, running out of change.'

'No need to shout.'

'Sorry, just meet me at the The Black Horse after work, say six.'

'Tell me what it's about?'

The pips sounded. 'Speak later.'

Danny was running out of cash, but had enough for a single rail ticket to London.

He arrived at the pub early and waited patiently, slowly turning his half-empty pint glass, while edgily glancing up at the regulars. Much to his relief, they seemed preoccupied with their own worries. Sara was punctual; clearly concerned by the tone of the call she'd received earlier in the day. She reluctantly laid her overcoat, garish green and dripping wet, onto the worn seating of the town drinking hole.

'Tried ringing your mobile all day,' she said. 'Did you leave it somewhere?'

'I've got shot of it.'

'Please tell me what's going on Danny, tell me it's nothing illegal.'

For fear of scaring her further, he said, 'Nothing's wrong, just need to chat to you about something.'

'What about the flat?'

'What about the flat?' Danny bounced the question back.

'You warned me not to go back there.'

'Oh that, I was just kidding, I had to make sure you'd turn up somehow. The amount of times I've been let down on a date.'

'This is a date?'

'Isn't it?' Danny's thin eyebrows arched.

'Are you feeling alright?' Sara asked, tilting her face like a perplexed dog he once owned.

Danny didn't reply, assessing whether he'd stalled enough for the coast to now be clear for them to return to the flat. *Once they'd found the box, surely that would be it.*

The pair was silent as they entered her block; Danny trying hard to mask his growing anxiety at what or who he'd find, while Sara exhausted from a long day working as a secretary in a busy solicitors.

'Wait here,' Danny whispered. He cautiously approached the internal front door leading to Sara's flat. As he'd expected, it was ajar. Splinters splayed from where the lock had been forced. The question running through his mind was: *had they already been and gone, or were they still there?* Danny couldn't take any chances, he mouthed to Sara, 'Stay there.'

'Why? Danny, you promised everything was okay,' she said, but Danny wasn't listening.

He prodded the pine door, it swung open with ease. At first glance, nothing was out of place.

The faint whiff of the overpowering aftershave took him straight back to the time he'd been held captive; this was definitely no ordinary burglary - they had been.

He tiptoed across floorboards which moaned under his weight.

Once he'd established the men had left, he made a beeline for the airing cupboard, which was open. The blankets and towels had been pushed to the side in a crumpled mess and there was no sign of the skippet box.

Danny hurriedly collected the sheets, and made the best job he could of folding them, before shutting the panelled door. He gulped a lungful of air, preparing to face Sara; the guilt was written all over his face. 'It's all clear. They've gone.'

'I don't believe this,' she cried. 'I'll call the police.'

'No!'

'Why not?'

'I think they'll be more interested in finding me than stray fingerprints of a few small-time burglars, don't you?' Danny turned to see Sara holding her head, eyes teary. 'I'm sorry, didn't mean to shout.'

'No, it's not that,' she wept. 'I'm just at my wits end.'

'I shouldn't have called on you.'

'It's not you, it's just-' she paused, swallowing back the tears. 'Everything.'

Danny offered his shoulder, she accepted willingly. His thoughts drifted back to happier times when they were an item. Perhaps it was through rose-tinted glasses, but those memories were mostly of Sara in fits of laughter. Danny loved the way she used to throw her head back in hysterics at just the littlest thing, sending a lovely scented wave of her perfume over him. He used to exploit this weakness when she was eating. He'd nail impressions of her pompous colleagues he'd met at hideous office parties in the law firm, particularly when they'd given her a hard time that day. She used to wave her hands in a shooing motion, face reddening, as she desperately tried to swallow what she'd been chewing. It usually ended with her leaving the room, as the mere sight of Danny set her off again. As soon as he picked up on something that tickled her, he wouldn't let go; bringing out the kid in both of them.

Looking back, he'd forgotten how he used to find lightness in the darkest of situations when with her. It came naturally, turning most things around with humour. But that old spark in his eyes had fizzled out since he'd put the job first. It dawned on him right then, he was a different man when not with her, *a lesser man.*

Later that evening, Sara sat on the lounge sofa, full glass of wine in hand. She said, 'One thing's bugging me, how did you know there was more than one of them?'

'What?' Danny pretended he'd not heard, but was really stalling time for a sensible answer.

'You said they were gone, as if you knew.'

'It's a phrase,' he said, raising his hands in protest. 'If it makes you feel any happier, he's gone. But that's presuming the intruder was a male, she's gone.'

'No need to get sarky.'

Danny felt bad going on the attack, but it was the only way he could stop the questioning. *Attack sometimes is the best form of defence.* They both sat silent in front of the television. She'd left the channel on BBC News 24 and both watched the moving pictures as if it were wallpaper until, fourth story in, what Danny saw on the 32" screen in the corner of the lounge made him choke on his lager. 'Turn it up, turn it up.'

Sara fumbled nervously with the remote.

The news reporter said, 'Simeon Lockhart's private research lab in Shropshire won a lucrative contract for the 'wonder drug' Definca successfully passed trials in the treatment of osteoporosis. However, many sufferers complained of painful side effects in the longer term and the drug, which had proved a lifeline for the ailing Simcorp Enterprises, was withdrawn four weeks ago. And now it was revealed through Mr Lockhart's solicitor on Tuesday that the Simcorp Group is filing for bankruptcy, another sign to Chancellor David Cromwell that the recession is beginning to take hold. Mr Lockhart was unavailable for comment in person today.' While the reporter spoke, film footage showed a man dressed in a dark suit, with shades to match, getting in a car - a Mercedes with blacked out windows. Danny recognised the man and the car instantly - their images still scarred his mind.

'Why do you want the business news for? Your share portfolio's gone down the pan?' she smiled to herself before standing for a fresh glass of wine.

'That man kidnapped me and killed my brother,' he said bluntly, jotting brief notes down.

Her smile vanished. 'Don't joke about things like that.'

A film glazed over Danny's eyes as he held the gaze, poker faced.

'You're not kidding are you?'

'I need to use your computer if that's okay.'

'Hang on,' she said, placing the glass on the table. 'I'm still digesting what you've just said.'

'My brother Rick - he's dead, partly because of me, okay!' Danny said.

Sara knew Rick from when she and Danny had dated. Although they'd met just the couple of times, a sympathetic mix of sadness and shock of someone dying well before their time pervaded her. 'How?'

'I can't deal with it right now. I need your computer.'

Sara nodded distantly.

The desk lamp splashed light over his navy t-shirt and khaki combats as he sat in front of the laptop. As the computer booted up and went online, he looked at the familiar name of the drug he'd jotted down from the news report. *The suspended drug Definca must have something to do with the ownership partnership of the same name.*

He typed Definca into a search engine and it threw up 216 matches. From what he could tell, most sites were news and reviews of the drug from medical websites, or text files and documents issued by the British Medical Association. He wasn't concerned with the drug itself. He needed to find a concrete link between those behind the drug and those behind the owners of the horses on the list found on Dean. It seemed the most unlikely coincidence, but, if he was to go to the police with this information, he had to make certain.

Danny could sense Sara approach from behind and resting her hands on his tight, cold shoulders, she said, 'What are you looking for?'

'I don't know,' he said, voice trailing off. He turned and looked up at Sara, who was nibbling at her lower lip. 'Anything that might implicate this Simeon Lockhart to the killing of Dean, the murdered stable lad.'

She wrapped her arms loosely around Danny's neck, and gently kissed the crown of his head. He smiled, it felt good. He looked up and, before words could escape his mouth, she'd backed off, sloping off to the kitchen as if suddenly realizing what she'd done. Perhaps she was embarrassed, forgetting they were no longer together or perhaps she was testing the water, Danny didn't know, though he'd hoped it was the latter. Even such a brief and subtle physical contact had left him glowing. Staying here made him realize just how much he'd missed her, those strong feelings having been reignited. He couldn't help wonder what would have happened if he'd chosen her over the job. He certainly wouldn't have been on the gallops that fateful morning and, as a consequence, wouldn't be in his current mess. *Probably happily married with a kid*, Danny reckoned, *that's where I'd have been.* 'Snap out of it,' he thought out loud. He hated people who wallow, what-if merchants, so he consciously derailed that train of thought. What's the point of worrying, his dad always said to his fretting mum, never was worthwhile.

Sara emerged from the kitchen.

'Sara?' Danny asked, concerned.

There was silence, before she sniffed, 'Yes.' Had she been crying? Danny swallowed. He felt uncomfortable from any outpouring of emotion, particularly from those he cared for. 'You okay?'

'Yeah,' she sighed. 'Fine, just a long day that's all and now this.'

'It's all my problem, this. Last thing I want is for you to fall apart.'

'But it's not just about that,' she snapped. 'It's you, turning up, unannounced, opening old wounds, it's too much to take.'

Danny turned to face her. 'I'll leave, right now.'

'No,' she snapped. 'That's not the point, you're here now. If you leave *again*, you'll only rub salt in the bloody wound. Leave me to pick up the pieces, again.'

'I just hate seeing you like this.' He paused. 'Just tell us what to do and I'll do it.'

She forced a smile, yet couldn't disguise the redness of her eyes. 'Nothing, Danny. Why do you think they are linked?' she asked, seemingly eager to change the subject.

'The drug this Simeon Lockhart patented was called Definca. I don't bet anymore, but I would lay you any odds he's also behind the owner syndicate of the same name. He has to be.'

'What's that got to do with anything?'

'Remember that list of horses found on Dean's body. Well, most of those horses were caught up in a betting scam and

114

all were linked to the owner syndicate Definca. This Simeon guy must've known Dean.'

'And you think he killed Dean?'

'Along with Dean's grandma, Elena.'

'Why?'

'He had something they were after.'

'Why on earth would they kill his grandmother?'

'Afraid she was in the wrong place at the wrong time.'

She sighed, 'But I don't understand, all over a small silver box?'

'You haven't met these people. Life ain't sacred to them. Their motive behind creating the wonder drug was money, not to do good. Wouldn't surprise me if they cut corners just to get it on the market.'

'And your brother, you think they killed him as well?'

'I know so, saw it with my own eyes.'

'I'm so sorry,' she said, her comforting arms wrapped around his neck.

Whether it was macho pride, or his unwillingness to accept his brother's death, or the guilt of knowing it was indirectly his fault, he couldn't deal with his emotions right then and pushed her away. He knew there was one man who was best positioned to tell him the answers and that was Michael Raynham. He stood. 'I need to use your mobile.'

She recoiled. 'Will it be traced? I know aiding and abetting a wanted man isn't smiled upon.'

'A wanted man, maybe, but also an innocent man.' She still seemed reticent. 'Don't worry,' Danny sighed with a thanks-for-nothing tone, 'I'll use the payphone.'

He pulled on his fleece, giving off a faint whiff of dirt and body odour. He left the flat and went in search of a payphone. He headed for Ilford's high street. He blew steam as he paced the ten-minute walk. Standing under the harsh light of the telephone box, he punched Raynham's mobile number, hoping not to get the answerphone again.

With every ring, his stomach sank. And then, silence.
'Hello?' Danny asked. Nothing. *Had the line gone dead?* 'Hello?
Michael?'

'Speaking,' a voice croaked.

'Michael, is that you? You sound bloody awful.'

'Who is this?'

'It's Danny.' Silence. 'You haven't hit the booze again
have you?'

'No.'

'Look, it must be a bad line. I need to ask you about
something to do with Dean's murder.'

'Go on.'

'What was the name of the main financial backer of the
yard? The one you mentioned loadsa times, but never named.'

'I can't tell you on the phone in case they're still tracking
my calls.'

'Who? The police?'

'Yeah.'

'Okay, we'll meet. Where?'

Another pause. 'In a quiet, yet public place. The multi-
story car park in Newbury town centre. Top floor at say . . . four
tomorrow morning, no one about then.'

'Okay,' Danny replied. He wasn't happy about returning
to Berkshire - the county where all this mess had begun – but he
knew that's where Raynham was based, and he needed to ensure
he would turn up. *Worth the risk*, he summed up.

'Don't let me down,' Raynham said. 'I know something
that might help you.'

The line went dead.

Danny pushed the receiver in its cradle and, cloaked by
darkness, retraced his steps back to the flat. There, he was met by
an atmosphere colder than the frosty air outside. Sara was curled
up on the sofa, not saying a word to Danny as he settled in the
armchair opposite. They both stared blankly to someplace beyond
the TV screen spewing out a repeat of *Only Fools and Horses*.
Normally the comedy would raise a smile on their faces, but both
sat there like mannequins, minds elsewhere. When the titles came

up, Danny broke the ice, saying, 'I'm sorry about all this, I'll be out of your hair soon, promise.'

'Your words mean nothing. It's not like you've never lied to me before.'

Danny was in no position to protest; a gambler's life leaves a trail of lies.

'I feel anxious, unsure of anything,' she said, shifting her weight to see Danny from the corner of her eye. 'Do you know the last time I felt this way?'

He knew full well what biting comment was about to shoot from her lips. 'Let me guess, when we were together, perhaps?'

She didn't respond; there was no need.

'I'm a changed man now,' he protested.

'We've both changed.'

'I've given up betting, and actually make good money from the sport now.'

'And that's why you're kipping round here,' she said.

'None of this is my fault.'

'It never is.'

The silence resumed.

'Can you turn it over?' she asked, pointing at the remote on the table. 'Make yourself useful somehow.'

Danny reached for the remote and fell back, flicking channels quickly, like a slideshow.

'Slow down,' she said. And so the evening dragged on with all the atmosphere of a wake.

Danny retired early and lay on the single bed in the spare room, staring blankly at the endless swirls of the Artex ceiling. A shaft of white light beamed into the room as the door slowly opened. Danny shot up. Had they returned for more? He let the air rush from his lungs as he saw Sara, dressed in a t-shirt draped over knickers, tiptoe into the room. Danny asked, 'What's wrong?'

'Everything,' she sobbed. 'Hold me.' She slid beneath the duvet. 'I'm sorry about earlier.'

Danny kissed her forehead tenderly and whispered, 'Everything will seem better in the morning. Get some sleep.' He'd detected Sara had not been her usual self since he'd arrived. If it was his fault, surely she'd have asked him to leave by now.

She held him tight, burying her head in his chest, her long chestnut hair cascading over the side of the narrow bed.

'Are you okay?' he asked, gently stroking her hair back away from her face.

'I've never felt so alone in all my life,' she sobbed.

Although facing away from Danny, he could see her eyes were open as they glistened in the reflection on the bedside clock face.

Many a true word had been spoken after a few drinks, Danny knew only too well. And he guessed, at some level, her real feelings were filtering through.

The pair lay perfectly still, relaxed in each other's arms, as the orange light from a flickering street lamp opposite streamed through a gap in the curtains. It was a comfortable silence, not awkward. Sara was the only person he could truly relax with, not feel the need to impress, or be 'on' all the time. He didn't feel the need to be on the go when with her, travelling the length and breadth of the country chasing the next winner. She always used to say, stop running away from your problems Danny.

Looking back, she was probably right, hiding any insecurities or worries he'd had by immersing himself in his all-consuming job. That defensive wall he'd successfully built up, particularly with work contacts, not letting anyone know his true thoughts and feelings, she'd slowly dismantled brick by brick over the years. She knew his weaknesses, flaws, and he knew how she ticked. And right now, he could sense her overwhelming sadness and it made him feel the same way. He could have stayed there comforting her in his arms for evermore.

Transfixed by the clock face, he saw her eyelids slowly droop and her face relax. He swallowed hard before saying, 'You know that promise we'd made, years back.'

There was a pause, before she replied distantly. 'What promise?'

118

Her eyes remained shut. Was she still awake?

'Our promise,' he said, barely above a whisper, 'to get back together.'

She remained perfectly still, like a mannequin. Danny could hear the patter of his heartbeat as he continued. 'Well, the things is, what I was thinking, would you . . . like to, if you still feel the same way.' She twitched ever so slightly, breaking his flow. Having rehearsed this question no end of times in his mind over the years, he couldn't believe how tongue-tied he'd become and what garbled rubbish had just escaped his lips.

Although he hadn't got his point across as he'd hoped, Danny still waited her reply with baited breath. But she said nothing, her breathing slower and heavier. Danny raised himself up and rested his weight on his elbow as he craned his neck to see her face. She was gone, drifted off; the alcohol had clearly gone to her head.

But had she heard what he'd said, Danny questioned.

'Sara?'

Silence.

CHAPTER 14

Danny drifted in and out of a light sleep, waking moments before the alarm went off; his body clock never failed. With almost imperceptible movements, like a safecracker, he released Sara's arms from around him before lifting himself from the sunken mattress, careful not to rock the rickety pine frame. He slipped on his t-shirt and, delving for a clean top in the wardrobe on the sidewall, was taken aback when seeing some of his old clothes. *Must have left 'em when kicked out without warning*, he thought. He'd assumed she'd burnt them or sent them to a charity shop. *Did she still hold a torch?* He looked over his shoulder at her, still clinging tight to the duvet, fighting the cold.

He unhooked one of his favourite leather jackets from its hanger and left the room. He glanced at his watch. 12.30 A.M.

He had time on his side. In any case, he knew Raynham was a man of his word and would wait if Danny hadn't made it on time. With no trains running at that hour, Danny made the trip by bus making several changes en route, allowing him time to run through the questions he needed answering.

Was Simeon Lockhart hiding behind this ownership pseudonym? If so, was he the big financial backer that'd helped Raynham strengthen his ailing squad? Did Raynham know of Lockhart's dealings with Dean? *He'd surely gotten wind of the betting scam surrounding the yard's runners.* Had he been party to it?

Danny knew times were hard at Millhouse Lodge and he also knew the former champion trainer was desperate to recapture the glory days. One thing stopped him – money. *Turning a blind eye to a few of his runners underperforming would've netted him substantial rewards*, Danny reckoned.

The clear navy-blue sky was lit by a faint moon and stars as the bus approached Newbury. His face was well known in these parts. The chances of him being spotted would be low at this hour, though. The distant shouts of delivery men arriving at the historic marketplace as traders set up their stalls and the faraway whine of a milk float broke the still morning air, as he casually walked the side streets, an out-of-the-way shortcut to the multi-storey car park beside the shopping centre. He knew he was early. 3.38 A.M.

Aside from a homeless man wrapped in a blanket sheltering in the alcove of a fire exit, the car park was ghostly quiet at ground level. He considered riding the lift, but, given the way things have gone in recent days, thought it best not to tempt fate. The last thing he needed was to get stuck in a lift and call for assistance at this hour. He climbed the concrete staircase. A heavy smell of damp and oil tainted the air as he slowly ascended, pacing himself, as one does when early for a meeting.

As he pushed the fire door at the end of the staircase, he sucked in fresh air and stepped onto the top floor, fully open to the elements. He looked up, the sky already a lighter shade of blue. Just a couple of cars were parked on this expanse of concrete, both wide apart and long-stay.

Seeing no one in either car, he decided to walk to the chest-high wall framing the car park and looked out over the flat urban landscape, off to the spire of the St Nicholas church – the spiritual centre of the market town for the past 900 years - in the distance and over to the large modern shopping mall partly obscuring his view to the right. As the minutes ticked by, the anxious glances at his watch grew more and more frequent. It was past the time they'd arranged, so Danny, using the payphone on the wall to the side of the fire door, called Raynham again to make sure he was on his way. The answerphone kicked in at once; Raynham had switched the phone off. A further ten minutes passed. *This is fucking ridiculous*, he thought pacing anxiously. Newbury was the last place he needed to be right now and he was close to cutting his losses by scarpering.

Running short of ideas, he called Gash, who'd not been in contact for three days, to check whether the betting syndicate was getting restless and to see if Raynham had called him to say there was a change of plan. After all, without a mobile, there'd be no way of getting hold of Danny. Before he'd got through to Gash, he dropped the phone to hang loose from the steel call box attached to the wall.

DCI Taylor, flanked by two armed officers, stood before him. 'Expecting Raynham were we?'

'Snitch,' Danny snapped, an air of resignation weighed heavy on his mind and shoulders.

'Far from it,' Taylor said smugly. 'Raynham is dead.'

'What?'

'Was found lying in a bath of his own blood, slit his wrists. Terrible mess.'

Danny whispered in disbelief, 'Jesus.'

'Looks like your luck has finally run out, Daniel.'

Danny's thoughts spiralled into oblivion as he stood there in the gloom. 'I've one last throw of the dice.' He turned and ran, bracing for the bullet in the back.

'Stop, or we'll shoot,' Taylor's voice barked from behind, as Danny hoisted himself onto the ledge. He then shifted his weight to look down at the dizzying 80-foot drop on to tarmac and certain death. He looked back over his shoulder at the approaching officers, AK-45s trained on him with a sniper's precision. 'Come on now Danny, let's not do anything stupid,' Taylor said sternly. 'Come back down, we want to hear your side of the story. Get this terrible mess sorted.'

Again, Danny shifted his weight on the narrow shelf. However, he knew if he jumped, the case would no doubt be closed and his brother's disappearance would never be solved. He was never one for the coward's way out. He dropped back onto the safety of the car park and followed orders to lie flat on his stomach, arms and legs stretched out like a star. Handcuffed and head bowed, he was led off in an unmarked police car.

'When did Raynham . . . you know, do it?' Danny asked through to the front passenger seat where Taylor sat.

'One of the work riders found his body two days ago. Suspicions were raised when Michael twice failed to turn up on the gallops.'

'That can't be right. I spoke to Raynham yesterday, last night.'

'Correct, you got through to Raynham's phone,' Taylor said. 'But it wasn't Raynham's voice.'

Danny shook his head, 'Who was it?'

Taylor swivelled in his seat to face Danny, still handcuffed in the rear. 'Don't let me down, I know something that might help you,' Taylor said with a mild Somerset accent. The armed officer fought hard not to smile.

'You bastard! That's entrapment, or . . . yeah, entrapment.'

'No it isn't,' Taylor replied, before returning his gaze to the road ahead. 'You'd left a message on his answerphone at the time Raynham lay there, dying. We found his phone in his trousers folded neatly beside the bath. When I heard your voice, you can't blame me for keeping the phone by my side, waiting for you to bite again.' Danny stared distantly out the window, he'd heard enough. 'When Raynham's phone blared from within a deceased possessions bag on my desk, I just had to answer, and hearing your voice, well it was too good an opportunity to miss.' Taylor turned and grinned like the cat that got the cream, before facing the road again.

Danny was led to the front desk to give his details once again and was held in a cell until the officers were prepared for the interview. He cradled his throbbing head. *Why would Raynham kill himself? Guilt perhaps,* Danny thought long and hard, running the events of the morning Dean had been found. Raynham had been drinking and didn't seem surprised Dean had been killed and was quick to point the finger in every direction but his.

Clunk. The bolt shifted across, releasing the lock and a uniformed guard entered. Danny was led to interview room two, this time with cuffs clasped firmly round both wrists. He was once again made to wait for DCI Taylor.

Danny idly adjusted the steel cuffs when Taylor entered and sat alongside a colleague already in the room. The digital recorder was flicked on and Taylor swiftly ran through the formalities.

'I'll lay it straight with you, Daniel. There's a pile of evidence connecting you with the murders of both Dean and Elena. Forensic evidence plus eye witness reports, including our officers, prove conclusively that you happened to be at both scenes, just hours after the killings took place.'

'Exactly, hours after, not at the time they were murdered.'

'How do you explain the skeleton key being on your person when last arrested?'

Danny's eyes lit as if being struck by a bolt of inspiration, 'Raynham must have planted the key on me. I remember him leaning against me, pulled me in close he did, thought it strange at the time. But that's when he pushed the skeleton key in my jacket pocket, must've.'

Taylor shook his head in disbelief. 'Why didn't you tell us this while Raynham was available for questioning? Seems a little too convenient, doesn't it.'

Danny pleaded, 'You've gotta believe me.'

'I want to believe you, but, as it is, we may never know, with Raynham now dead,' Taylor said. 'You're a clever man, Daniel. But you're easily led and you have a temper.'

'If you think I'm that clever - why would I leave the key on me? Surely that would be the first thing I'd sort. After all, I was in the Lodge for a good half-hour waiting for you lot to arrive. Plenty of time for me to return the key to Raynham's office.'

Danny had raised a doubt that Taylor didn't want to hear. In Danny's eyes, Taylor thought he'd got his man.

'Raynham's office was locked,' Taylor said.

'And I supposedly had a skeleton key!'

'But you couldn't lock the door on the way out, Raynham had the only other key and, in his interview, stated that he always locked his office as he didn't trust his staff.'

Danny let out an exasperated gasp. 'Then ask yourself why Raynham should want to end it all? Guilt, that's why, cos he had a hand in the murder of my good pal Dean McCourt.'

'We've questioned many of Mr Raynham's employees and all of them agree that his diagnosed drinking problem had gradually worsened in recent months. He was on three different anti-depressants, since his wife left him. When the training operation fell heavily into debt, he took what he considered to be the only way out. No suspicious circumstances, case closed.'

Out of sheer annoyance, Danny pushed back forcefully in his chair, *they just weren't listening.*

'Enough about him, we have more pressing matters concerning your good self. I must remind you of your right to a solicitor.' Danny shook his head, blood still simmering to the boil. 'Tell me, if you are innocent, why you left the murder scene at Elena's house, assaulting one of my officers.'

'I knew how it would look and panicked.' Danny paused. 'Look, I've told you all I know. It's not me you should be questioning.'

'I've heard enough of this nonsense.'

'I tell you, you're barking up the wrong tree. You'll get more luck with Simeon Lockhart. He's the man you should be questioning, not me.'

'How do you know of his name?'

'I've been doing some investigating myself. Christ knows, no one else will,' Danny said, a remark that thickened the chilled atmosphere. 'He killed Dean McCourt, then he killed Elena and not content, he killed my brother. He's a friggin' psycho.'

'These are very serious allegations, Daniel.'

'Do you think I'm joking?' Danny fumed.

Taylor passed a note to his colleague who stood and left the room. 'Let me get this straight, where did your brother enter the equation?'

'I was kidnapped by Simeon Lockhart, dragged to his labs, where I saw my own brother being given a lethal injection.'

'Your brother's name?'

'Richard,' Danny replied. 'Richard Rawlings'

'And when did this alleged incident take place?'

'The day before yesterday.'

'Time?'

'I dunno, I was blindfolded. Early morning, six, seven,' Danny said. 'At Simeon's research labs in Shropshire.'

'You actually saw the act taking place?' Taylor asked incredulously, clearly struggling to treat Danny's revelations seriously.

'Yeah. At last we're getting somewhere. He was injected with something.'

'We are obliged to investigate your allegations, of course, but I warn you that a charge of wasting police time will be made if these turn out to be false.'

An officer stood by the door was ordered to leave. *Off to bring Simeon in for questioning*, Danny hoped.

'Say this Lockhart was guilty of killing these people, what would possess him – a respected businessman – to do such a thing?'

Danny asked, 'What was his motive?' Taylor nodded. 'It's a long story.'

'I'm ready and waiting,' Taylor said. He seemed to be intrigued by what Danny could possible concoct.

'Dean entrusted something with me, he asked me to take great care of it in a letter.'

'What is it?

'A box.'

'A box?'

'Yeah, a silver box.'

'And Lockhart was after this . . . box.'

'Yeah. He killed Dean and painted the silversmith's mark on the wall – GH - a kind of warning to whoever possessed it. To say they were willing to go to any lengths to get it.'

Taylor shrugged his shoulders. 'Enough to kill three people?'

'Yeah.'

'Danny, you can surely do better than this.'

'It's the truth, I tell ya,' Danny barked. 'I know it sounds crazy but I couldn't make something like this up.'

'Go on then,' Taylor reclined in his seat grinning, as if to say I'm going to enjoy having a laugh at this.

'Dean linked up with Lockhart, who owned most of the horses on the list found on Dean, in some sort of betting scam.'

Taylor raised his hand, like a traffic cop. 'We investigated the initials of the horses on the list and the Jockey Club verified that all of the drug tests returned with negative results.'

'There are other ways of getting a horse beat. And I saw on the news that his company, Simcorp I think it's called, is filing for bankruptcy, desperate times lead to desperate measures and all that.'

'Okay, say this Lockhart was paying Dean to pass on information, or to ensure these horses were getting beat. Why should he want to kill him? It's a drastic measure, don't you think, whatever the lad had done.'

'At some point, Simeon got wind of the box and demanded it. But when Dean refused, he paid the ultimate, his life.'

'This box is valuable?'

'I dunno, guess so.'

'And Elena?'

'She was the bait to attract me to this mental hospital in Devon.'

'Wait a minute, slow down. Why on earth would she want you to go to a mental hospital?'

'Dean had left me this box in a sort of will. He told me to look after it, guard it with my life.'

'Let me guess,' Taylor said knowingly. 'You haven't got it now.'

'No, Lockhart's got it. I gave into pressure when he threatened to kill my brother.'

'But you say he did kill him.'

'He executed my brother for the hell of it, after I'd told them the box's whereabouts.' Danny started to break down.

'Please, spare me the crocodile tears.'

Danny made a ball with his fists and slammed the table hard, the metal cuffs clattering the veneered surface.

'Settle down!' Taylor barked. 'Or we'll terminate this interview and have you returned to the cell.'

'But you're just not listening.' Danny took a deep breath.

Taylor continued the questioning. 'Why was Elena killed?'

'You haven't seen these people in action, they're ruthless. She was a feisty old dear who wasn't afraid to go to the police as a witness. They couldn't risk it.'

'As I've mentioned before, two of my officers witnessed you running from her house on the day she was murdered, your prints were all over the murder scene.'

'I don't deny being there, but I arrived well after she'd been killed.'

'An angry message was left by you on her answerphone,' Taylor said. Danny swallowed hard. 'We've just witnessed your temper, Daniel. Do you sometimes have trouble keeping a lid on it?'

'I was angry because I thought she'd let me down, led me into a trap. And I was foolish enough to take the bait.'

'Are you saying she knew Simeon?'

'I dunno,' Danny sighed. 'All I know is – Simeon as good as admitted to me that he was the one who killed Dean, that's when he had a gun pointing in my face.'

'And all for this precious box?'

'I know this all seems crazy, but these people are crazy.'

'Where is it now?'

Danny's gaze fell to the smooth, dull surface of the table. 'They've got it. I couldn't take any more. For crying out loud, they killed my brother!'

Taylor started jotting notes. *He surely wasn't treating this seriously*, Danny thought, *at last*.

'We'll terminate the interview there, the time is 2.14 P.M.' Taylor's colleague flicked a switch on the digital recorder.

'Am I free to go?'

Taylor smiled. 'I'm not aware that your situation has changed. You are still under warrant for questioning.'

'So what's gonna happen?'

'We will look into these claims,' Taylor said. 'Until then, you will remain in custody. You'll stay in one of the remand cells within this station. We may need you to visit Simcorp labs to tell

128

us where exactly these alleged events took place. Off the record, if I have found that you've been lying, you'll be grey and old before seeing the light of day again.'

Taylor's empty threats weren't of any concern to Danny, who, having told of the anguishing chain of events, felt a great weight lifted from him, as if revealing his innermost, darkest secret.

Danny was sat still in his cool, whitewashed cell when the door unlocked and two officers entered, one uniformed, the other plain-clothed. The tallest of the pair said, 'We need you to come with us.'

'He won't be there. The body of my brother will have gone, long gone.'

Neither reacted, clearly used to the unhinged ramblings of arrested inmates. Danny was left with an unsettling feeling turning the pit of his stomach.

He was led away from the station in a three squad car convoy, driving the fifty-minute journey to the headquarters of Simcorp Enterprises. On leaving the M4, Danny observed his surroundings. The distant peal of church bells flashed him back to the morning of the kidnapping. Although returning with police protection, he couldn't settle on the rear seat, sandwiched between two detectives.

The car slowed to cross a cattle grid. *Must be getting close*, Danny thought. They were met by a security guard, the same one that'd tried collaring him the day before. Surely he would recognize Danny? The guard looked at the papers handed to him by Taylor in the front passenger seat. His furtive eyes skated over the documentation without saying a word. The stout man wore a blazer that creased when leaning over to peer through the rear window where Danny was slouched, but, on staring directly at him, the guard failed to react. *Probably under orders from his superiors*, Danny thought, *forewarn those in the lab that they'd arrived*. The car passed through the electric gates and rolled up to the grand facade of the research labs. The main building looked like a converted manor house, from which single-level modern buildings spread outward from either side. A pillared entrance was topped by a white sign with Simcorp Enterprises written in bold black.

Danny stretched his legs, as if preparing to escape again. This was the last place he wanted to be, but he knew it had to be done. He was led into the darkening reception area, its cooling marble floor framed by sterile white walls. Sat behind a broad counter was a plump lady. Metal chains fell from either side of her thick-rimmed spectacles.

'My name is Detective Chief Inspector Taylor.'

'Yes,' she replied, a tense smile spread across her face. 'We were expecting you. I'll call someone down to show you around.' She pressed an intercom buzzer on her desk and said, 'The police have arrived.'

Shortly after, a whey-faced young man, late twenties, emerged from behind electronic doors that glided open with ease before hissing shut. He carried himself awkwardly, as if his shoulders and neck muscles had knotted, and his furrowed brow was glazed with a beaded film of sweat, despite the cool air-conditioned surroundings. His eyes briefly scanned the group of five collected in reception, lingering on Danny. A spark of recognition fired Danny, before the man swiftly averted his gaze. Danny was sure the man before him was the same person who'd set him free. He wasn't so sure whether to tell the police, or keep quiet. After all, he wasn't the mastermind behind all the killings. He thought it best to keep quiet.

'We have a warrant to search these premises,' Taylor said.

'I have to warn you certain areas are forbidden, for health and safety reasons,' the man replied. 'Only trained personnel are allowed in those restricted areas.'

Taylor frowned, clearly not used to having his requests rebutted.

'You will need to wear these passes at all time. Security is a priority as I'm sure you can appreciate, particularly given the recent unrest with animal protestors.'

Internal CCTV cameras whirred as they tracked the visitors' every move.

'Big Brother is watching,' Taylor said to one of his colleagues.

The guide remarked, 'As I said, security is paramount.'

'Is it true that Simcorp is filing for bankruptcy?'

'I'm not here to discuss financial matters.' The man stopped and turned, arms now crossed. 'You'll have to speak to the owner.'

'Is Simeon Lockhart about?' Taylor asked, though it failed to elicit a reply.

The harshly lit corridor looked and smelt familiar to Danny. Progressing deeper into the building, he noted a door with the same sign he'd seen when last there: Toxic Waste – Restricted Area.

'In there,' Danny said. The officers ushering him stopped abruptly, as if shot. He continued, 'I escaped through there. You'll find wheelie bins full of black stuff, reeks like hell it does.'

Without having to be asked, the man coaxed a key shaped like a credit card from the large pocket of his white overall and swiped it through a slot next to the door handle. 'Would you like a look?'

The visitors stepped into the dark, cool room. The breezeblock walls were as he'd remembered. This time, however, the wheelie bins were not to be found. 'I swear to ya, they were here, right here,' Danny said. Taylor scanned the empty space. 'They must've been moved, as soon as he knew we were coming.'

'Part of the more sensitive side to our research is the experimentation,' the young employee said. 'This man is correct, we do store dead animal matter for a short space of time. I can assure you, it is dealt with as toxic waste in the correct manner, following all environmental and health laws. You can check our files if you like.'

'That's okay, I trust you,' Taylor said.

Danny groaned.

131

CHAPTER 15

Danny endured a sleepless night pacing the police cell. His mind kept going over what had happened at the research lab the previous day. *Perhaps tweaking the story would do the trick*, he thought, but soon banished that idea. After all, he knew he was telling the truth. *Justice would be served.* A change of tack would extinguish what little credibility he had left. Although his watch had been confiscated by the duty sergeant, the brightening light seeping past the reinforced glass and bars of the cell's sole window high above told him enough.

The grinding clang of keys turning the lock echoed the room. Danny shook his head and struggled to his feet. He was ushered back to the now-familiar interview room at the opposite side of the police station.

Taylor, who was now accompanied by another suited detective type, introduced the persons present before recommencing the interview.

'Daniel Rawlings,' Taylor said, rather more formally than their last interview. 'Picking up where we'd left off, there was nothing to glean from our visit to the Simcorp laboratories in Shropshire to corroborate your side of events. Have you any explanation for this, or would you rather start telling us the truth, it will be easier for all of us in the long run.'

'It's a cover-up,' Danny said. 'And they've disposed of my brother's body, probably with the rest of the chemical waste.'

Taylor afforded him time to reconsider his answer, but Danny held firm.

'Check Rick's house.'

'We already have.'

'And? He's not there, right?'

'But the neighbours say he's away on work much of the time anyway, it means nothing.'

'You're not listening.'

'Daniel, your prints were found at both murder scenes of Dean and Elena. This is what really happened: suspecting

132

something was going on, you search Dean's jacket while he's working on the gallops. You discover the list of horses, your fingerprints having been found on the sheet. He was working your patch as it were, taking trade off you. You argue, witnessed by Michael Raynham. The mother of all arguments. And in one of your fits of rage, picking up the nearest weapon at hand - the farrier's knife - you finish him off. That would sort it, wouldn't it?'

'This is complete bullshit,' Danny interjected.

Unmoved, Taylor continued, 'You thought the matter would end, but then Elena contacts you, suspects you of killing her precious grandson and threatens to go to the police.'

'No,' Danny protested. 'No!'

'And you couldn't risk it,' Taylor continued. 'She needed to be dealt with too.'

Danny lunged forward, pleading, 'I've done nothing wrong.'

'Settle down!' Taylor growled, fixing an icy glare on Danny. His face reddened, fine veins visible on both temples, ready to explode. 'Or you'll be fully restrained, permanently.'

Danny sat back down. 'I'm sorry, but this is all getting too much.'

'Daniel Rawlings, currently residing at Flat 11 Ocean's Crest, Cardiff Bay,' Taylor read from a sheet of paper. 'I am formally charging you with the murders of both Elena McCourt and Dean McCourt. You are not obliged to say anything. Anything you do say will be taken down in writing and may be used in evidence in a Court of Law.'

Danny sat speechless, stunned into silence, shellshock.

Handcuffed and head bowed, he was taken back to the cell while the detectives prepared the paperwork involved with charging him for such a serious crime.

Danny shook his head as he paced back and forth in the cell, like a polar bear mentally scarred from being kept in captivity for too long; except Danny's days of captivity may have only just begun.

Subsequent days saw him regularly meet with solicitor James Royston - recommended to him by Sara, who worked as a secretary in the same law firm. However, with forensic evidence from both murder scenes stacked against Danny, together with his angry message left on Elena's answerphone, the prosecution's case was formidable.

Given the violent nature of the crimes and the previous criminal history of the accused, the initial hearing saw Danny refused bail. He was therefore sent to Ringwall Prison for the intervening lengthy remand period until the court case.

CHAPTER 16

Arriving at Ringwall Prison, Danny was stripped of all his clothes and possessions. The officers made him walk to his cramped cell naked, holding just his sky-blue prison uniform to cover his embarrassment. The jeers and laughter from those inmates playing pool and on the card tables on ground floor were only a glimpse of things to come, Danny feared. 'It ain't that cold in here lads,' one of them shouted. The rest laughed.

Danny self-consciously lowered his uniform to cover his dick. He felt his face burn and urged the officer who led him like a dog to get a move on, but the guard was also grinning, seemingly relishing this moment where Danny kissed goodbye to any dignity. This was an initiation done to put newbies in their place, he reckoned, so they didn't get ideas above their station. He'd seen it done to others when last inside and tried not to take it personally, though it still felt as if the world was against him right then. And this would be his world until he was old and grey.

He would later know that heckler as Dagger, on his fourth year of a life sentence. Danny never found out how he got tagged with that nickname, though he knew soon enough that Dagger was in for unprovoked murder and it didn't take much to assume the two were linked.

The officer slammed the cell door shut. The grinding noise of the lock turning reverberated off the grey walls and flashed back harrowing memories of when last banged up. He sat on the edge of his bed fingertips pressed firmly against his temples, trying to fathom where it all went wrong. He then stood and faced the far wall. Leaning forward, his hands and forehead pressed against the wall, he started to bang his fists and skull against the cold painted brick, light taps at first but increasing with force as his anger fired him on. Whether it was to knock himself out or knock some sense into him or just out of the sheer frustration of the injustice, he didn't know. Perhaps it was a vain attempt to cover the emotional pain inside with physical pain. He could deal with physical pain. But it did no good, he just felt bad both inside and out. Ironically, although innocent of any crime, he felt more guilt than most in here, as his brother's needless execution continued on replay in his mind. *Got to get out of here, clear my name and get some justice for Rick.*

But he knew any idea of him escaping this high security establishment was the stuff of dreams once convicted. He needed to find a means to prove his innocence.

The early days inside were just as harsh, if not worse, than his previous stay at Her Majesty's pleasure. Bullying was rife and, given Danny's slight build, he was an easy target. There was a kind of playground hierarchy, but these thugs – mostly doing long stretches for murder and rape - weren't interested in tripping you or calling you names. If the lead honchos didn't take a shine to you, they wasted little time making it known. And, in Danny's case, they didn't.

Initially, Dagger made his life hell. Events came to a head when Dagger forced Danny's face in his toilet bowl swamped by floating faeces and used bog roll. And the reason, he later found, was that Dagger was convinced Danny had nicked one of his ciggies, even though Danny had given them up for good. He was left retching for the rest of that day and he knew it could go on no longer. He didn't want to be dependent on anyone or anything in a place like this. That low point fired Danny on. *Have to do something, or die trying.*

Danny knew from his school days that the best way to stave off such bullying was to either try to ignore and avoid it or deflect the anger with a defensive mechanism like humour. He knew the first option was a non-starter confined within prison walls and he was in no mood to joke and have a laugh with these guys, particularly Dagger, who, in Danny's eyes, was nothing more than oversized knuckle-scraping waste of skin. He did, however, have an ace up his sleeve.

All forms of gambling were rife in the prison, with many of the guards, and even the top dog Governor Simmons, turning a blind eye. Danny had heard a rumour that Simmons was partial to the odd flutter himself. Presumably they felt it was an easy way to keep these captive animals tamed, a distraction for them. Word soon got around that Danny was in the business of making serious money from the horses and, working hard to keep up to date with all the form, thanks partly to Sara making daily visits with a *Racing Post*, he set about finding winners to keep the inmates sweet. It was his only survival mechanism, so he made sure he put the work in. In total, he was working for twenty-two inmates, who used their rationed phone calls to loved ones to relay bets for them on the outside. However, Danny knew it was only a matter of time before it got out of hand.

One Tuesday morning, a guard popped his head around the door and told Danny that there was a visitor. He thought this unusual as Sara visited after midday and his mother on Fridays. He joined the steady flow of prisoners funnelling through to the visitors hall. On clocking who'd turned out to see him, Danny thought seriously about turning on his heel and returning to his cell. Sat at the third table in was Gash, stooped forward above the plastic surface of the table, his fingers fidgeting.

Out of a morbid curiosity, Danny approached and dropped his weight on the seat opposite Gash, who looked a shadow of his former boisterous self. He'd lost weight. Danny could see it in his gaunt face.

Gash looked up and said, 'Danny, how are you mate?' Having never heard Gash voice a thought for anyone but himself, Danny quickly became suspicious of his motives.

'I need to link up with you,' Gash pleaded. 'Start getting results again, like the good old days. I'm still in touch with the betting syndicate.'

'Can't be done,' Danny replied curtly.

'But we were good together.'

'True,' Danny said. 'But that was before my solicitor told me you've refused to attend the court case as a character witness for me.'

'I can't. The case is being reported in all the papers and I haven't declared some of my incomes, you understand.'

'Oh that's just fucking marvellous, I'm probably in 'ere until I'm old and grey once they find me guilty. The most you'd

137

have got was a ticking off and that's even if they bothered investigating it. It was always me, me, me with you.' Gash held his hands up, but Danny wasn't finished. 'Wait a minute, you said you were still in contact with the betting ring. How come?' Gash dropped his hands and stared blankly back. 'I haven't given you a selection for ages.'

'Look, it's like this. I kept dishing out tips in the hope that you're gonna be let off.'

'But I've been in here.'

'I couldn't stop,' Gash said. 'They would've suspected something.'

'So they should. For Christ sake, Gash, you couldn't tip a wheelbarrow.'

'I know, but I had to try,' Gash protested. 'The bills weren't gonna pay themselves.'

'And let me guess, you're on a losing run.'

'Worse than that.'

'You haven't been chasing losses, have you?'

Gash nodded shamefully.

'You fucking fool!' Danny said, burying his face in his hands.

One of the guards looked over, but didn't move. He just cast a cautionary glare in Danny's direction.

'I know, I know,' Gash said. 'But I had no choice. If I'd told 'em the truth, I'd be dropped like that.' He clicked his fingers. 'I'd lose my flat and, with no qualifications or experience, I wouldn't get another job for love nor money.'

'I'm sorry, I left the violin back in my cell.'

'I'm not after sympathy.'

'Good, because you've come to the wrong place.'

Gash had become a sorry sight since he'd last seen him attend the bail hearing.

'Why have you really come here?' Danny asked.

'As I said, I need help. Get me out of this hole.'

'How big is the hole?'

'It's all gone.'

Danny ran his fingers through his hair and sat back into the contours of the uncomfortably moulded plastic chair. 'Let's get this straight, the whole of the betting bank has gone.'

'Afraid so.' Gash pinched the bridge of his nose, tears not far away.

'For fuck sakes. Five years' work, up in smoke.'

All his hard work in accruing the betting bank had gone due to the fantasy world lived in by the pathetic excuse for a human being hunched before him.

'Leave out the crocodile tears,' Danny said. 'You've got yourself in this mess and it's up to you to get out of it. And if I hear you've revealed my name, I know people in here who know people on the outside that can make your life hell.'

'So that's a no.'

'What would I do with any extra money?'

Gash broke down. Seeing the thirty-something man sob before him, Danny had had enough. 'I'll give you the name of a horse expected to win on Saturday. But that's it, I never want to see you again, ever.'

Gash leant forward, visibly trembling, a desperate man looking for one last roll of the dice. 'What's its name?'

'The horse is called Land Of Glory,' Danny said, recalling a horse he was going to pinpoint to his inmates later that week. He thought about saying the name of any old donkey to get his own back, but it wouldn't give him any real satisfaction – *what's done is done* - and it would only serve to aggravate Gash into making a return visit. 'It's being laid out for a maiden at York on Saturday.'

'What price?'

'I dunno. But a winner's a winner, whatever the price. And remember, no more visits.'

Gash slipped Danny his calling card, marked with the Phoenix symbol. A guard approached and inspected the card before allowing Danny to take it. And he did, just to appease Gash. He stood to leave and was escorted from the visitor hall by a guard.

Later that afternoon, he was playing cards with a couple of inmates, quiet types keeping a similarly low profile, that he'd befriended during his short time at Ringwall Prison.

A guard approached the trio crouched over the small bedside cabinet that'd been dragged into the centre of the cell.

He was pulled from the table mid-game. He exchanged concerned glances with his card-school pals before being led by the muted guard to the west wing of the jail housing staff quarters alongside the infamous isolation block. He tried to stem growing nerves with steady breathing and steered his thoughts away from what hideous punishment Governor Simmons had planned for him. It was like being sent to the headmaster's, but only a whole lot worse.

Danny was led through security doors and down a corridor. Carpet replaced the cold concrete of the jail and framed pictures adorned the walls; a small oasis in an otherwise barren building. Danny caught glimpse of one picture, a photo of the Governor shaking hands with a portly gent in regalia and gold chains and surrounded by councillor types, clearly thriving on the perks and the power that came with the job. He turned the corner and waited while the guard knocked on the Governor's door. There was a pause before a muffled 'yes' came from within. Danny had only met Simmons a few times, the first being in the initiation on his first nerve-wrecked day inside. He seemed firm but fair, though his stern, creased face and erect posture was that of someone who wasn't to take any liberties with.

'Sit,' Simmons commanded, scanning paperwork on his desk.

Danny mumbled something incomprehensible, tongue stuck to the roof of his mouth.

Simmons eventually finished scrawling something on a sheet in doctor's hand and, after placing his fountain pen on his desk in what seemed like slow motion, his eyes fixed on Danny, who shifted his weight edgily on the leather seat opposite.

'Do you know why I've brought you here?'

Danny ran through his time there in fast-forward, trying to recall any misdemeanours. Surely he hadn't been framed for something again. 'No.'

'You're a rookie here,' Simmons said, studying what looked like Danny's custodial papers. A rookie, Danny had learnt, was a term covering those in their first year of a stay at Ringwall, like a fresher at Uni.

'Yes, I guess . . . sir.'

'I like to weed out the troublemakers early on,' he said. 'Teach them a lesson, keep order.'

Danny didn't like either the tone or content of Simmons's remark.

'My guards tell me that you are passing on horseracing information to other inmates.'

'Yeah, can't deny it, been giving tips to my fellow inmates,' Danny confessed, confident that it didn't breach prison rules, 'but not for money.'

'Why then?'

'To save my skin. Keep 'em happy, off my back,' Danny said. 'I've done nothing wrong.'

'Not the way I see it,' Simmons said, looking down on Danny with those piercing eyes. 'Encouraging gambling is strictly forbidden within my prison regime. Do you understand?' Danny nodded attentively.

There was a pause. Simmons removed his glasses and sat back in his executive leather chair, making a steeple with his fingers. 'I sense you're not one to respect rules. I'm going to make an example of you.'

Averting Simmons's searching eyes, Danny glanced down at the desk. Something grabbed his attention. Lying innocuously on the maple desk was a letter addressed to Simmons. It wasn't the typed body of text on the sheet that seized his attention, but the symbol embossed in the top right corner. The fiery red plumage of a bird stretching its wings, Danny would recognise that image anywhere: *the Phoenix betting partnership.*

His gaze locked on Simmons again, barely masking a look of surprise. Danny was aware of the governor's penchant for

141

gambling, but could he really be a member of the Phoenix mob? Before the punishment was dealt, he rolled the dice. What had he to lose? 'I can give you the info instead, I don't mind.'

Simmons's eyes widened but his mouth remained tight shut. Whether the reaction was that of surprise at the sheer audacity of the offer or anger at the pushy request of this rookie, Danny didn't know, but felt sure the answer was coming.

It was Simmons's turn to glance at the embossed letter in front of him. He said, 'I don't need your money.'

'I can see,' Danny said, looking up at the gallery of photos colouring the walls. 'You clearly enjoy living the high life.'

Simmons frowned, but said nothing.

Danny continued, 'Whatever dividend you've been promised from 'em, I'm afraid you can forget it.'

'What?'

'The Phoenix betting syndicate. I was the informant behind it and, since I've been stuck in here, some clueless fool has gone 'n blown it all.'

'What?' Simmons repeated, fuelled by a mix of anger and confusion this time.

'Want proof?' Danny asked. 'Phone numbers, names. I got 'em. Cos I'm the man they used.

'Nonsense.'

The pregnant pause that followed seemed to last forever. Danny sensed he now held the upper hand and felt like saying, *in your own time, I'm probably only in here for two life stretches*, but thought better of it.

'Fair enough, no skin off my nose,' Danny said. 'It's just, from where I'm sitting, it's a no-lose deal. For you, I mean.'

Simmons's creased brow began to glisten in the afternoon sunshine beaming through the sole window to his right. He stood, walked to the window and opened it. 'If this . . . is true.'

'I swear on my mother's life.'

'So what? Half of them in here would sell their mother like that.' Simmons turned and clicked his fingers. 'I still don't believe you.'

142

'Don't believe me, or don't want to believe me,' Danny said before offering Gash's business card to Simmons. 'Speak to the guy who blew the lot, his name's Gash.'

Simmons sat down, as if struck by hammer blow, and ran his hand over his face, as though on the verge of a breakdown.

'I'm giving you a lifeline,' Danny said. 'I can help you carry on living in the manner you've become accustomed.'

Instinctively, Simmons sunk his face in his hands, before looking up, as if suddenly aware he still had company and didn't want to reveal his predicament.

The governor's apparent overreaction left Danny slightly off-guard. There was more to this, but what?

'If what you've told me is the truth and, be clear, I will check, well . . .'

'I'm sorry, truly I am,' Danny said. 'This needn't happen, I can help fill the financial hole, just you see.'

Simmons remained slouched over his desk, the demeanour of a beaten man. He growled, 'If this is some sick joke, you will be sorry.'

Danny wasn't counting on such an extreme reaction, clearly a release of tension that had been brewing for some time. Mixing with the gambling fraternity, he'd witness enough people on the verge of a financial precipice in the past to know that there was another one sitting before him.

'It's no joke.' Danny paused. 'Let me help you. We'd make a good team.'

'Get out,' Simmons barked.

Danny feared he'd pushed too hard. 'But-'

'I need time to think,' Simmons said. 'Now get out!'

Danny needed no more encouragement. He'd sewn the seed of doubt and was willing to wait for it to grow.

Indeed, at first light, Danny was dragged to Simmons's office.

'Had time to think?' Danny croaked.

'Quiet.'

Sorry, Danny mouthed, before pressing his lips together, mindful of his habit of saying too much when nervous.

143

'I spent last evening considering your offer,' Simmons said.

And through the night, Danny reckoned, noting the governor's bloodshot eyes.

Simmons stood and said, 'What I'm about to say to you is in the strictest confidence. If I so much as hear a word spread to anyone, and I mean anyone, I will come down on you like a ton of bricks.' He clenched his fist and hammered it on the finely polished surface of his desk. 'And your life will not be worth living. Understand.'

Perplexed, Danny asked, 'So you want in?'

Simmons's tone softened. 'Sole rights to this . . . information.'

Danny struggled to hide the smile, a mix of relief and surprise. *Had he heard right? The big fish had bitten!*

He guessed there was always a degree of corruption at every level in the prison system, but this took a bit of digesting. So much so, he thought he'd misheard.

'What's in it for me?'

'Name your price,' Simmons said guardedly. 'There are limits, of course.'

'My freedom,' Danny replied.

Simmons brow lowered, awaiting a serious offer.

'For this to work, I'd need all the latest form books, access to the internet and a private phone.' Danny paused, but didn't get the negative response he was awaiting. 'Of course, to obtain the greatest long term profits,' Danny continued, 'I need to be on the gallops, see 'em in the flesh, like.'

'I cannot allow such liberties. It would be more than *my* job's worth if the Board of Governors found out.'

'Okay, leave that for now,' Danny said, keeping the deal alive. 'But, if I'm to stop handing this information out to the guards and the other inmates, I'd need some form of protection, or segregation.'

Simmons jotted something down on the paper in front of him. Danny craned his neck but couldn't catch sight of what the

Governor had written. 'I'll see what I can arrange. But if a word is breathed about any of this, you know what will happen.'

Danny raised both hands, 'Don't have to tell me, it's just as much in my interests as yours.'

Just two days later, Danny was ordered to gather what few things he possessed and was moved from the main G-wing to the isolation block. Those aggrieved inmates making a mint from his tips were told Danny's sudden disappearance to another wing was a punishment for his gambling activities - 'a bad influence on others' was the official line sent down by Simmons.

He knew less experienced gamblers such as Simmons had a short patience span and would soon get cold feet if initial signs weren't positive. Much to Danny's relief, he got off to a flyer. The opening trial month with Simmons saw him give twelve selections, five of which won, netting the governor just over £30,000 to level stakes. Needless to say, Danny was flavour of the month when Simmons saw the money roll in.

Despite Danny's cautionary note that results could dip at any time, Simmons remained ebullient about their agreement and, as far as either was concerned, suspicions about the setup were not raised. The guards were told these allowances were afforded for good behaviour. Arrangements were made for him to be moved to a regulation cell whenever an external audit of the prison was planned. The Governor was apparently given plenty of warning before such visits were arranged, allowing ample time to ship him over to the main wing.

On Sunday, Danny glanced up at the clock on the wall. 11.16 A.M. He sat at his desk, watching recordings of the previous day's racing on his small portable TV, featuring the comfortable win of Land Of Glory at York. He was also taping the races for future form study. They provide an invaluable record of each horse's true performance, one that doesn't always correspond with the form comment in the racing publications, and it gave him a further vital edge over most punters.

Potted plants were scattered around the cell, including on the windowsill, and pictures of champion racehorses of the past adorned the flesh coloured walls.

Soothing classical music from his iPod helped created an ambient mood. He stretched his arms. A knock at the door broke his dreamy, passive state. 'Come.'

A guard poked his head around the door and requested his presence in Simmons's office immediately. He quickly grew suspicious of this slightly unusual request. Simmons rarely called on him during the week and never in the morning. He knew Danny would be hard at work searching out the next winner. He frowned at the possibility of his current lap of luxury disappearing.

Simmons was sat at his broad desk to the far side of the room. He wore a Saville Row suit and a sallow expression. 'Sit.'

'What's this about?' No response. 'Results have been good, right?'

Simmons replied, 'More pressing matters have come to my attention.'

Danny's heart and mind began to sink. *Was the honeymoon period over?*

'Yesterday, at the monthly meeting of the Board of Governors, two of my colleagues on the committee took me aside and confronted me about allegations surrounding the special treatment of a particular inmate.'

'Go on, hit me with the goods,' Danny said, 'or should that be bads.'

'Somehow, rumour had got to them about our *agreement*.'

'Shit,' Danny muttered.

'And, as a result-' Simmons paused. 'They want to come on board.'

'What?'

'They want to be party to this information.'

Danny laughed.

'Quiet!' Simmons barked.

'Hang on, what's in it for me, I'd need something extra, a reward. And, before you ask, money's little good for me cooped up in 'ere.'

'So what are you angling for?' Simmons asked suspiciously.

'To keep results good, I need to be on the gallops at Lambourn and Newmarket, keep my finger on the pulse. There's a new generation of horses coming through each year, see, results will suffer in the long run, I need to see 'em live.'

'Daniel, you're in for double murder.'

'I'm awaiting trial, whatever happened to innocent until proven guilty,' Danny protested. 'I didn't do it.'

It was Simmons's turn to laugh. 'Along with ninety per cent of them in here.'

'Surely you've the power to sign for day releases,' Danny said. 'I'm willing to be tagged if you don't trust me.'

Simmons pursed his lips, considering the options open to him; all of them highly unethical and unprofessional. Both knew if their secret was uncovered, the cost to Simmons would be far greater than for Danny. The Governor had more to lose, farther to fall. After all, Danny was already disgraced in the eyes of the public. However, the powerful drive fuelled by greed and his current financial mess could never be underestimated and Danny, being a compulsive gambler in remission, knew this only too well.

'I'll see what I can do,' Simmons said. 'But if I agree to this and you fail to return by a specific time. You will be caught and your life will be made hell!'

'I'd never do a runner,' Danny reassured, but the Governor's attentions were now drawn to piles of paperwork on his desk. Danny stood and said, 'Oh and by the way, I need my jacket cleaned if that's possible. It looks shabby and smells as bad as it looks.'

Simmons sighed. 'Very well, leave it with me. I'll pass it on to prison laundry. Now go.'

Danny was led back to his cell by the guard who'd waited the other side of the door. Three days and a 4/1 winning selection later, Danny was once again summoned to the Governor's lair.

Simmons sat upright at his desk. 'Sit.'

Danny entered and dropped on the seat opposite.

'I've considered your proposal and I'll agree to it in the short term,' he said. 'But if there is *any* indication that suspicions are being raised either inside or outside prison walls, I will terminate the agreement and we'll have to reconsider our deal.'

'There won't be,' Danny reassured, though, deep down, he was equally uncertain of what the future held for them both.

The following morning, Danny was once again ushered to the Governor's office.

Simmons disappeared beneath his desk and reappeared with Danny's fleece draped over both arms, as if about to present an award.

'Oh you got it done, thanks.'

'They found a scrap of paper and a twenty pence piece in the lining of the jacket. There's a hole in one of the pockets.'

Danny grabbed the coat and then took the scrap of paper. 'Thanks, again,' he said and glanced at the paper. 'Father of the sun!' was written in blue ink, faded and blotchy. Beneath was a telephone number, the one he'd jotted down from the phonebook in Elena's house. The number had completely slipped his mind under the extreme pressures of being on the run and during the lead up to the court appearance. 'Must be an old friend,' he said cagily.

Simmons replied. 'Now, do you mind?' He motioned with his hand towards the door.

Returning to his cell, he dropped the fleece on his bed, flattened the torn scrap of paper on his desk and sat staring at the number.

Over the next few days, Danny pondered hard about whether or not to ring the number he'd rediscovered. Eventually, he thought it best to let sleeping dogs lie. What good would it do? *Probably just some distant relation or old friend*, he thought, as he placed the crumpled slip of paper in the desk drawer.

A week later, Danny was allowed on his first day release and, true to his word, he made a beeline for the Limekiln gallops at Newmarket before returning punctually. For the first dozen or so releases, Danny was electronically tagged as a precaution until trust grew over time. He ventured further afield, making regular visits to his old haunts at Lambourm, under strict orders to limit contact purely to those who could provide information.

He soon familiarised himself with the latest crop of juveniles and glued broken links with entrusted contacts from the past. Few of them batted an eyelid on seeing him, much to his surprise and bemusement as, at the time, the murder of Dean McCourt made big news in the racing community throughout the country. Most were so wrapped up in their own business, they had little care for how or why Danny still had his freedom. On the rare occasion where his presence was queried, he shrugged it off with the response, 'Managed to get bail.'

The impressive run of results ensured status quo during subsequent weeks. As Danny became more accustomed to his new regime, which wasn't far away from his life when on the outside, he pushed himself harder than ever to maintain the flow of winners.

He regularly spent three hours work-watching on the gallops before returning to his cell via a back door used by prison staff. There, he would study form during the afternoon while watching the live racing on the specialist satellite channels, picked up via a receiver in the Governor's room. He ate better than any other prisoner, the Governor ordering extra portions off his own menu.

Occasionally, the Governor would ask his opinion regarding bringing more in on the betting syndicate, but Danny was wary. The more on board the greater the risk of a member inadvertently spilling the beans. Simmons made it clear he didn't share Danny's caution. *Clearly taking a cut of their winnings also*, he thought.

CHAPTER 17

Danny stood at his usual spot on the Newmarket gallops in Suffolk watching attentively as a group of three horses approached. Steam shot from their nostrils, like pistons, as they stretched out in an easy piece of work on that hazy morning.

He couldn't help noticing that one of the threesome lagged behind, despite some serious urgings from the work rider in the saddle. Normally, he'd merely dismiss this as a moderate recruit lacking ability or a rogue who just doesn't try on the gallops and at the track. However, he was taken aback by this well-made burnished chestnut colt with a lovely conformation and distinct ewe-neck. He wore four navy socks to protect his short, light-boned fore and hind legs. Against the other two working alongside, he stood out as a physical specimen. He couldn't be certain but, from their lack of size and maturity, they gave the impression of juveniles.

He sidled up to Jeremy Gibbs - who was standing further along the gallops - one of the leading lights in the training brigade at Newmarket, and the rest of the country for that matter. He'd regularly provided Danny with information about his string for a small remuneration, but that was before the murders. Gibbs's eyes were glued to powerful zoom binoculars fixed on the next Lot carving up the gallops.

'Any stars to look out for?' Danny said tentatively.

Gibbs dropped his binoculars and turned. His face went fish-white, as if seeing a ghost.

'Don't worry,' Danny assured. 'Got granted bail until the trial.'

'What are you after?'

'Gonna be found innocent, so thought I'd better keep my eye in.'

Gibbs swallowed hard before eyeing Danny up and down, as if not convinced. 'What is it, Danny? I'm a busy man.'

'What's the name of the horse with the blue socks?'

'Why do you ask?'

'Just took my eye, that's all,' Danny said. 'Can't put my finger on why, seein' as it was just thumped by the other two in its work, but there's something about it.'

'It's bone idle,' Gibbs replied. 'But, boy, when he gets to the track, he's a serious talent. Potential star.'

'What's he done?'

'Placed in a maiden and then won a good sprint at Ascot.' The binoculars again met with Gibbs's broad chest. He looked at Danny, who stood to his side. 'The colt's name is Hyper Tension; a name you'll be hearing a good deal more of, that's for sure.'

'No offence, but he doesn't look like a speedball.'

'Sprinting won't be his game. I'm under strict orders from the owners. The long term goal will be next year's Derby.'

'Epsom?'

'Correct,' Gibbs said, 'the one race that's eluded me.'

Danny couldn't quite believe that one of the country's most astute handlers would dream of classic aspirations with the colt just trounced on the gallop strip before him. Given the youngster's appealing conformation and athleticism, he continued to probe. 'When's he out next?'

'We're saving him for an autumn campaign. The Dewhurst has been earmarked.'

'And you think he'll stay seven furlongs?'

He afforded Danny a knowing glance. 'He'll stay.'

Danny knew the Dewhurst Stakes at Newmarket was one of the most prestigious juvenile races that normally lived up to its Group 1 billing. He made a mental note of the horse, though he was still to be convinced he would stay the extra two furlongs, particularly over the stiff undulations at the historic home of Flat racing.

Days led to months and, as the Governors' bank balance continued to swell, greater effort and more stringent measures were put in place to prevent the recently formed gambling ring being exposed. Regular visits from his mother and Sara provided the emotional backbone, helping to maintain Danny's level-headed approach to the all-important betting decisions and, as

151

results continued to go his way, he was kept in the manner he'd grown accustomed to.

With the Flat turf season drawing to a close, Danny was concerned by how he would keep the Governors happy during the winter, so he started to study the National Hunt scene. Danny often swerved the All-Weather meetings as they were generally low-grade fare and could produce unpredictable results. He feared the privileges would be stripped from him until the spring when the Flat campaign started up again on grass. After all, he'd accrued some reliable contacts from dual purpose yards - those who train on the Flat and over the jumps - in preparation for the winter months and diligent form study would help ensure the profits continued to grow.

The following day, Danny rang Simmons from his cell and told him to place a maximum bet, which equated to £12,000, £4,000 from each of the Governors involved in the betting ring.

The betting forecast from the Press Association and the *Racing Post* agreed Hyper Tension would start at roughly 3/1 for the feature juvenile race - the Dewhurst - at Headquarters, dishing up a monster payday if the colt were to live up to the hype and form.

Minutes before race time, he watched the small screen of the portable telly in his cell. The race was being covered by a terrestrial channel. He saw them stretch down to post on the sweeping lush green grass of the expansive Suffolk track. Hyper Tension strode to the starting post with some purpose and looked alert. The colt's ears were pricked while circling patiently behind the stalls, though Danny had noticed he'd lathered up between his hind quarters. It wasn't unusual for a horse to sweat in the prelims, particularly amidst the buzz and tension during the build up to a big race, but on such a cool autumn afternoon it signified the horse was under some stress.

Danny rested his hand on the receiver of his phone, preparing to call Simmons and tell him to hedge off the bet. The price of Hyper Tension had shortened to 9/4 and, having already taken odds a fraction over 3/1, there was a no-risk profit – which Danny knew in bettors' slang as an arb (short for arbitrage) - to be made by hedging the bet off at a shorter price and saving the money for another day.

The horses continued to circle, waiting for the starter to give the order for the first to be installed. Danny swiftly logged on to the internet to scour over the form and pedigree of the horse one last time. The clock was ticking if he was to change his mind. He brought up a window housing Hyper Tension's stats and, on seeing the owner of the juvenile, his heart quickened a pace; it was the Definca Partnership.

'Oh shit,' Danny whispered. Given that the very same ownership was involved in the laying off of horses on the list found on Dean, there was every chance they'd be up to similar no good with this one. Danny couldn't take the risk and picked up the receiver. He punched the direct link to Simmons's office, but the line was engaged. 'Oh fucking shit.'

Four of the nine runners had been installed by this point. He had no access to the betting exchange account in which the bet was placed; only Simmons knew the username and password. With no way of laying off the bet, he sat back in his chair and prayed the owners, presumably headed by Simeon Lockhart, had gone straight and the days of corruption were behind them. With Dean now dead – the source behind the mysterious defeats of the previous horses - perhaps the Definca Partnership and Lockhart had turned over a new leaf.

Either way, it was too late for Danny to chicken out; the last horse had now been loaded and all that he could do was to watch and deal with the consequences of his actions. Not to notice the owners of the selection was an uncharacteristic oversight for Danny, given the size and importance of the bet. Having been so engrossed by the horse's appearance and form on the track, he'd simply forgotten to check out the connections. Not normally a vital factor, but, in rare circumstances like this, it proved crucial to the selection process.

'They're all set, and they're off!' said the racing commentator.

Hyper Tension, who was drawn three off the rail, was soon tucked in behind the leading pair, a couple of lengths off the pace. As they swept past the three-furlong marker, the pacesetter and second favourite, White Petal, an unbeaten filly from Stuart Martin's yard, had extended the lead to three lengths, causing the packed crowd in front of the grandstand to roar in anticipation.

Danny gripped the arms of his wooden chair seeing Hyper Tension embroiled in a barging match as his jockey Michael O'Bourne tried valiantly to create some space and get out of the pocket he'd found himself in. Once clear of the traffic problems, Hyper Tension's power-packed muscular quarters kicked into action, propelling him into second in a matter of strides, sending the crowd to fever pitch as the duel between the two most fancied runners began to unfold before them.

Danny stood, eyes fixed on the small screen as he listened intently to the commentator who said, 'White Petal has first run on Hyper Tension, but the favourite has closed the gap to a length, with Martooth well held in third. A furlong to go and White Petal is strongly pressed by Hyper Tension. Well inside the final furlong and now Hyper Tension hits hyper-drive and goes on. Hyper Tension wins it by just over a length to White Petal. Martooth holds on for a remote third.'

Danny fell back on his chair and breathed a huge sigh of relief. He'd made an error and, by a stroke of luck, he'd got away with it.

'Some horse,' he muttered. He felt a warm smile spread across his face, heart still pounding, as he watched the horse canter back to the winners' enclosure.

That buzz, however, provided a mere brief break in the dark cloud that hung constantly over him. Feelings of remorse as the realization of where he was and how he'd got there still cast a great shadow over his mood. More than anything, he wanted his freedom back; a return to how things used to be. And, while he'd made the best of a bad situation on remand, he was still nowhere closer to finding how he could possibly prove Lockhart's guilt.

154

CHAPTER 18

Danny kept a low profile during the winter months, making steady long term profits from backing on the All-Weather tracks and over the jumps to smaller stakes. The scaled down bets appeared to work well as Danny found his feet with two codes of racing that he'd not specialised in on the outside. The routine of form study, keeping record of speed ratings and the occasional visit to both track and gallops helped keep his mind alert. Although he would have been lying to say he wasn't glad that the turf Flat season was now in sight.

    Danny sat in his cell. There was a good hour before the first race was off and he'd finished all his form study for the day. With nothing better to do, he glanced down at the pages of the *Racing Post* lying open on his desk. His eyes casually scanning down page eight, full of news snippets alongside a naps table of all the newspapers - national and regional - vying for the coveted title of becoming champion tipster. But that wasn't what had caught Danny's eye. A small piece headed: Hyper Tension Bids to Further Emulate the great Hyperion. The article occupied a single column strip running down the left of the page. A seemingly insignificant piece, probably just a filler, but Danny was nevertheless drawn to it having continued to be impressed by the physical presence of Hyper Tension on the gallops over the winter. Danny read:

Hyper Tension had quickly emerged as a leading light among an ordinary crop of juveniles last year, culminating in a ready win in the Group 1 Dewhurst Stakes at Newmarket. The son of Burgundy had already recorded impressive wins in the Listed New Stakes run over 5f at Ascot before narrowly winning the Prince of Wales's Stakes over a furlong farther at Goodwood. The last horse to achieve such a feat was the legendary Hyperion, who went on to land the Epsom Derby the following season. The rising star is a timely boon for owners in the Definca Partnership which was forced to switch its fifteen-horse team to Newmarket trainer

Jeremy Gibbs after the sad death of former champion handler Michael Raynham.

'To bag a prestigious Group 1 like the Dewhurst was a great fillip for all concerned with the horse and I'm glad to report he's wintered well since,' Gibbs said. 'He's not big and takes a bit of getting ready for his races, but he's all heart and has clearly got a Rolls Royce engine.'

Regarding Gibbs's newly forged and successful relationship with the Definca Partnership, he said, 'I'm delighted with my involvement with these owners, as they haven't always enjoyed the best of luck in the past and it's always great when a good one comes along. It makes it all worthwhile.'

Yeah, they've been really unlucky, Danny scoffed. He thought he'd heard the last of the Definca Partnership. Was it still being run by Lockhart? With Dean McCourt dead, perhaps he was actually playing to win with his horses. Funds were clearly short following the liquidation of Simcorp Enterprises.

Danny's enquiring eyes narrowed as they focused on the emerging star's name Hyper Tension; the letters making up the name Hyperion sprung from the page. *That's odd*, he thought. Was this merely a coincidence? Danny didn't believe in coincidences. He logged on and typed a search on Hyperion. The syndicate was clearly a fan of the great horse and appeared to be following the same career path with this rising star.

If they were mapping out the same races, which one would Hyper Tension be going for next?

The search engine threw up a myriad of results, a mix of horseracing websites and those concerning the Greek Titan of the same name. His eyes scanned down the screen until coming to an abrupt stop. A familiar phrase had caught his attention and it wasn't from one of the horse sites. A sharp bolt of pain shot between his shoulder blades as he read the words: 'father of the sun.' It took him straight back to the horrific scene at Elena's cottage, the sights and smells still seemed only too real. But what could it mean? Why did she write it above a telephone number in her phonebook?

He clicked on the web address and it soon became apparent that, according to Greek legend, Hyperion was the father of the sun, the dawn and the moon, whose name literally read 'the one above' taken from the text *Theogony* by Hesiod.

He fished for the scrap of paper that he'd left to fester in his drawer and unravelled it, bathed in light splashed from the desk lamp. *Father of the sun! This was no coincidence*, he thought, *but what the hell did it mean?* He picked up the receiver from its cradle and punched the number beneath the writing scribbled in his own hand.

The rings stopped. 'Hello?'

'Who is this?' came the reply, an elderly man's voice.

'I was a friend of Elena and her grandson Dean.' Danny paused. 'You knew them.'

'Who is this?' the voice demanded, more sternly this time.

'My name's Danny, I was a good friend of Dean. I know you were connected to his grandma Elena in some way.'

The line went dead. Danny pressed redial. 'Please don't hang up, hear me out, please.'

'You've been charged with their murders,' the man raged. 'Listen, I don't know how you got my number, but don't you ever call again! Do you hear me?!'

'Wait, I can explain,' Danny couldn't spit the words out fast enough. 'I didn't kill either of 'em, but I know who did and why.'

There was a moment's silence. *A good sign*, Danny reckoned, *at least there was no dial tone*. 'Dean left an object for me, which I now reckon was the reason for his death.'

The voice at the other end of the line began to break with emotion. 'Meet me.'

'Name the place and time, and I'm there.'

'At the Winchester Pub in Stevenage. Say two, tomorrow afternoon.'

'On the dot,' Danny replied. 'Like I said, my name's Danny and I'll be the one with a *Racing Post* open.'

He would miss tomorrow afternoon's racing, but he knew the potential reward would far outweigh any gains from watching

157

the nags, if there was the slightest chance he'd find out a vital clue. What was the underlying reason behind his brother's death? Why he faced, if convicted, serving successive life sentences? *It had to be worth it.*

CHAPTER 19

Danny lay on his bed, awake. He half-opened his eyes on hearing the rustle of a *Racing Post* being forced through the serving hatch in the door. He sighed as the slightly torn tabloid spread to the stone floor in a mess. It had been posted by Simmons on his way back from the morning inspection tour of the prison.

He rubbed his eyes and laid the paper on his desk as he tried to shift his mind into gear for a form-studying session before leaving for the rendezvous with Elena's acquaintance. However, having read the front cover, his eyes and mind were already open and receptive. The headline read:

MARY ROSE SUNK WITHOUT TRACE!

In a sensational Shergar-style raid, the world's leading broodmare, Mary Rose, was snatched from her base at Barton Manor Stud in Derbyshire late yesterday afternoon. Police have confirmed that the nine-year-old mare, whose progeny have amassed 26 Group 1s between them, was taken from her box at just after five o'clock under the noses of staff.

Owners and employees at the stud were unavailable for comment, but were said to be shocked and deeply upset by the incident and pleaded for the mare's safe return. But one insider said, 'All concerned with the mare are distraught and left speechless by the audacity of the raid. Needless to say, we're desperate for her safe return and plead with whoever has taken her to search their consciences.'

Danny was well aware of the stories regarding Shergar's unruly behaviour probably causing his ultimate demise after the kidnappers lost patience and shot him dead. However, the insider commented, 'Thank god there's no problem on that score, she possesses a lovely temperament that can only help her chances should she be held against her will.'

Fucking hell, Danny thought, *is nothing sacred no more*. The tactical manoeuvre of jockey Ryan Cross on Mary Rose in the King George six years previous – the root cause of Danny's premature retirement - was still painfully raw in his mind.

Although smart on the track, she'd since come into her own at stud and he knew the disappearance would send shockwaves through the horseracing industry.

He turned to page three for the remainder of the story.

Danny read on:

It is an undisputed fact that Mary Rose is the finest broodmare for many a decade and boasts the highest ever recorded fee per successful covering.

Rupert Lacroix a spokesman available at the Jockey Club was quoted as saying, 'It is with great regret that we announce such a callous incident and, rest assured, every effort will be made to capture the culprits. I must remind you, however, it is an isolated incident and breeders and owners should not be overly concerned for the security of their horses, though we do have to emphasise the importance of basic security precautions at all times. We cannot confirm as yet what the motive behind the abduction is, though I can confirm the owners have yet to receive a ransom demand.'

Later that day, Danny arrived at Stevenage with time to spare. He felt a tingling sense of anticipation. The Winchester was a quaint country pub dressed with baskets of budding flowers outside and oak beams traversed low ceilings with uneven wood and brick floors on the inside. A grand Inglenook fireplace was the centre piece of the bar area and an array of real beers were on tap. Danny opted for a lager.

He grabbed a spare table and placed his jacket over an empty seat opposite. He stared blankly at his pint, watching the endless streams of tiny bubbles rising to the top. He opened the *Racing Post* brought along to identify himself and started to check out that afternoon's action – minor Flat meetings at Newcastle and Lingfield, plus a spring jumping card at Ludlow.

It had passed the time they'd arranged to meet and Danny began to fear that the stranger had lied, just to get shot of him. And then the door opened. A distinctive man walked in wearing a long black raincoat and carrying a closed umbrella. He briefly scanned the room. On seeing Danny reading the *Racing Post*, he stopped in his tracks and approached. 'Daniel?'

Danny nodded. 'I'll get 'em in.'

'A half of best bitter,' the man said.

He returned and placed the pints carefully on the small circular wooden table. The man's bald head reflected the bright wall lights in the bar area, like a finely polished billiard ball, and he bore a thick coarse beard of grey. *Early eighties*, Danny guessed.

The man took a sip and then offered his hand, guard seemingly lowered. 'John Tavistock.'

'Danny Rawlings.' Danny reciprocated the gesture.

'I know,' Tavistock said. 'What I don't know is why have you contacted me after all this time? Bringing back painful memories.'

Danny finished off his first pint and shifted the fresh one to the same beer mat. 'I'll cut to the quick. I dunno whether the police told you, but there was a list of horses found on Elena's grandson Dean and, aside from the fact that they all got stuffed at short odds, get this, they're all owned by the same people.'

'Shouldn't the Jockey Club be looking into this? Or the police?'

'The Jockey Club did, but, as luck wouldn't have it, they found no wrong doing. As for the police, they ain't interested. It's all circumstantial, I need hard evidence,' Danny said. He lowered his voice, 'The name of the syndicate is the Definca Partnership which also happens to be the name of the drug this guy called Simeon Lockhart patented, see. Lockhart must've used Dean's position as stable lad in Raynham's yard to get his horses beat in a betting scam. With the drug being withdrawn not long after hitting the market, Lockhart discovers a back-up plan to cover growing debts and was willing to kill to get the job done. The words money, root and evil spring to mind.'

'What plan?'

'I dunno, but there's a silver box, passed on to me from Dean.'

'What?' Tavistock spluttered.

161

'A silver skippet box,' Danny confirmed. 'It's a curse. Why? Do you know of it?'

'Elena gave it to Dean,' Tavistock croaked, his face now creased and blanched. 'As a gift.'

Danny's blue eyes widened. 'So you do?'

Tavistock didn't reply, deep in reflection. 'You are too young to remember a horse called Hyperion.'

Danny leant forward. 'Go on.'

Tavistock adjusted his weight for comfort, as if about to tell a life story, 'In 1930, a chestnut colt was born that would have a monumental impact on the horseracing and breeding industry to this day. His name was Hyperion.' The man's eyes lit up just saying the name, as if it triggered a flood of memories still fresh. 'At the time, there was nothing remarkable about his physical appearance. In fact, he was weaned late and, with short cannon bones and a far from robust constitution, he barely reached 15 hands. So he, along with another small foal were left at Side Hill Stud, while the more forward types were sent on to Liverpool. But his owner/breeder, Lord Derby, had faith in him you see. Hyperion was sired by a Triple Crown winner called Gainsborough out of a prolific winning mare, and possessed the brutish strength of a wrestler. The horse was a street fighter. His trademark long, level conformation and ewe-neck were stamped on his progeny for generations to come. Legends of the game like Mill Reef and Nijinsky, real superstars, can all be traced back to Hyperion.'

Danny wasn't sure where this was going, but felt he should humour the old man with his memories. But then he recalled the engraving on the side of the skippet box. 'Gainsborough. You said Gainsborough.'

'He was sired by a champion, but his future record, both on the track and at stud, would surpass his father countless times over.'

'But what's this got to do with the box?'

'Elena was married to Hyperion's vet, they separated and she remarried, he didn't.' Tavistock took another gulp of his bitter. 'Over the ages, a few with foresight, mainly landed gentry types, kept, as mementos and keepsakes, a token of their cherished champion racehorses, often a lock of mane. The Earl of Monmouthshire kept the skin of his champion and hung it from his wall, way back in the eighteenth century. Hyperion was no exception.'

'How do ya know all this?'

Tavistock's eyes bore into Danny with a laser-like intensity, as if about to unburden a long-held secret, 'I was his vet.'

'I don't. . . I don't understand, you said the colt was born in 1930.'

'Not only was he successful, he possessed a strong heart and virile loins. He kept his prolific stud career going right up until his death at 30 in 1960. In human years, he was 120. There's hope for us all.' A Mona Lisa grin spread across Tavistock's face, only to dissolve almost immediately.

'I knew the tipster name for The Independent was Hyperion, but, until this, I'd never heard of the horse,' Danny said.

'The breeding community is well aware of the legacy of Hyperion. His skeleton is at the National Museum of Horseracing at Newmarket. And the Jockey Club even honoured him with a life-size bronze statue by Skeaping outside their headquarters in Newmarket. The monument was bequeathed to the racing authorities by the now late Lord Derby in 1996. The pint-sized legend now watches over his many descendants as they walk off to the gallops.'

'I'd seen it many times, but had never bothered to look at the plaque,' Danny said, slightly ashamed to admit. 'But I still don't understand what this has to do with the box.'

Tavistock said, 'Firstly, describe the box to me.'

Danny recalled the time he'd held the box up to the light in the watchtower. 'Um . . .it was oval, it had a picture on its enamel lid, what looked like silver sides, possibly solid silver.' Tavistock nodded. 'And a ruby base.'

Tavistock stopped nodding. 'Wrong.'

'What?'

'The base was glass.'

'Coloured glass?'

'Plain glass, two strengthened sheets.'

'I don't understand.'

'There's a thin gap between them,' Tavistock said, 'encasing the blood of Hyperion. The base of the box provided an airtight vacuum and, choosing a fairly valuable box as a container ensured it would never be discarded. That was a fatal mistake, as it turns out.'

'Was it to keep his memory fresh?'

'You could say that. I missed the old sod and longed for the day, when I'm old and grey,' Tavistock ran his hand over his gleaming head, 'well old, when I could see him again.'

'By saving his DNA?' Danny asked.

'I had no idea that it would cause such misery. I took a sample of Hyperion's blood when his health was failing, thinking little of it. I sorely wished I hadn't now.'

'You're not to blame,' Danny said, seeing Tavistock on the verge of breaking down. 'But couldn't Lockhart have just stolen the skeleton at Newmarket?'

'He could have, there would be some remnants of DNA, though, given its exposure to air over such a lengthy period, after years of degradation, the condition wouldn't be sufficient to clone, not with today's technology.' There was a pause. 'Wait a minute!' Tavistock pushed back on his seat, the legs scraped the wooden floor, as if preparing for flight. 'Why so many questions? Tell me you're not one of them?'

'No,' Danny said, faintly insulted. 'Do I look like a killer?'

Tavistock didn't reply immediately. 'Why have you asked me here?'

'You knew Elena McCourt, she had your number written in her phonebook.'

'God rest her soul.' Tavistock drew a cross in the air with his hand.

'As I said on the phone, I knew Elena's grandson, Dean, who asked me to take care of the box,' Danny continued. 'There was a letter he'd written, as if he knew his life was in danger.'

'But where is the box now?'

'I can't say for sure, but I'd bet any money you like it's with Lockhart.'

Tavistock glanced scornfully.

'I had no choice, the madman had already killed my brother, threatened to kill me and, for good measure, framed me with double murder,' Danny fumed. 'And if we're pointing fingers here – why on earth did you allow the box to reach your grandson? Knowing what it contained.'

'I kept possession of the box and told few of its meaning, significance – to possibly clone the ultimate horse for thoroughbred racing. When Elena and I split, she laid claim to the box. Seeing no use for it, I didn't protest, but when I heard she'd passed the box down to Dean, my heart sank. I begged Elena not to and I didn't have the heart to take it back off him, he didn't have much you see. Instead, I told him never breathe a word of the box's true value. He agreed.'

'And you think he told Simeon Lockhart?'

'Just two days before Dean's death, I received a call from him. That bastard had bullied my boy endlessly.'

'You called him: 'my boy.' Were you close then?'

'We - Elena and I - treated that boy like our own son, as his parents weren't around to care for him. I repeatedly asked for the box back, to protect him, but he refused, saying he could deal with it. I cannot understand why,' Tavistock said, as if to cleanse his conscience.

'I can help you with that one. As I said, Dean was boosting his measly wages by passing on info to Lockhart.'

A look of concern was now etched on Tavistock's face, so Danny thought it best to protect his feelings and change the subject. 'One more thing that's bugging me - did Hyperion have foot problems?'

'No,' Tavistock replied. 'Why do you ask?'

'Could cloning cause a kinda physical defect with its replica?' Danny asked, mindful of the four blue socks worn by Hyper Tension on the gallops and the tracks.

Tavistock replied, 'All I can tell you is Hyperion had four distinct white socks, white pasterns in front and similar markings just above the ankles behind.'

'They must be covering 'em up,' Danny said distantly.

'What do you mean?'

'I know Lockhart's got the set-up to clone from DNA and reach his goal,' Danny continued to think aloud.

Tavistock asked, 'How are you so confident?'

'Let's just say, I've been on a guided tour of his place.' Danny paused. 'But I'm still having a hard time getting my head around this. Surely cloning is just a fantasy, stuff of the future.'

'You're right, it's still in its infancy,' Tavistock replied, his veterinary interest still evident. 'There will be significant glitches along the way and you would need the strongest DNA sample to successfully carry out the procedure. Having said that, a lab in Italy became the first to successfully clone a thoroughbred horse in 2002.'

'I hadn't heard,' Danny said. 'Only all that fuss about Dolly the sheep in Scotland.'

'It made the headlines, but cloning a different animal like a horse was largely considered old news by then. However, what the scientists failed to publicize was that it took many failed attempts along the way and the health of most successful implants was moderate at best, with clones often stunted in growth and suffering other serious health problems later in life.'

'But what bad will come of it?' Danny asked. 'In the long run, I mean. When they've ironed out the teething problems.'

Tavistock leant across the table and, almost spitting the words out as if they were poison, said, 'The implications on the breeding industry are unthinkable. That's why, although cloning is allowed under certain codes of competition like show jumping, it's completely prohibited in horseracing. Throughout the breeding world, there would be mass redundancies as the big shot owners revert to replicas of their favourites from the past. Not to mention, the decrease of the gene pool. It wouldn't be long before the clones would struggle to fight off infection and diseases, threatening to wipe out the whole species, destroying hundreds of generations of selective breeding with it. It would be a catastrophe. I fear that day.'

And then Danny sat back, he'd heard enough to convince him of Lockhart's intentions. 'I think that day has come.'

'What do you mean?' Tavistock asked.

'Do you still follow racing closely?' Tavistock nodded. It was Danny's turn to move in close, 'The current hot favourite for the Derby, Hyper Tension, I reckon, is a clone of Hyperion.'

Tavistock didn't rubbish the seemingly outlandish claim. He just sat there, perfectly still, waiting for Danny to elaborate. 'As a juvenile last year, Hyper Tension followed the exact career path of Hyperion, campaigning and winning the same races for the Definca Partnership. Top it all, the bloody arrogance of Lockhart, they gave it a name containing the letters of Hyperion.'

'Let's not be hasty, if he is an exact copy of the original. The breeding industry has moved on a lot since the mid-nineteenth century. They're breeding faster and stronger horses year on year,' Tavistock reasoned. 'We can't just assume a copy of Hyperion would win the same races over seventy years on.'

'You said yourself, Hyperion was one of a kind, ahead of its time.'

Tavistock continued to raise doubts. 'But there would be other factors that could easily prevent this Hyperion Mark II making the grade.'

'Like what?'

'For a start, the trainer.'

Danny said, 'Hyper Tension has been placed with the champion trainer Jeremy Gibbs at Newmarket, no better man, no better location.'

Tavistock's wariness was beginning to wear off on Danny, though. They sat there for well over a minute absorbing the facts. The silence was broken by Danny. 'Having said that, a few things don't add up. Watching Hyper Tension in his homework, he can barely muster a gallop. Certainly doesn't shape like the replica of a champion.'

A glow of familiarity lit Tavistock's face. 'Hyperion was a very intelligent horse, he knew where and when it mattered, and that was on the track. He was a notoriously hard horse to get fit and required plenty of exercise. Something Lambton – his trainer, who incidentally got the very best out of him – knew only too well. Hyperion's results went downhill when he was switched to another trainer, Colledge Leader, as a four-year-old.'

'So why didn't Lord Derby send him back to Lambton?'

'It was too late by then, Lambton's failing health meant he couldn't do the horse justice. Some say, the horse only gave his all for Lambton. Parading in the prelims for the Ascot Gold Cup, it was reported he'd seen the then wheelchair-bound Lambton and stopped, steadfastly refusing to go on.' Tavistock paused, reliving the memories of better days. 'I had the box donated to me by Lord Derby himself as a present for all my hard work with his little hero over the years. He even held a wake in honour of the horse which I attended. We drank from the bottle originally opened for Winston Churchill. Lord Derby called them: 'The two greatest grand old men of our time.'

'But surely the officials would detect something was iffy about Hyper Tension's pedigree, even if they've managed to cover the distinctive marks on his feet,' Danny said.

'Daniel,' Tavistock said, 'What these evil people have achieved will not only net them millions in prize money, it could yield nine-figure sums in future breeding rights. If they get away with it, in today's terms, they can expect to be billionaires within ten years. Do you really think the minor stumbling block of an entry in the General Stud Book will get in the way?'

'No, I guess not.'

'Everyone has a price son, perhaps even officials at the Jockey Club, something I'm sure you will learn in time,' Tavistock said. 'My question is: how on earth they will find a mare worthy to carry and fertilise such blue-blooded seed?'

'I'm not sure,' Danny said.

There was a pause, leaving the ambient background noise of conversations unfolding on the tables around them. And then it suddenly occurred to Danny. He swallowed hard. The answer was right in front of him, literally. He closed the *Racing Post* and pushed it to face Tavistock. Danny asked, 'Would she do?' His forefinger pressed against the face of Mary Rose, pictured large on the front page.

Tavistock sunk his face into his hands. 'Oh Jesus.'

'We must do something,' Tavistock continued. 'Expose this piece of dirt for what he is. We must tell the police.'

Danny nodded. His love and loyalty for the sport of kings could not be questioned and not because he earned a good living from it. He cared for its future. He well aware, like any sport, it had to compete as part of the leisure industry, but the ruling bodies had been slow in adapting to the new market and the devastating impact this revelation would have on the breeding industry would no doubt bring about the collapse of the racing industry, along with thousands upon thousands of livelihoods.

Despite this strong desire to act quickly, Danny had to tread with caution. 'It's not that simple. I can't go to the police and, even if I was a free man, they're sure to think I'm crying wolf again. In any case, Lockhart has covered his tracks well and will continue to do so. He's no mug.' Danny sank his second pint and asked. 'Another?'

'Not for me, I'd best be off.'

'One more thing,' Danny asked. 'Your number in Elena's phonebook was under Father of the Sun, S-U-N.'

A regretful frown befell his already sallow face. 'That was my 'pet' name, when our marriage started to fall apart. With all my attentions placed on my beloved Hyperion, she was left out in the cold. I regret that to this day.' He paused. 'In Greek mythology, Hyperion was one of the Titan Gods, he was father of the sun god Helios. It was an ironic swipe at me, as she didn't want anything to do with me in the end, only to look after the welfare of our grandson. Funny, eh?'

Neither smiled.

Tavistock asked, 'What now?'

'I dunno,' Danny replied. 'I'll get back to you, I need to think. Don't go anywhere. You'll be on that same number?' Tavistock nodded.

The pair parted and Danny returned to the secure unit back at Ringwall Prison in time for Simmons not to suspect he'd been anywhere but the races.

CHAPTER 20

With renewed interest, Danny continued to make regular visits to watch Hyper Tension in his Newmarket workouts through early spring. While gallop reports in the trade press slated the leading light for his sluggish homework in the build up to an eagerly anticipated second term, Danny knew otherwise. Although the colt hadn't made significant physical progress and his work continued to disappoint - both hallmarks, according to Tavistock, of the great Hyperion - he remained prominent in the ante-post markets for both the 2000 Guineas at Newmarket and the Epsom Derby.

Just a week before the Guineas meeting, Hyper Tension was scratched from the opening classic at Headquarters, a race he'd been backed into 7/2 second favourite. Gibbs stated that, after discussions with the owners, it was decided the colt wasn't sufficiently forward enough to tackle the big race at this early stage in the campaign.

The weekend after the prestigious Newmarket contest, which for most true racing aficionados marks the proper start of the turf Flat season, it was revealed to the press that connections were preparing for a tilt at the Chester Vase. Danny was unsurprised by the twelfth-hour switch as the great Hyperion had also missed Newmarket in favour of an opening assignment in the Chester showpiece as a three-year-old back in 1933.

The Chester Vase is one of two recognised Derby trials on the three-day May Festival at the tightest and oldest Flat track in the country, commonly known in racing circles as the Roodee. Set in an amphitheatre-style arena within the historic town, besides the walls left by the Roman occupation, the Chester Vase sees the runners cover twelve furlongs, for the most part on a left-handed turn.

One of the most popular tracks in England, Danny knew it would be a sell-out and had arrived plenty early enough. He loitered within earshot of the owners' and trainers' bar, occasionally looking at his watch, pretending he was waiting for someone. In fact, behind mirrored shades, he was on the lookout for Lockhart. *Surely he'd wanna see his 'wonder horse' complete the Derby prep with a win,* he thought, or maybe he'd be scared off by the media spotlight, with the terrestrial Channel 4 covering the five big races on the card. Given their audacious plan, Danny guessed Lockhart would want to keep a low profile, for the time being at least. Nevertheless, he remained posted like a regimental guard on the paved area surrounding the members' bar on the off chance he could catch a glimpse of Lockhart and thereby cement his association with Hyper Tension.

Two and a half hours later and there was still no sign of Lockhart, who, since Danny's imprisonment, had become as elusive as the Loch Ness monster. His reverie was disturbed by the distant ring of a brass bell, a signal for the runners in the first race to enter the parade ring. The first three races were of no interest to him; he was at the Roodee for one purpose and one purpose only.

The Chester Vase was due to go off at 3.30 and Danny whiled away the hours moving from the grandstand to the paddock in the middle of the track, trying to look inconspicuous. He'd booked his pitch overlooking the parade ring in plenty of time, but Lockhart was still nowhere to be seen. He could, however, see Jeremy Gibbs and Mick O'Bourne, the trainer and regular jockey of Hyper Tension. From the big screen, Danny could see Hyper Tension open up as the 4/7 favourite for the feature contest. Within thirty seconds of the opening show, the odds had shortened to 1/2, despite fears by the tipsters in the trade papers regarding the rain-softened surface. Would he handle the juice in the ground? Danny had no such doubts. After further research, he knew Hyperion dead-heated in the Prince Of Wales' Stakes at Goodwood and then ran away with the Dewhurst at Newmarket as a juvenile, both in mud-bath conditions. With a winter's growth both mentally and physically there was no doubt his replica, Hyper Tension, would sluice through the good-to-soft ground encountered today with comparative ease.

There were just the five runners set to line up for the established Group 3 race – also known as a Pattern race - and

Hyper Tension stood out in both physical appearance and on the formbook.

With no sign of Lockhart, Danny gave up his prized position against the white plastic railing bordering the paddock enclosure and left to gain a decent viewpoint to watch the race from in front of the grandstand. With no way of connecting this champion elect with Lockhart, he was starting to doubt whether he'd concocted the whole story and it was merely a figment of his imagination. Perhaps Hyper Tension really was a natural born son of Burgundy out of the mare Let It Be, like the racecard stated, and perhaps the Definca Partnership had been bought out to pay off debts owed by Lockhart's ailing company Simcorp. It could have been a mere coincidence that the letters Hyperion glaringly stood out from that of Hyper Tension.

Doubts continued to filter into his subconscious as he watched the five colts canter down to the start. Hyper Tension was the last to stretch out on the way to the post, the stalls positioned to the far side of the track. Given the almost circular American-style configuration of Chester, runners would need to complete over a lap of the track to cover the race's one-mile and four furlongs distance. The betting suggested it was a two-runner contest, between Hyper Tension, who was now a well backed 4/9, and second favourite No Difference, who had drifted from 11/4 out to 7/2, with 6/1 bar the front pair.

'And they're off!' the course commentator bellowed to the roar of the packed crowd. The cauldron of sound gave Danny a rush of adrenalin. He'd thrived on the buzz of going to the track, but he also knew there was business to be done. With the runners still out of view, Danny's eyes were trained on the large screen erected in the middle of the course before they swept into the home run for the first time after just two furlongs.

The green and yellow quartered silks of No Difference were the first to come into view, holding a two-length lead. The rank outsider, Sore Loser, disputed second with the free-pulling Maverick, whose jockey struggled to keep him settled, not to waste energy. Danny's focus on Hyper Tension didn't waver. The hot favourite had relaxed well in the capable hands of O'Bourne in last place, just four lengths off the leader. *Clearly mirroring the hold-up running style of Hyperion,* Danny thought. As he'd seen on the gallops, the colt wore four distinct blue athletic socks. He also noticed white sweat coating the colt's ewe neck and between his fetlocks, also a trait of Hyperion.

The quintet gathered pace as they powered past where Danny stood, packed like a sardine against the rails. As the runners progressed to the far side of the track, his gaze reverted to the big screen. Passing the six-furlong pole, there was an electric atmosphere in the grandstand, further charged by Hyper Tension's effortless move to pick off two of his rivals, pilot O'Bourne sitting perfectly still in the saddle.

'With three to go, No Difference still holds a slender lead over Maverick, who's travelling the better. Hyper Tension is covered up, stalking the front pair and ready to pounce,' the commentator sounded, above the crowd. 'Two to go and push comes to shove on No Difference and he starts to back-pedal, leaving Maverick with the lead, but for how long? Hyper Tension is swinging on the bridle in his wing mirrors, maybe just a question of when he'll strike. The others look beat.'

Danny swallowed, accepting the inevitable. Both horse and jockey exuding confidence, it was merely a matter of time before Hyper Tension would strike for home.

The commentator continued to narrate the unfolding drama, 'The hot favourite Hyper Tension draws alongside Maverick, who's now flat to the boards passing the furlong marker. And now O'Bourne says 'go' and the response is immediate, Hyper Tension drawing a length, make it two, three, four lengths clear in a matter of strides. This is impressive! Maverick left standing in second, a further three back to No Difference in third. But it's Hyper Tension – the easy winner of the Chester Vase. Have we just seen the Derby winner?'

Yes, Danny thought knowingly. He backed away from the rails; he'd seen enough. He carved his way impatiently through the milling crowd, towards the growing presence swarming around the winner's enclosure. He waited for the connections of the winner to meet the horse and collect the trophy. Would it be

Lockhart, or had his fervent imagination taken over? Polite applause grew to a loud roar as the horse was led in by both stable lass and trainer Gibbs. Jockey O'Bourne, who still sat tall in the saddle and was blowing harder than his mount, smiled as he exchanged words with his boss walking alongside, still no sign of any owners. Danny's mouth became dry. If Lockhart was no longer an owner, how could he possibly track him down?

Gibbs was taken to one side and faced the media, with the TV crew plus several newspaper reporters taking notes and pointing handheld recorders in his face. Danny craned his neck to see O'Bourne dismount, remove the saddle and begin to make his way to the picturesque weighing-in room, decorated with floral baskets around a white wooden veranda. There, he'd be met by the clerk of the scales, who'd ensure each jockey placed in the race carried their declared weight. Anything significantly less and disqualification was inevitable.

Lockhart had clearly swerved the occasion, avoiding any undue public exposure and watched it on TV instead. Danny wished he'd done the same. *A wasted journey*, he thought. He started to turn on his heel when, from the corner of his eye, he caught sight of a familiar figure. His blood ran cold. Lockhart had stepped into the circle and was patting his champion elect. A grin plastered across his flushed face, as if to say another hurdle cleared. Shrewdly, Lockhart had waited in the wings until the press's attentions were focused on the trainer. He'd quietly entered the winner's enclosure, wearing a neatly cut suit with salmon pink shirt and matching tie. Despite impenetrable shades pressed tightly against his face, there was no mistaking; it was the man who'd killed his brother for the sheer hell of it and, without remorse, left Danny to rot away in prison for murders he hadn't committed.

Lockhart stood there talking to a corpulent gent alongside, also dressed for the occasion with white hair swept back, before being called up to collect the Waterford Crystal vase on behalf of the Definca Partnership, at a small temporary podium plastered with the sponsor's name.

The unsuspecting crowd responded with rapturous applause. The punters around Danny, many of whom had backed the hot favourite, cheered as Lockhart lifted the vase above his head. The warmth emanating from the bustling crowd towards this man - this evil man – made Danny sweat with rage.

He turned and left the winner's enclosure, pushing his way passed the densely packed racegoers. He'd heard relatives of murder victims suggest they felt no anger for the killer but pity and sorrow instead. At that moment, Danny couldn't empathise with such emotions. He felt pure anger and bitterness. He wanted to shout at the top of his voice *murderer!* But he knew only too well no one would believe him, security would pick him up and it would soon become clear that it wouldn't need the impending court case to have him back behind bars. Instead, he left the track and stewed over the day's events on the train back to Ringwall Prison.

That evening, he punched Tavistock's number, one of only three on the memory dial of his new phone. The other two were his mother and Sara.

'Hello?' Tavistock answered.

'It's me,' Danny said. Tavistock, who'd watched the big race at home on TV, was expecting his call. 'Just as we thought, Lockhart owns Hyper Tension. We need to act and quickly.'

'The old man in shades collecting the trophy was Lockhart?'

'Yep, no mistaking,' Danny replied without hesitation. 'I'd recognise him anywhere. Also, there was someone else hovering around Lockhart.'

'I didn't see, the cameras cut away for an ad break,' Tavistock said. 'Who was it?'

'I dunno for sure,' Danny said, 'but I recognize his face from somewhere.'

'Well, it's time for action,' Tavistock said. 'Meet me tomorrow morning at Ramon's Café on the high street in Stevenage.'

'I'll have to get the nod from Simmons, but there shouldn't be a problem. About eleven? I'll say I'm off to Folkestone.'

'Make sure you do, I think I may have something that will interest you.'

The line went dead. Intrigued, Danny sat back on his narrow single bed pushed against the cell wall and stared up at the low ceiling.

CHAPTER 21

The following day, Danny woke early. Escorted by a guard, he paid a visit to Simmons's office. He told the governor that there was a potential big payday in the third race at Folkestone and he needed to be on course to see how this betting proposition took the prelims; a bare-faced lie that proved sufficient incentive for Simmons to give the okay for a day release. He arrived at Stevenage on time and made his way down the high street, glancing into the odd shop window. He turned onto a side street where he'd arranged the rendezvous.

Through the café window fronting the cobbled street, he could see Tavistock pouring a piled spoonful of white sugar into his tea before stirring. He then aligned the cutlery and condiments with military precision, as if it were a daily ritual. Danny dropped onto the seat opposite.

Tavistock beckoned a waitress by the name of Sam to their table three rows in. *He was a regular here*, Danny reckoned. *Clearly hadn't remarried since his divorce from Elena*, though he didn't pry to find out. There was hollowness behind those hazel eyes magnified through silver-rimmed glasses, as if something was missing in his life. *Could well have been the ghost of my future*, a thought that sobered Danny, making him pine for Sara yet more.

A heavy blend of grease, stale cigarettes and coffee hung in the air, left by the early morning rush of predominantly students, unemployed and truckers passing through. Danny tucked into his full English breakfast like it was his last.

Tavistock smiled, 'Home cooking not up to much.'

'Could say that,' Danny muttered between mouthfuls.

He'd wiped the plate clean with the last piece of fried bread and sat back with a warm, contented glow on his face.

Tavistock ordered another pot of tea. 'Down to business.'

'What have you got for me?'

Tavistock fished deep into the pocket of his corduroy jacket and removed a piece of paper. He handed it to Danny, who unfolded the sheet to reveal a handwritten five-figure number.

'What's this?' Danny asked, trying hard to mask his disappointment.

'Our way of proving Simeon Lockhart is a murderous fraud.'

'Go on.'

'It's the code to deactivate the security alarms at the Jockey Club.'

'And?'

'The main headquarters have now moved to London, but the Suffolk premises are less well guarded. Also, it's where they store the breed registry of all thoroughbreds foaled in Great Britain and Ireland. The original pedigree form submitted by the veterinary officer overseeing the foal Hyper Tension will be there, along with the General Stud Book. They may reveal something, it's a good starting point.'

'Where d'ya get this?' Danny asked, waving the scrap of paper in the air.

'An old friend from my days as a racecourse vet. He's now on the BHA and I managed to obtain the security code for the Jockey Club from his diary.' He afforded Danny a knowing look.

'Couldn't you tell this friend of yours what's really happening?'

'You know as well as I, we have no hard and fast evidence. To anyone else, our story is merely fanciful, we'd be laughed at.'

'So what do we do?'

'That's where the security code comes in handy. You will have to break in, take copies of the pedigree of Hyper Tension and anything else that could prove our case.'

'What about you?' Danny argued. He'd promised his mother that he'd never do another break-in again.

'You're slimmer and younger than me,' Tavistock replied. 'Anyway, it's your name that needs clearing and then there's your brother's death.'

'What about the death of your wife and grandson? You're in this just as much as me,' Danny said. But, deep down, he knew he only had one option. There was little to lose and everything to gain, however improbable.

'Okay,' Danny sighed.

'Okay what?'

'Okay, I'll do it. I'll need equipment: hammer, chisel.'

'Already thought of that,' Tavistock said. 'Plus here's a camera to record what you might find.'

'Bit presumptuous,' Danny said. 'Might not have said yeah.'

'You know as well as I that we have few other options right now.'

Danny sighed. 'Tell me about it.'

'Look, I've been there on several occasions during my time as a vet,' Tavistock said. 'I know the layout, where to go. We need to discuss plans. What to look for.'

CHAPTER 22

Darkness had descended by the time Danny arrived at Newmarket train station. He was anxious about breaking rules with Simmons being out so late, but there was less chance of being exposed at this hour. He hopped onto the platform and glanced at the large white face of the station clock. 10.12 P.M.

Surely no one would be there at this hour, Danny hoped, as he made the short walk to the heart of Newmarket - the historic Suffolk town associated with horseracing since the rule of King James I in the early 17th century.

Danny walked the main thoroughfare through the town, past the glow emanating from The Stable pub alive with music and chat, and the old Jubilee Clock Tower standing proud in the centre of the widened street.

He soon reached the Jockey Club Headquarters, number 101, further along the High Street. A mix of cold and apprehension pricked the hairs on his arms and the back of his neck as he stood and looked up at the impressive red-bricked façade of the building.

Railings separated the courtyard of the Jockey Club from the pavement outside, from which five ornate Victorian lamps splashed light over the area. Tall Georgian windows overlooked the courtyard from all sides. Danny felt conspicuous as he stepped towards the fringe of the light.

Seeing the coast was clear, he quickly jumped over the railings and ran across the courtyard. Halfway across, however, he heard the distant banter of two men. They were leaving the building via the main front door, files tucked under both arms. He ducked instinctively, crouching behind the solid sandstone base of the courtyard's centrepiece, a life-size bronze of a horse, standing like an emperor. Danny pushed himself against the stone engraving: HYPERION 1930-1960. He heard one of them turn keys in the heavy oak door and held his breath as the members neared, skirting the monument to the left. *Please don't look around*, he prayed, as the two portly men, dressed in pin-striped suits approached the gates, still engrossed in convivial chat. Danny remained crouched perfectly still in the shadow cast by the imposing statue, heart thumping like a battle drum. An uncomfortable feeling that shot him straight back to some of the close scrapes he'd endured as a housebreaker.

The men soon disappeared from view, a signal for Danny to kick into action. He poked his head around the base of the statue and his furtive eyes scanned the black windows, some with drapes pulled and others in darkness. With no obvious sign of life, he darted for the front of the building. Back against the wall, beneath the cover of pillared arches, he was safely out of shot from the security camera fastened high above and to his right. From his belt he coaxed a small chisel and hammer. He positioned the chisel at the sill of the smaller sash window to his side. He waited a moment to clear his thoughts. He knew only too well, once the alarm sounded, the clock would be ticking; there was just one minute to find the reception area and type the code to deactivate the alarm. With one sharp stab, he prised the wooden window frame from its sill. He pushed up the window as far as it would go and wriggled his way through the gap. He picked himself up, face creased from the harsh siren of the alarm, getting louder by the second.

Through the gloom, he ran through what looked like a boardroom, as Tavistock had described, banging his leg on a chair along the way. He opened the door which led on to the reception area. Heart still thumping and sweaty gloved hands shaking, he searched the reception area for the security alarm. Panic started to set in when he saw there was clearly no alarm system there.

Was Tavistock lying? Had he set this up in the belief that Danny was the killer of his wife and grandson?

Paranoia consumed him as he frantically swiped the shelves with both hands. And then he turned and saw a door marked PRIVATE: STRICTLY NO ENTRY, he glanced through the small window, but to no avail; it was like a black hole. He looked again at his watch, twenty-two seconds and counting. He grabbed the phone on the desk and, cranking it up behind his head like a baseball pitcher, he cracked it against the glass, again and again, until it shattered. He hooked his arm through the window, his leather jacket snagging on the shards of glass.

Turning the Yale lock, he pushed the door open and felt for the light switch. He blinked as the lights flickered on and, seeing the alarm system directly ahead, rushed forward. Eight seconds. His shaking index finger pressed the green 'enter code' button and started punching the five digit code, knowing there was no time for a slip up. The digital timer on the machine counted down three . . two . . . one. With one swift movement he punched the deactivate button, just as the counter reached zero. Had he made it? He waited. Silence. He exhaled loudly out of sheer relief. The alarm was off.

He stepped over the thousands of glass fragments, scattered like diamonds on the marble floor. He left the reception area and, following Tavistock's instructions, climbed the sweeping staircase leading to the first floor. Light from the reception area slowly faded as he carefully ascended. Once on the landing, his hands traced over the wall and flicked the switch, illuminating a long corridor with plush blood-red carpet, plants and oil portraits. The place exuded affluence.

He progressed further along the corridor and pushed open a door marked The Coffee Room. He crept cat-like across the balcony that overlooked a big banqueting hall, complete with three elegant chandeliers. Long drapes hung from the windows, maple panelling scattered with old oil paintings of important members and a long dark wood table fit for a king; all on the site where in 1750 the initial rulers of the sport – some of the richest, most powerful gentlemen in the country - formed the Jockey Club and wrote up the complete rules of the sport.

The lavish surroundings were clearly used for more commercial, corporate and private parties now. The wooden floorboards groaned under his weight as he passed through grand oak doors opening up to the Committee Room that, in turn, led on to The Stewards' Room. Through the shadows, Danny could see a grandiose fireplace dominate the wall to his left, surrounded by tall-backed leather chairs. Danny's fears grew as he searched deeper into the labyrinth of exquisitely furnished rooms.

The one room he was after - The Meeting Room – was strangely elusive. Had he mixed up Tavistock's directions? He continued his search; there was no point in turning back. And then he saw it, the door ahead, leading off The Stewards' Room, was marked: MEETING ROOM. Danny's face lit up like a child spotting his pile of presents on Christmas morning. He wasted no time in making his move and found himself stood in the centre of the room. He scanned his surroundings, stopping at a small door next to an oil painting of an early Club member. He twisted the handle of the door marked Private: Jockey Club Personnel Only; the one Tavistock mentioned to him in the café the previous day. The door slowly glided open. Danny grimaced, bracing himself for tripping another alarm. Silence. He turned a dimmer switch on the wall to reveal an office with two computers, one on the main oak desk and one to the side of large filing cabinets.

Danny tugged on the metal drawers but they were firmly locked. He turned to the imposing oak desk and, on Tavistock's instruction, tried the drawers which, much to his relief, opened invitingly. *At least Tavistock was true to his word.* He plunged his hands into the mix of files and stationery. At the bottom of the drawer was a small set of keys. He tried them in the cabinet and blew a sigh of relief when the lock turned. He wiped beads of sweat collecting in the ridges of his brow. Within each deep container were racks of files, seemingly endless. Clearly administrative staff kept both manual and computer files. With no way of tapping into the Jockey Club database, he knew the only way to find Hyper Tension's file was to sift through them. He started leafing through the documents, mercifully filed in alphabetical order. *Got it!*

He held the birth certificate of Hyper Tension before him. From within his leather jacket, he withdrew a miniature camera and took shots of the pedigree form. He held the sheet up against the light and could see the name of both sire and dam had been changed by hand. He took another photo against the harsh light. He went to the adjacent filing cabinet which contained details of both jockeys and trainers who currently held a licence with the Jockey Club for riding and training respectively. Once again, he

184

flicked through the hundreds of files until reaching the one of three marked R. He pulled the first one out. Three sheets in was his file marked Daniel James Rawlings. The sheet had all his personal details - date of birth and when the licence was taken out. Also, Danny's address in Cardiff was there along with details of any bans or suspensions during his brief career in the saddle. He took the sheet as a memento and, fearing he'd pushed his luck already, he replaced the keys and decided to leave the way he'd entered, swallowed by the darkness. He was well aware that it was closing time at The Stable pub, so took the backstreets on his way to the train station, avoiding drunken jockeys and stable staff spilling onto the high street.

CHAPTER 23

Early the next day, Danny arrived at Tavistock's semi-detached house on the outskirts of Stevenage.

From the inside pocket of his leather jacket, he withdrew the photos he'd taken of Hyper Tension's pedigree form and placed them onto the lounge table, next to a glass of lager Tavistock had poured him from a can. As he removed the photos, his jockey licence he'd taken fell loose onto the sofa next to him.

'The blueprint behind it all,' Danny said. He sat back, pint in hand, feeling proud of what he'd achieved the previous night.

Tavistock examined the photos.

Danny added, 'As we'd suspected, they've amended the forms, covered their tracks.'

'Looks like it,' Tavistock said, distantly.

'Reckon that'll be enough to clinch it?'

Tavistock didn't reply, his attentions had been distracted by the loose sheet on his couch. 'What's that?'

'Oh just my jockey's licence. Took it while I was there, a memento of my time in the saddle.'

'You were a jockey?'

'An apprentice, but my weight got the better of me, after an accident,' Danny said. 'But you didn't answer my question.'

'No, it's not enough. We need more.'

The pair sat quietly for what seemed like an age. The silence was eventually broken by Danny. 'I've got it.'

Tavistock leaned forward. 'Go on.'

'We'll block the Definca Partnership before they get chance to build a breeding empire.'

'How?'

'Hyperion won the Epsom Derby, probably the world's most prestigious race, in a record time, right? It made his career and was a licence to print money at stud, yeah. Lockhart is relying on his superstar clone repeating the feat. It's gonna be at the heart of their plan. Bypassing the Guineas and then failing in the Derby would mean the colt ends the campaign without a Classic under

186

his belt, as the St. Leger, the final Classic, has become less fashionable in the breeding world these days. And with no Classic wins, it would put their breeding plans back at least a couple of years, until Hyper Tension proved himself to be a leading sire in his own right, further down the line.'

'And how do you suggest we get Hyper Tension beat? Security around the horse will be like an iron wall,' Tavistock said. 'We wouldn't be able to get close to it and, even if we did, you'd be thrown into isolation for good by Simmons if he found out, from what I've heard of the man.'

Tavistock stood and stretched his legs as he approached bay windows overlooking his small, well-tended front lawn.

Then a spark lit Danny's eyes. He said, 'Wait a minute, we don't need to drug the horse. We don't even need to go near the horse, not in the prelims in any case.'

Tavistock said, 'I don't understand.'

'My licence is still kosher.'

'Your driving licence,' Tavistock said.

'Riding.'

Tavistock turned and said, 'You must be joking. We've a better chance dressing up as Hyper Tension in a pantomime costume than getting the ride on him. Anyway, Lockhart knows you only too well.'

'Who said anything about riding Hyper Tension?' Danny asked rhetorically. 'I know people that could help. I reckon these contacts could wangle a spare ride, one of the no hopers, like.'

'Gambling contacts, may be,' Tavistock said dismissively. 'Not riding contacts. Not anymore, surely.'

Tavistock sat down, seemingly exasperated by the whole situation. But Danny was steadily warming to the idea. It was his last chance to foil Lockhart's plans. 'I'd have to somehow reinvent myself with a new name.'

'Any ideas?' Tavistock asked.

'I could change the details on this,' Danny said, waving his riding licence.

Tavistock's brow became even more furrowed. 'This is ridiculous, who would let you on a horse now. I mean, come on, what do you weigh?'

'I was,' Danny paused to recall, '10st3lb going into prison and, with the extra food handouts from Simmons, I reckon I've put on a few pounds since. There's a month to the Derby, I think I could shed the weight. Done it before.'

'What's the maximum weight for the jockeys in the Derby?' Tavistock asked, still seemingly entertaining the farfetched scheme.

'They race off nine-stone level weights, so 8st7lb would be a target weight if you include saddle and saddle cloth.'

Danny took another gulp of his pint when Tavistock reached forward and wrenched it from his mouth, spilling some down Danny's shirt. 'Great, cheers.'

'Until we dismiss this idea, I don't want you to touch anything with calories.'

Danny reached for the open packet of crisps, only for Tavistock to swipe them from his grasp. 'I'm serious,' he barked.

'And I was joking. So let's get this straight,' Danny said, slowly revolving his glass between his forefinger and thumb. The monumental task he was considering was beginning to sink in. 'I need to lose 24lb and get fit enough to ride the gruelling mile and a half of Epsom's undulations, a track I've never ridden I might add, and conjure the tactical race of the decade on a three-legged outsider to get the hot favourite beat. If the racing bigwigs and police don't lynch me, the punters on course surely will.'

'Perhaps, if we can pick up a spare ride on one of the pacesetters, one with good early speed to gain the best tactical position, we could pin Hyper Tension in on the rails,' Tavistock said. 'Long enough to destroy his chances.'

'It would mean I'd only be racing competitively for a mile at most,' Danny reasoned.

'Exactly, just ease off once you've run your race.'

Danny added, 'And connections I'd be riding for won't be too narked, seeing as they had little chance in the first place.'

'Even if they did, who cares? Our objective will have been achieved.'

'Not entirely,' Danny said. 'You forget that we still have to get a platform to spill the beans on Lockhart.'

Tavistock's grin vanished.

'Wait,' Danny said. 'What if the interference was bad enough to earn an enquiry at the Jockey Club. It could get us a hearing and give me a chance to tell all.'

'I don't know,' Tavistock said.

'What's there not to know,' Danny said. 'I'm the one putting it all on the line, I just need you to back me up if needed, sort out the red tape. You've nothing to lose.'

Tavistock paused, 'I'll regret this when it's fully sunk in, but . . . okay, I'm in.'

Danny forced a smile. 'It's not gonna be easy, but I reckon it's our only hope.'

'And a pretty slim one at that,' Tavistock added. 'I'll amend the details on your licence and fax them to the Jockey Club for filing if, I mean when, you're booked for a ride.'

CHAPTER 24

Back in the comparative safety of his cell, Danny sat and sketched out a plan with a view to losing weight while gaining strength. Having spent three years struggling to maintain a decent racing weight as a jockey, he was well-versed in the art of shedding the pounds.

Deep down, he knew the task facing him in such a short timeframe, barring chopping a limb off, was virtually impossible. His hopes lay with gaining access to a sauna in order to sweat off any excess condition on the mornings leading up to the big race on Saturday, June 4.

He knew the two main areas of physical fitness needing serious attention was cardiovascular and building strength in both arms and legs. He set about a rigorous regime of push ups and leg presses. At night, he was granted access to the prison courtyard, out of view from the main wing. In the cool night air, he would do, at first, just a dozen laps of the concrete rectangle, equating to a couple of miles in total.

As the days rolled by, he knew time was running out and it would be tight whether the target weight was reached. The saving grace – whoever owned his mount would have no time to desert him for another jockey if he failed the pre-race weigh in. *Restrict carbohydrates,* he thought. Last thing he wanted - he'd learnt from an instructor from of the riding schools set up by the BHA - was to build excessive muscle as that weighed more than fatty tissue. However, that meant his energy levels were constantly low. He knew staying awake for longer would burn more calories and during the twilight hours, he would force his eyes open and meticulously run through pre-race preparations in his mind. He'd started smoking again, helping to temper the food cravings that ravaged him during the night.

However, with just ten days to go and all potential avenues of getting a ride exhausted – ringing the trainers of potential lower-profile runners in the Classic - Danny felt resigned to the fact that his efforts had gone to waste. He consoled himself with the fact that he'd lost 17lb in just under three weeks and was feeling brighter, more alert both physically and mentally from all the intensive exercise. He'd even mimicked a workhorse by throwing stirrups, brought in by Sara, over the pommel horse in the prison's gym.

During the day he not only kept his agreement with Simmons, but also steadily worked down the trainers with potential Derby runners. Danny posed as an agent, putting on a phoney Scottish accent. The trainers were steadily finalising jockey plans with some of the leading pilots in the land. Danny wasn't getting any joy with the false story of representing an up-and-coming jockey practising his trade in South America.

Danny requested to see Simmons.

He knocked and entered.

'Yes?' Simmons asked, busy with paperwork.

'I've been feeling slightly unwell in recent weeks.'

Danny was Simmons's main source of income now, far outweighing his prison wages. He could see the look of concern wash over the face of the Governor, who saw him not as a human, but as a money printing machine, nothing else. *Like the dog dreaming of the chicken on a spit-roast in one of those old cartoons,* Danny reckoned. He smiled, but then realized he had to feign illness.

'What do you need, the prison doctor?'

'No,' Danny said tentatively, bracing himself for the favour. 'You know the sports club you've talked about.'

'No way,' Simmons barked. 'Too risky.'

'They've never met me. And you've said there's a gym and a decent sauna there. Healthy body, healthy mind.'

'You're taking liberties now. Take an aspirin and be a man.'

Danny lay the cards on the table by saying, 'I could easily stop this cosy agreement we've got. I'm sure Mrs Simmons will be delighted by the massive slump in income.'

Simmons stood and, with face turning puce with rage, barked, 'This is a two-way agreement, you knew that from the

191

start. I've held my side of the bargain and you *will* continue as before,' he growled, spittle escaping from his mouth. 'Otherwise, I will withdraw all perks, you will be sent back to the main wing and, believe me, I will ensure you continue to provide the goods. There are ways and means. Now get out!'

Danny returned to his cell, head bowed. He'd yet to even get close to securing a ride for Epsom. With one last throw of the dice, he called his good friend back in Cardiff.

'Hello?'

'Stony, it's Danny. I need another favour.'

'What is it?' Stony asked, somewhat reticent.

'I need a ride.'

'Where to?'

'Not a lift. A ride, in a race.'

'You are joking?'

'D'ya hear me laughing?'

'But you've long given up. You'd be rusty as hell and you're too heavy, lad.'

'I'm back in shape and, anyway, it's like riding a bike. I'll soon be back in the swing of it.'

'April 1st has passed ain't it?'

'I'm deadly serious, emphasis on deadly.'

'I don't know what you've been up to now Danny and, to be honest, I don't think I want to know.'

'Will you help or not?'

'But how can I?' Stony asked. 'You're inside.'

'Managed to get bail at the last minute before the trial in a couple of months.'

'I dunno, Danny,' Stony said. 'I'm not happy 'bout this.'

'Please,' Danny said. 'I'm begging you, just think of all those dead certs I'll line up when I'm free again.'

Stony emptied his lungs. 'Tell me where and when.'

'Ah, that's the real hurdle,' Danny said, fearing Stony's reaction.

'What?'

'It's the Derby.'

'Epsom!'

'Yep.'

'Now I know it's an April Fool's.'

'Come on Stony, you owe me countless unreturned favours over the years.'

There was a pause. 'Alright, alright. I'll make a few calls, but I can't promise anything,' Stony said. 'And then we're even, right?'

Danny didn't raise his hopes, he knew Stony's past record in delivering promises. 'Something else, I'm using false ID; my new name is Frederick Daly, I'm a promising rider from South America.'

'Good God,' Stony laughed. 'Better get down the tanning salon.'

'I'm of European descent, just been riding out there, that's all. Just talk me up as much as possible. This is vital.'

'Why South America?'

'They've no link with the BHA, so there's no way of 'em tracing my past record, or no inclination of finding out. Why should they? By the time I'm rumbled, the deed will have been done.'

'What deed?'

'You'll have to wait and find out.'

It was just five hours later when Stony called back, hardly containing the excitement in his raspy voice, 'You sitting down?'

'Why?' Danny asked.

'I've struck gold.'

Danny raised his spare hand to steady the receiver. 'With who?'

'Rhys Reynolds, trains in the Vale of Glamorgan. Wasn't easy but I've known him since my riding days, see, won a few big races for him too. The colt's called Hope Springs.'

'Eternal,' Danny added. He quickly picked up his well thumbed *Racing Post* and checked the odds grid with all the ante-post prices for the big race. Hyper Tension headed the field at 6/4, stretching down to Hope Springs near the bottom of the page, 500/1 rank outsider. Danny swallowed. 'When do I have to meet the trainer and owner.'

'Well, there's good news and bad news.'

'Hit me with it,' Danny said, bracing himself.

'The good news is, Rhys is the owner/trainer of Hope Springs, so you've only to convince him that your worthy of the ride.'

'I don't understand,' Danny replied. 'I thought you said it was in the bag.'

'That's the bad news; he wants to see you ride the horse out, a trial for you more than the horse.'

Danny sighed. He hadn't sat on a horse for many years and, although he'd been stretching the sets of muscles used for strenuous race-riding on the pommel horse, keeping control of a real thoroughbred in convincing fashion was a whole different ball game.

'I told him you could meet tomorrow. With Epsom just nine days away, you can hardly blame him wanting things sorted straight away.'

Danny didn't reply, frozen. He knew it was too late to back out now, the chances of him finding another opportunity at such short notice was virtually non-existent. 'What time?'

'Eight.'

'In the morning?'

'Yep. Just arrive as you are, he'll have the tack and saddle waiting.'

Danny thanked Stony and hung up. His palms glistened from the light of the desk lamp as he tried to convince himself that he'd still got the bottle to ride again for the first time since the accident. *Just like riding a bike,* he reminded himself, *never leaves you.*

He logged on to the internet and brought up the form-file of Hope Springs. He'd heard of the horse through his daily form analysis, but wasn't aware of what he'd achieved. As it turned out, very little. The colt was a son of Daydreamer, a little known sire, who'd produce a couple of maiden winners, out of a mare who was a half-sister to a Guineas winner. Touch of class on the female side of her pedigree, but no guarantees of him staying the distance. His eyes were then drawn to Hope Spring's achievements on the track. As a juvenile, he'd run three times, finishing second in low-key maidens at Salisbury and Chepstow, both over seven furlongs. He made it third time lucky in a backend maiden on a return to Chepstow, all out to beat an ordinary type by a length. Despite a comment in the write-up suggesting he'd had a few niggling problems with his legs during the winter, the colt managed to finish a respectable fourth off a mark of 87 over a mile on his return in a spring handicap at Doncaster's Lincoln meeting. Although the form was solid enough in its own right, it was virtually unheard of for a good handicapper to contest the Derby let alone win the thing. *Against some of the best blue-blooded equine talent in the world, he's going to be sunk before the turn for home,* Danny reckoned, *leaving about seven furlongs to interfere with Hyper Tension's progress.*

Danny was only too aware that a typical Derby winner would be rated at a mark of 120, which in layman terms means that if the race was a handicap, Hope Spring's would need to shoulder 33lb less than the winner to have a chance of plundering the £1 million Classic. On a level playing field, with each runner carrying the same weight, Danny's prospective booking had no chance, borne out by the bookies offer of 500/1. Initial promise had clearly spurred on Reynolds to supplement the colt for the Derby last autumn, fuelling the dream of Classic glory, but it was merely a dream.

CHAPTER 25

At break of dawn the following morning, Danny was let through the fire door in staff quarters. He paced through misty rain on his way to the station and, head bowed, bought a return ticket to Cardiff with a sub from Simmons, who allowed him £130 a week travelling expenses. *Knowing the Governor, it was probably claimed against tax.*

From the capital of Wales, he switched trains to make the twenty minute journey to Rhymney in the picturesque Vale of Glamorgan. No point in going back to his apartment in the bay, it was being let out by his mother at Danny's request. He then caught a cab to the estate run by Reynolds amidst lush green rolling hills about ten miles north of the capital, near Rhymney.

He arrived at the stables just before eight and was met by a young stable lass, who led him to the trainer's house situated alongside the stabling area. It was a small establishment. Reynolds had just fifteen horses currently in training, with only three boxes left empty; hardly a threat to the likes of Gibbs, whose Newmarket outfit housed over two hundred thoroughbreds, featuring Hyper Tension.

'Morning,' Reynolds greeted with a melancholy expression.

'Fred,' Danny said, offering his hand.

Reynolds didn't reciprocate the gesture, he just said, 'You'd better get changed, he's round the back.' He disappeared into the cottage and closed the door behind him.

'Man of few words,' Danny muttered, which came as a relief to him; the fewer questions the better.

Having kitted out in riding gear, he was led by the young stable lass to Hope Springs, who was stood proud. The bay colt's physique and conformation failed to inspire Danny with much confidence. He did, though, have alert eyes and large ears, a sign of genuineness.

Reynolds emerged once again from the rear of the farmhouse, wearing jodhpurs and knee-high boots. 'The gallops are through there. Get on and we'll see what we're dealing with.' Danny assumed the trainer was referring to him and not the horse.

He held his breath as he approached the horse, praying the colt would stand still and not play up at the arrival of a stranger. With the help of two stable staff anchoring the colt perfectly still, Danny hopped into the saddle. The stable lass said, 'Saddle fit okay?'

Danny adjusted his weight until comfortable and slid his feet through the irons. 'Like a glove.'

She beamed a smile up at him.

The pair walked steadily from the yard, Danny consciously trying to recapture the feelings and confidence he'd gained from his riding days. Last thing he wanted to be was nervous, as horses soon pick up on these anxieties and fail to perform or behave.

'Do a half-mile canter up the slope there and get a feel for him, before coming back at a more serious pace.'

Danny gripped the reins like they were his only lifeline and urged Hope Spring's forward. The colt quickly broke into a canter. *So far so good*, Danny thought. Confidence began to flood back and his limbs moved with the self assurance of a professional.

The pair swept past the watching connections at three-quarters speed. Danny was charged by an electric buzz of adrenalin from being back in the saddle, a life-affirming experience that had long been missing. *This felt great*, Danny thought, as the breeze brushed over him and the ground rushed beneath, *just great*.

Despite an urge to glance at the onlookers to see for any reaction, his focus remained dead ahead. Slowly, he wound down the piece of work and soon found himself trotting back to meet Reynolds and the rest.

The trainer smiled, 'Good little sort, isn't he.'

With no point of reference for many years, Danny had no answer. 'Yep, sure is,' he said, keeping the prospective boss sweet.

'I've seen enough,' Reynolds said. 'Lead him back and I'll talk to you back in the farmhouse.'

Danny wasn't sure whether to take that as a nod or a rejection, he just kept quiet for now.

'You speak good English,' Reynolds said.

'I was born and raised here, but switched to South America a decade ago.'

Reynolds eyes narrowed, as if trying to work out where he'd seen Danny before. 'Have we met before?'

'I used to take the odd ride in Britain many years ago, before moving abroad. Perhaps you saw me at one of the tracks.' There was a pregnant pause. Danny stood awkwardly, not sure where to put his hands, as Reynolds eyes looked him up and down. Danny felt like he was in another police ID parade.

'Doesn't matter, sure it will come to me. I liked the way my horse responded to you and, with that in mind, I'm willing to book you.' Reynolds shook Danny's hand firmly and continued, 'He'll need one more serious piece of work on Thursday. I want you here to ride him and we'll also discuss tactics.'

'Sure,' Danny said. He'd have agreed to virtually anything, such was his relief at Reynolds's answer.

Despite his train departing late, he comfortably made the 6 P.M. curfew set by Simmons.

He was doing push ups when the cell door opened. Simmons appeared, on his way home. He'd come to see what Danny had done during the day, a spot check to ensure liberties weren't taken.

'Went to see a horse workout on the Newmarket gallops.'

'And did it impress?'

'Nah, ran like a drain.'

'So a wasted day,' Simmons huffed.

'Not exactly, I think he might be worth laying for its next outing.'

Once Simmons had gone, Danny fished for his riding boots from beneath his bed and set about gluing a passport photo of Sara, kept safe in his wallet all these years, onto the inside of the left boot. He then started reading the instructions on the hair

198

bleaching packet that Sara had leant him. He had to change his appearance as much as possible. *Saves going under the knife.*

His thoughts drifted to how exciting his Dad would've been in the lead up to the great day. *Perhaps he was looking down and would be cheering on,* Danny hoped.

With the big race looming large, he needed to meet up with allies Stony and Tavistock.

CHAPTER 26

Danny was sat in front of the TV with a video set up on a shelf below. Tavistock was busy sorting through tapes of past Derbys in his dining room.

Tavistock entered and said, 'I've sifted out recordings of recent renewals, see if we can glean anything from the tactics of those finishing prominently.' He turned to face Stony, who'd entered from the kitchen with cup of coffee in hand, and continued, 'Feel free to contribute with any points regarding the way the track rides.'

Stony nodded.

Tavistock pushed one of the tapes into the VCR and sat back with the other two. 'This is North Light winning in 2004 for Sir Michael Stoute. It's the leggy colt tracking the leaders in pale blue colours.'

All three were glued to the screen, watching the joint favourite produce a textbook performance. Having stalked the leaders, champion jockey Kieren Fallon pushed on at just the right time. His mount quickened to the lead and had daylight to spare over nearest pursuer Rule Of Law with two furlongs to run.

Tavistock froze the screen and rewound in-vision. He paused again as the runners were about to exit Tattenham Corner. 'This is where Fallon begins to make his move, and that's where O'Bourne is likely to go for home, over three furlongs out. I want you glued to his side, wherever he goes, you follow.'

Danny said, 'With a couple of lengths lead, given that Hyper Tension's got more gears than my mount Hope Springs.'

'Exactly,' Tavistock said. 'The ferocious pace set from the off means they'll be going a stride too quick for Hope Springs, blunting the turn of foot he normally possesses come this stage. If you see Hyper Tension getting away from you, do anything, whip O'Bourne, anything that could slow him down. But you must remember, it's likely you'll have until this point.' Tavistock pointed a marker at the TV screen just before the three-furlong pole. 'Beyond there, you can kiss goodbye to foiling Lockhart's breeding empire.'

'Cresting the rise at the end of the back straight,' Stony added, arms crossed, 'you need to be handy to have any chance of landing a serious blow. It's all about momentum from then on, you see, as the ground starts to fall away from you on the decline. It takes all your strength getting the horse organized at this crucial point. Back in '87, I remember like it was yesterday, my horse refused to settle on the steep climb for Tattenham Corner and, by the time we were on the homeward stretch, he was legless, drifting to the far side. If the rail wasn't there, he'd have wandered off into the funfair in the centre of the track.' Both Danny and Tavistock smiled. 'It made no difference, though. The winner, Reference Point, was different class that year.' Stony also smiled, as if memories of the occasion flooded back.

They sat and studied tapes of other winners, including Galileo's impressive drubbing of the opposition in 2001 and Motivator's demolition job in 2005, both implementing similar prominent racing tactics as North Light.

Tavistock pulled the tape from the machine and inserted another. '*And the piece de resistance.*'

Danny's eyes widened. 'What is it?'

'Old Pathe news footage of the great one, Hyperion.'

The video recorder whirred into action.

'A record crowd came to watch and savour a new champion being crowned king of the Epsom Derby,' sounded the film's commentary, voiced with an impossibly posh and high pitched English accent. 'As the runners come hurtling around the world famous Tattenham Corner, the great race looks between King Salmon and Statesman. But, wait a minute, here comes little Hyperion, nipping up the inside rail to take the lead! The result is no longer in doubt as Hyperion pulls clear of his rivals in astonishing fashion. He crosses the line in a new record time to the delight of the packed crowd, a performance that makes him something of a public idol.'

Danny glanced towards Tavistock, eyebrows raised. He started to doubt how he could possible stop Hyper Tension, who'd

201

been shaping in similarly imperious fashion to his original he'd just witnessed in the grainy black and white film.

Tavistock said, 'He won in record time, two minutes 34 seconds. The official winning margin was four lengths, though seeing this it looks like more. Judging by all previous career starts of Hyper Tension, they appear not to be taking any risks, following the exact game plan of its DNA blueprint Hyperion.'

Although he never reached the top echelons of the game, Stony did ride in a couple of Derbys and boasted a wealth of track knowledge that Danny hoped to tap into. Over his career, Stony had ridden 32 races at the world renowned Surrey track and won four – one of which was over the rollercoaster that was the course and distance of the Derby. Its severe undulations scared off many international jockeys as it provided a major culture shock to any foreign raider used to flat, less daunting, configurations.

'To win there, the horse not only needs pace at both ends of the race, but has to be well balanced; one that could switch lead legs without losing momentum and accelerate out of the inevitable trouble as they crowd up in a concertina effect turning into the straight,' Tavistock explained. 'Swinging off Tattenham Corner, the tightest of turns on the apex of the horseshoe shaped track, runners face a predominantly downhill home-straight with a pronounced camber towards the far rail.'

Danny nodded. He knew, come the business end of the race, even the classiest horses in the land will show a tendency to roll off a true course, gradually veering towards the lowest point of the track. Potential winners of the prestigious classic, open to three-year-old colts, are usually well-made and possess more than enough stamina to last the mile and a half trip. 'So if Hyper Tension follows the same race-plan as Hyperion, O'Bourne will probably go for a run on the inner.'

'Particularly as he's been drawn low, number three of 16, on the inside,' Tavistock added. 'From the Derby start which is about level with the grandstand on the far side of the course, there's about four furlongs' climb to the highest point of the track. Hope Springs will have to climb a hundred and forty feet during that stretch.'

'Have you ridden Epsom at all?' Stony asked Danny.

'Only in an apprentices' sprint on the straight track, never had to go on the round course.'

Stony continued, 'When you pass the shoot for the seven-furlong start, you'll know it's virtually downhill from then on until the last hundred yards or so, where it rises again, but you'll be a spent force by then.'

'There's a slight kink to the right along the back straight,' Tavistock added. 'When the going is on the easy side of good, runners tend to group to the far side where trees border the track, their overhanging canopies can shelter a strip of ground from rain. The surface tends to be a degree faster there and you'll find it's a magnet for the jockeys. Something to bear in mind.'

'If there's traffic problems during the race,' Stony said, 'that's where you're most likely to get it.'

Danny asked, 'What about Tattenham Corner itself?'

Stony said, 'And remember, momentum can force runners to fan out on the bend. If he nips through, you won't catch him.'

'What do you recommend?' Tavistock sat back, open to suggestions.

Danny said, 'I reckon the only way is to keep him penned in on the rails and stay there. If O'Bourne tries to force his way out, which he probably will given he's a champion and hungry for success, I'll have to somehow stand my ground, throw my whip at him if I have to. Perhaps the folding pacemakers will help by blocking him as they fade back through the field.'

'Remember, you're on a nag with gas for about nine furlongs max at this level. From then on, you'll be running on empty, freewheeling,' Stony added, a sobering thought. 'You'll only have one chance and one chance only.'

'Once Hyper Tension has cleared any trouble caused by you,' Tavistock said, leaning forward, 'he may well be good enough to claw back the deficit in any case. All you can do is try your best and keep him in as long as you can.'

CHAPTER 27

Danny had been granted special dispensation to be released on Derby Day. In return, he advised Simmons to significantly lay a horse to get beat, promising the greedy Governor a big payday. He couldn't resist advising Simmons and the other members of the prison board to lay Hyper Tension for £20,000 at odds of Evens. Not least because it helped add focus, if it were needed, that Hyper Tension had to be stopped. Given the good run of results of the syndicate, he hoped the luck would rub off on the big occasion.

The Derby used to be run on the first Wednesday in June but, with so many London businesses suffering from workers taking a day off midweek, organizers decided to switch it to the first Saturday instead.

Danny was well aware of the pomp and ceremony of the big race, with the men dressing up in morning suits and the women in colourful summer outfits. It was a special day out on the Flat racing calendar, one that Danny made as a kid with his dad.

Walking alongside the racecourse, Danny could see the world's media occupy a large area running beside the grandstand, a sea of temporary buildings and vans with satellite dishes, from which sprouted miles of thick cables. A long hospitality tent was located nearby to meet their culinary needs.

Even though it was just gone eleven, Danny could hear frantic activity in some of the vans and tents. There was a press conference about to take place in the Shergar suite in the Members Enclosure, but Danny wasn't invited. Much to his relief, the sponsor – an insurance company called Dorstones - was only interested in the big-named jockeys; the ones riding the leading fancies for the race. *O'Bourne was no doubt there*, Danny thought, *probably revelling in the limelight of riding the hot favourite.*

For small fees, other jockeys would be called up to do TV interviews, trying to assess their chances for the watching punters, in the build up to the race. Danny walked pensively towards the towering concrete grandstand, his royal blue silks with yellow epaulets folded neatly in a kit bag slung over one shoulder. He'd have to hand them over to the jockeys' valet, who'd hang them from the appropriate peg, before each race.

The racecourse was already teeming with ground-staff and connections of the sixty-four runners on the card, sixteen of which were set to line up for the Derby; a big field for a Classic of any description at home or abroad. A stream of early racegoers were funnelling through the turnstiles on the grandstand side, heeding the warning to arrive early and avoid the inevitable traffic chaos later in the day.

As Danny approached the jockeys' changing room, he glanced across to the centre of the track. He saw rows of open topped double-decker buses, catering for champagne swilling racegoers, mostly overdressed and already half-cut from the copious free drink on offer courtesy of their companies. Although he'd visited regularly as a child, his memories were distant and he was glad Stony had refreshed them; where to go and what to do.

He wore a green peaked cap embossed with the Epsom logo which had been sent to him in a gift bag, reserved exclusively to those riding in the premiere Classic. He'd pulled the cap down to cover much of his face and shades masked his eyes. *Surely no one would clock me*, he thought, *not after such a long time away from the scene.* Not with hair bleached white and two weeks' stubble growth.

The jockeys' room would be full of new faces, Danny hoped, none of which would recognize his. Nevertheless, he knew most riding in the feature race were early thirty-somethings who were booked for their superior experience and more substantial rolls of honour. They would have been kicking around when Danny was a burgeoning apprentice, climbing the ladder and establishing their names. He needed to keep as low a profile as possible. Speak as little as he could to as few people as possible. Swerve all interviews. Just get the job done and be gone.

He entered the jockeys' quarters and felt his heart quicken. He dropped his kit bag in the corner of the changing room, alongside several others. A handful of jockeys - a few of which were journeymen pros - Danny knew by sight, were chatting casually to the far side, three seated, another stood resting his extended hand against one of the rows of hooks on the wall. Another was pacing, whether through nerves or excitement of what the day had in store. Danny felt like pacing as well, so he left to walk the track.

The plastic pass he'd been handed by a course official at the entrance allowed him access to the course. He felt a strong breeze sweep across the course, sending shivers down his spine, as he traced a path from the furlong marker to the finish line. The closely cropped grass turned different shades of green as the short blades swayed in the swirling breeze. There was a steep climb from the dip 100 yards from the finish line; Stony was right on the money.

He glanced down at his watch - 12.03 P.M. – before looking up at the modern grandstand shimmering in the summer haze. Below, punters were now milling in the betting ring, partly shaded by a Perspex overhang high above. Rows of private boxes booked by firms for corporate days out looked down, like lords over the manor.

Further along the course was the recently built Queen's Stand, an impressive glass-canopied banqueting, conference and media centre where business deals were struck, and journalists scribed and emailed copy for their editors, mostly in nearby London.

Danny turned and soaked up the atmosphere, trying to tame the butterflies flapping wildly in the pit of his stomach. He looked towards the far side of the track where the distant white starting pole for the Derby could just be seen, like a needle. Beyond the trees, on the horizon, Danny's eyes caught sight of the London Eye and the pyramid roof of The Tower at Canary Wharf – home to the *Racing Post*. *Wonder what the reports will say tomorrow*, Danny feared.

The mere thought of what lay ahead made him retch. He needed the toilet, quick. He ducked under the plastic rail separating grass and concrete, and past the various fast-food outlets to the side of the grandstand, heading straight for the public toilets. He made a beeline for one of the cubicles. He didn't want to use those in the Jockeys' Room, the less time he spent in there the better.

The race time fast approached and, once changed into the pristine colours of Hope Springs, Danny, along with a handful of other jockeys, stood and waited for the pre-race parade. A television set in the corner showed live pictures from the BBC. O'Bourne came on. One of the rival jockeys in the room, Terry Regan, said, 'Turn it up, Micky.'

The jockeys' valet, who held the remote, turned the volume high enough for O'Bourne's thick Irish lilt to bounce off the walls of the changing room.

The reporter asked, 'Are you confident as the punters are?'

'I'm on the best horse, I won't lose.'

'Cocky twat,' escaped Danny's mouth. The surrounding jockeys laughed like hyenas, clearly jealous of O'Bourne's success. Prickly heat rose from his neck to his cheeks as he realised what he'd done. He'd just broken Tavistock's rule number one: before the race, keep as low profile as possible.

The reporter continued, 'The Chester Vase was run on an easy surface, do you think he'll handle the much drier conditions at Epsom?'

'The best horses go on any ground, and are versatile regarding trip. I have no doubts whatsoever.'

The interviewer signed off with, 'Best of luck, Mick.'

When the speaker system in the changing room ordered the jockeys to the parade ring, Danny felt his stomach tighten.

CHAPTER 28

Reynolds, a small fry in the training establishment, stood quietly by his stable flagbearer Hope Springs. As Danny had hoped, press and public attention largely focused on the leading lights in the Classic, featuring the extraordinary presence that was the ball of muscle called Hyper Tension, who was on his toes and clearly pumped up for the big day as he circled the parade ring under the steadying influence of a handler each side.

Gibbs was chatting to Lockhart. Something made them both laugh, perhaps nerves. Danny was just thankful that their thoughts were for the safety of the hot favourite and neither had even looked in his direction, let alone cast a suspicious glance.

Danny tugged on his gloves as he approached Reynolds, whose face bore a studious expression. He gripped Danny's hand with a vice-like hold. 'How are you feeling?'

'As well as could be expected.'

'Well, this is it.'

Hope Springs handled the parade in front of the grandstand like an old pro. Unfortunately, so did Hyper Tension. As Danny steered Hope Springs to the starting post on the far side of the course, the noise from the public enclosures became muted.

Circling behind the stalls, Danny glanced across at the packed grandstand, rippling in the heat haze. When the jockeys' banter quietened down – each most likely playing out the race in their heads - there was a kind of serenity down at the start. Just the ambient crackle of the distant crowd, reminding him that this was no rehearsal, as he circled patiently. The starter began to read out the jockeys' names, together with the stall numbers. Danny knew it was a signal for the stall handlers to start the loading process. He felt his stomach cramp to the size of a tennis ball.

The biggest race he'd contested was the Ayr Silver Cup – a 6f handicap for the reserves who'd failed to make the Gold Cup at the Scottish venue. Although a big handicap in its own right, it paled into insignificance with the world's most prestigious race.

He listened out for his pseudonym Fred Daly as the starter continued down the list of sixteen runners.

'Daly, stall eleven.'

The first few had already been installed; the race time 3.45 P.M. had clearly past.

Danny was ninth to be installed. Initially, his mount was reluctant to move, *not a good sign*. The handler bent to rip a tuft of grass, trying to entice the animal forward while patting and gently stroking Hope Springs's neck, now glistening with sweat. The colt duly responded to the encouragement, walking forward willingly, much to the relief of Reynolds watching through powerful binoculars from the stands and Tavistock staring intently at the live television coverage in his living room.

Danny sucked in a lungful of clean fresh air as the chestnut three-year-old beneath him slotted in the stall marked eleven.

'Good luck,' a high pitched voice came from his right. Danny turned. It was Tom Sayers – a vastly experienced jockey who'd done him many a favour in Danny's betting days.

'And you,' Danny replied. 'I need a quick start, can you give us some space.'

'After you,' he replied with a faint smile. 'Mine needs holding up.'

'Cheers,' Danny replied, though not sure whether it was a bluff. After all, he knew all of them were out to get first prize, except him of course.

Danny glanced over his shoulder. Only two left to load. He felt his gloved hands tighten around the reins. He adjusted his tinted Perspex goggles and gulped deeply again, swallowing back fiery bile rising like molten lava in his gullet. Danny's heart felt like it was about to explode, he could hear the machine-gun patter in his ears. He reached down to touch the lip of his riding boot where Sara's photo had been pasted.

'One to go,' shouted the starter. Connections of the last few were usually given special dispensation to go in late as they normally had a history of playing up at the start and could easily be left if refusing to enter the stalls. He heard a metallic thud and was momentarily jolted forward; the last horse had swiftly entered, hitting the front gate with his nose.

'Jockeys!' growled the starter.

Danny felt like shouting back, No!

And then the gates violently swung open. At which point, the diligent pre-race planning and instinct took effect. With adrenalin flowing, he rousted Hope Springs with all his might, growling at his charge's big ears to make sure he got the message. The colt soon found his stride and, as they passed the first furlong pole, he glanced over at those on the inner. He could see a trio of pacesetters, jostling for an early pitch on the rail – one of which was Dream Catcher, stablemate of Hyper Tension.

Breathing hard from the early rowing, Danny again briefly glanced to his left. Sayers was nowhere to be seen, clearly a man of his word. There was, however, a runner moving up on his inner. Two furlongs covered. He glanced at the silks of the one on his inside, moving up to Hope Springs's quarters. He caught a glimpse of bottle green and yellow stripes. From recalling the runner's colours, he knew instantly it was the third favourite Rewind. But where was Hyper Tension?

The main body of the field had settled to a sensible gallop as they continued the gruelling ascent to the seven furlong offshoot. As planned, Danny had gained a prominent pitch in fifth, three horse widths off the rail.

Hope Springs's breathing had softened and the feel he gave Danny was comfortable, plenty left in the tank. Half a mile covered. Further back in the field, he caught a blurry glimpse of the red and black quartered silks of Hyper Tension tucked in on the inside about three lengths behind where Danny was placed. He wanted to close in on Hyper Tension while maintaining a lead. Given the superior tactical speed and stamina of his target, he knew falling behind would just about seal his fate. However, Rewind had blocked his path.

As they continued to climb the backstraight, he didn't panic. His years of controlled thinking under pressure with the betting syndicate were paying off. *Plenty of time*, he thought, though he knew Hope Springs would start floundering after a mile. He needed to make a split second choice. Whether to pull back and let Rewind pass, or push on and round him from the front. Either way was a risk, but he knew sitting so far wide would mean he'd fan even further into the course turning Tattenham Corner. He recalled Stony's words: think positively and always move forward, momentum is everything.

Danny slipped his whip through to his right hand and gave Hope Springs a few reminders, tapping his shoulder with the air-cushioned persuader. The game colt responded instantly, finding a length on the imposing rival to his inner. But how much had the tactical move taken out of his mount? After all, Hope Springs was already racing faster than he was used to. *Having run with his choke out for so long, he would soon be out on his feet,* Danny reasoned. Without fear of his own safety, he slotted in two off the fence, partly blocking Rewind's path and forcing Sayers to check for a beat.

'Fuck off!' barked Sayers from behind. Danny didn't flinch; he wasn't there to make friends.

He glanced across once again, keen to shadow Hyper Tension, like a driver urgently crossing lanes to avoid overshooting a turn off. He was relieved as the ground levelled off at the seven-furlong marker. They'd crested the rise and it was largely downhill from then on. They were now galloping at over 40mph.

Danny had reached joint-third, racing alongside Dream Catcher, who was already showing early signs of fatigue from forcing such a furious early gallop.

Six furlongs to go, they'd passed the farthest point from the stands and were now on their way home. Despite his 5'8" frame, Danny kept as low in the saddle as possible, reducing air resistance and improving balance as they continued to eat up the ground around the tricky apex of the elliptical Tattenham Corner.

Danny felt the horse beneath start to wobble slightly. With every stride, Hope Springs was working harder to bravely maintain his prominent position. The loud snorts escaping the horse's flared nostrils became more frequent and erratic. Danny knew it was now or never. He glanced over his left shoulder.

211

There was a procession of five horses tracking Indian file on the rail, stretching to the back markers. Dream Catcher had quickly beaten a retreat and, Danny surmised, Hyper Tension had been switched wide to avoid his ailing stablemate. They swept past the five–furlong marker. Danny looked over his right shoulder, hoping not to see Hyper Tension on his heels and in the clear. There he was, flashes of blue from the athletic socks as the clone's rounded action drew closer. O'Bourne poised with a double handful, sat perfectly still ready to pounce.

There was another furlong before Hyperion was sent on for his decisive burst in the 1933 Derby. Danny guessed Gibbs's racing orders would be similar. Just over two hundred yards before Hyper Tension would be out of his grasp. They entered the home straight and the excited roar of the crowd grew louder with every thunderous stride. Danny looked again and heard the commentator say, 'Jockey Daly moves confidently on Hope Springs, looking over both shoulders to see the dangers.'

There was only one danger, Danny thought, and that was tracking his coattails. He started to move his arms in a rowing action. Shaking the reins, he asked for Hope Springs to find some more. Although his mount lacked class, he was a tough brute that relished a battle. Danny knew he needed to find similar tenacity from the saddle. And then his stomach sank as he heard Hyper Tension draw alongside. Half a mile to go. He looked over at O'Bourne, who returned the glance, mouthing something inaudible and then smiled smugly, still motionless in the saddle. With open space ahead, Danny knew the game was almost up.

Tavistock's words reverberated in his mind: get him beat, at all costs.

Danny sat lower in the saddle and with all his might, worked the reins vigorously. Hope Springs kept finding plenty, digging into reserves he'd never called upon before. The onlookers lining the track began to grow, as did the cheering and hollering, sending a rush of adrenalin to Danny's fatigued, aching limbs. He edged ahead of Hyper Tension a half-length and then a length.

He glanced back. O'Bourne appeared unconcerned by the outsider's bold bid for home, oozing confidence that he could pick Danny off as and when he wanted. Even wider, a couple more challenged, including Rewind, who'd regained his equilibrium and was travelling reasonably well. Two and a half furlongs to go. Hope Springs was racing beyond his capacity, like a car starting to rattle and groan. The three-year-old started to roll into the camber, away from Hyper Tension, towards the far rail. The pre-race plans went out the window.

Tavistock and Stony hadn't counted on O'Bourne going for a wide assault. Danny switched his whip. He'd been rather clumsy at the fiddly manoeuvre in his riding days. Maybe it was the intense pressure - knowing what was at stake - that made him focus and find the zone, but he threaded the rubber whip through in one seamless motion and started to strike Hope Strings on his gleaming hind quarters. Once again his mount kept responding, edging away from the whip back into the centre of the track, enough to cross Hyper Tension's path. He once again heard a fuming screech from just behind. Had he hampered Hyper Tension and halted his momentum? He looked around and saw the hot favourite being switched to his inner. Danny, still frantically pushing his mount, pulled down on his left rein and his mount, through tiredness more than anything, started to loll towards the far rail again, this time taking Hyper Tension with him.

'Get back,' Danny cried, passing the two furlong marker.

The densely packed crowd either side of the track, produced a deafening roar, with hats and newspapers flying high in the air as the favourite challenged for the lead again. Danny caught glimpse of the tall grandstand to his right, packed to the gunwales with punters, most hoping to hail a great champion – Hyper Tension. None of these distractions derailed Danny's tunnel vision as he continued to lean into Hyper Tension, who couldn't gather enough momentum to get past the nuisance outsider.

The commentator's raised voice described the drama unfolding. 'Hyper Tension is struggling to get a clear passage, as the pair drift to the far rail. Meanwhile, up the centre, Rewind and Cartography, are finishing to good effect. As they approach the furlong marker, Hope Springs has done Hyper Tension no favours, dragging him half the width of the track to the far side. Nearside, Cartography takes a slender overall lead, closely pursued by Rewind.'

Danny squeezed Hyper Tension up against the rails, forcing O'Bourne to check and then switch, losing valuable momentum as the ground began to rise.

O'Bourne, face puce and eyes fiery, threw everything at his charge to make up the ground lost after the altercation. Hope Springs began to make a spluttering noise, as he desperately tried to fill lungs already stretched to capacity. Danny knew his valiant mount was now running on empty. He also knew his job was done and started to ease his mount as it tired in the dying strides, fourth, fifth, sixth.

The home-straight was a deafening corridor of sound. But Danny heard nothing. His eyes were fixed on the big screen in the centre of the course. Just fifty yards to go.

The commentator continued to build the drama, saying, 'Cartography and Rewind in a titanic battle, and here comes Hyper Tension back for more. Cartography. . . Rewind, nothing in it, Hyper Tension a length back and closing.'

Like watching a car crash, Danny felt it hard to look away as he saw Hyper Tension grab the ground in the dying strides, performing miracles to recover from such a mauling.

'That's a photo!' the commentator shouted. 'Hard to call. A classic in every sense of the word, with inches separating Cartography, Rewind and the gallant Hyper Tension.'

'Photo . . . photo,' the steward called almost instantly over the tannoy.

Followed soon after by the inevitable, 'Stewards' enquiry . . . stewards' enquiry.'

Danny dropped his hands and let his legless mount freewheel across the line in eighth. The initial relief that he could have done no more was overshadowed by an anxious wait for the outcome of the big race. Although normally an eagle-eyed judge of photos, from the unsteady perch on his handkerchief sized saddle, he found it hard to gauge the result.

A sudden unexpected wave of emotion washed over him. He fought back the tears as he remembered his father and his unerring belief and support in his riding. One day you'll ride the Derby winner son, he'd say. Danny glanced up at the sky, feathered with wispy clouds, and opened his mouth to speak, but the words he so desperately wanted to say failed to escape his mouth. Instead, he just thought, *I did it, dad. I did it!*

The exhilarating buzz from just riding in the race he'd always dreamt of as a child was soon wiped by the fear of what the angry punters might do to him. *The lynch mob will be baying for my blood*, Danny feared, pulling his sweat laden goggles away before running his hand down his redden face, desperately trying to catch his breath.

Whatever the result, he knew he had a lot of talking to do, mostly to the stewards. And his stomach sank further once remembering he had to face the music from Reynolds, who'd watched his prize animal meander throughout the home straight as his seemingly inept pilot got embroiled in an extended barging match with the favourite. *This could get ugly*, Danny feared.

He trotted his mount back to the grandstand where the offshoot to the unsaddling enclosure was situated. Hope Springs had begun to recover from his exertions, though he was still panting heavily in the summer heat. He badly needed hydrating and a hosing down.

A peculiar silence befell the enormous crowd as they awaited the result, almost like the quiet before the storm. Confusion as to who had won the heavily hyped race sent the world's press into a frenzy, scurrying around the connections of the first three as they filed off the main track on to the rouge asphalt pathway. Danny sat back, away from the hubbub up front. He knew the spotlight would soon turn on him – the villain of the piece. The normally frightening scenario of the stewards' room would seem like a refuge with the ensuing chaos outside. *As long as my cover ain't blown before the case goes to Portman Square*

215

in London, he thought, *just keep the mouth shut while eyes and ears open.*

A three-note chime came over the racecourse loudspeakers. 'Here's the result of the photograph for the 2007 Dorstone Epsom Derby . . . first number twelve Rewind . . . second number three Cartography . . . third number six Hyper Tension. Starting prices to follow.'

Danny buried his head in his chest, overcome by the sheer emotion of the occasion. His thumb and forefinger pressed against his tired eyes, forcing back the tears. He'd done it.

He gently patted Hope Springs's neck as he trotted sedately back to unsaddle. The colt felt heavy beneath him, clearly a spent force after running his heart out. The pair was met by the stable lass near the offshoot. She led them to Reynolds, whose flushed face and waving arms told their own story. 'What the fuck were you playing at?'

'To be fair, the horse hung with me left and right. I could do no more,' Danny said, practising his excuses for the interrogation he was about to receive by the stewards shortly.

'You rode him too close to the pace. He could have made the frame. Jesus, Daly, you won't be riding for me again!' He ran his hands through his thinning grey hair. 'We went over the race plan. My boy had a real chance if you'd listened. Jesus!'

'I'm sorry. Prize-money down to tenth,' Danny said, trying to calm the situation.

He dismounted and removed the saddle with saddlecloth. As he was in the prize-money, he was needed at the weighing room before being ushered to meet the stewards. Given the sort of questioning he was about to face, he didn't feel as stressed as he thought he might, the adrenalin clearly helping him through it.

He turned and instinctively stepped back when confronted, within arm's reach, by O'Bourne, who's normally fish-white skin was now puce. 'You're fuckin' dead meat,' he growled. 'I'll make sure you never ride in Britain again, d'ya hear.'

Last thing Danny wanted was a scene. The world's press and photographers were prowling and a shot of his mug on the back pages was all he needed. 'I tried my best, but the horse drifted badly. I'm sorry.'

'You will be,' O'Bourne barked. 'Fucking waste of space. Go back to the donkey derby racing you're used to.'

'Let off your steam in the stewards' room,' Danny said and began to pace towards the building to the side of the grandstand.

Most of the media were milling around Rewind and his connections. Until one caught sight of Danny, and hollered some of his colleagues to leave the winner's story and focus on the reason behind the controversial defeat of the favourite – Danny Rawlings a.k.a. Frederick Daly.

'Daly, what have you got say about your ride?'

'No comment,' Danny said, pushing away a handheld recorder thrust into his face. 'What will you say to the stewards?' another asked.

'That's for the stewards.'

'Have you an apology to the connections of Hyper Tension and the thousands of punters who've done their money?'

'It's not my fault. He had the whole track to get past me.'

'But you appeared to do your best to stop his progress and there's a lot of angry punters who think they deserve an answer.'

Danny signed off with, 'That's racing.' A flippant reply that would have riled him had he still been a punter himself, but the boot was on the other foot now.

He kept the thoughts of his brother firmly to the forefront of his mind as he leapt up the four steps and swept past glass doors. He took refuge under the shelter of the red-bricked building housing the stewards' room. O'Bourne and Sayers, who both finished on the podium despite being affected by the wayward path Danny had taken during the race, were already there. Neither spoke, their faces expressed more than enough.

Danny exchanged the briefest of eye contact with O'Bourne, who growled, 'I meant what I said.'

'I meant what I did.'

'You what?'

Danny kept his mouth shut.

'You'd better fucking say that to them in there.'

The trio then stood and waited in silence, preparing their side of the story before they were called in to meet the course officials on the other side of a windowless pine door. Danny felt like a lamb to the slaughter and, though his conscience was telling him otherwise, he kept running over in his mind the comforter: I meant it to be this way, this is for my brother and for justice to be served with Lockhart behind bars.

The pine door opened. A suited man with thinning, wispy hair and angular glasses resting near the tip of his nose, poked his head around the corner and beckoned the threesome in.

Danny drew a calming breath and led the way.

The three jockeys, still wearing their silks minus the helmets, turned on the marble floor and faced a long table covered by a plain white cloth behind which sat a panel of four stewards plus a secretary. The windowless room was airless.

Silence except for the distant whir of the air conditioning. *Turned low to make us sweat*, Danny thought, as he pulled at his royal blue collar from his neck.

There was a camera on a tripod pointed accusingly at them. Although stewards' enquiries weren't televised to the betting public, unlike other countries such as Australia, the evidence was filmed to supplement the case in any further enquiry at Portman Square in London.

A gallery of four 42" plasma screens hung from the wall to their right showing the various camera angles of the race at their disposal. In this high-tech age, there really was no hiding place on the track and, with at least four angles covered by Racetech, there was no escaping a charge of reckless or dangerous riding.

Danny noticed that two were frozen at different stages of the race, while a third screen provided a head-on shot of the home-straight to help distinguish if any interference had taken place, or whether any paths were crossed. *Things have changed since my former riding days*, Danny thought, recalling the few times he'd been called to explain his riding. During just under three years riding, he'd been banned merely the once for

218

intentional interference in a juvenile race. Unlike the real judicious system, racing laws can take into account past riding offences in the sentencing procedure. But he knew only too well, the stewards would have no record of this, having adjusted his personal details on Fred Daly's fictional jockeys' form, amended by Tavistock and faxed through to them from Newmarket.

'My name is Samuel Davis, the stipendiary steward employed by the Jockey Club and these are my colleagues.'

From his previous experiences with these enquiries, Danny knew that there was a senior steward – the stipendiary – plus three non-paid members to ensure that fair racing has taken place.

'Our first point of interest is the manoeuvre made by Mr Daly aboard Hope Springs passing the mile marker, cutting across the path of Rewind. As a result, Mr Sayers was forced to stop riding and take a pull to avoid a collision. Mr Sayers, could you please explain your side of the story?'

'Yes, sir. I was travelling sweetly on the heels of the leaders on the climb for Tattenham Corner. Hope Springs was on my outside and was given some reminders to kick on. But the jockey didn't allow enough room.'

'He cut across you?'

'And I lost all momentum and it could have cost me the race. As it turns out, I managed to get up, but, in my eyes, it was a dangerous act and one that could have brought me down and caused a fatal pile-up.'

'Mr Daly, could you respond to this?'

'I was aware of the horse on my inner and I admit full responsibility for my mistake.'

'You are admitting to one count of riding with intention to cause interference?'

'I am.'

The stewards' secretary confirmed, 'Riding across a rival to prevent a horse from going up the inner is deemed as a dangerous act, one of the most serious riding offences.'

The secretary scribbled shorthand notes. The senior steward muttered something to the colleague sat to his side, appearing somewhat taken aback by Danny's honesty. 'Moving on to the second more prolonged piece of interference. This occurred in the home straight from just after the three-furlong pole until inside the final furlong. For the record, the interference involved Hope Springs ridden by Frederick Daly and Hyper Tension ridden by Michael O'Bourne. I would like both of you to look at the middle screen as well as the one to the right.'

The steward to the left looked down at the laptop. His fingers skated over the keys, prompting the race footage to unfold. 'We can see that Hope Springs veers violently left.'

Danny said, 'My horse was beginning to tire and started to roll on the camber, sir.'

'You make no effort to counter the wayward path,' the senior steward said. 'In fact, even though you look over your left shoulder now.' The recording was paused again. 'And you've seen Hyper Tension just behind, you proceed to use your whip in your right hand, further accentuating the drift to the far rail, dragging Hyper Tension with you,' the secretary said. 'Can you put forward any extenuating circumstances for your irresponsible actions?'

Danny glanced across at O'Bourne, who struggled to conceal a contented smile, stood alongside. 'I saw him and tried to peg him back – I was out to gain my best possible position, at all costs. I admit my race-riding tactics were overplayed and I apologise for my actions.'

'Very well. Robert, could you move the footage on,' the steward said to his colleague directing the film. 'Here, having drifted half the course width, we see Hyper Tension run out of room on the far rail.'

'Mr O'Bourne, could you talk us through this passage of the race?'

'Yes sir. Having been pushed across the course, I have no option but to rein Hyper Tension back, losing all momentum at this critical stage, and then switch to the outer to gain a clear run. By which time the pair down the centre got first run on me. Without the traffic problems, I would've won the race, no doubt. I was on the best horse and still had plenty left to give when it happened.'

'Daly, care to add anything?'

'I've nothing to add, sir,' Danny said, though he felt further insurance was needed to ensure the case would be treated seriously enough for Portman Square to take a look. He added, 'But I would do exactly the same if given the chance.'

They all looked up. The stipendiary steward's unkempt eyebrows arched. 'Mr Daly, here in Britain we like to play by fair rules and your apparent disrespect of these is of great concern. May I go as far to say that you've flouted the rules set out by the Jockey Club and having shown no remorse for your actions, it's just not acceptable. On two occasions, by intentionally causing interference, there's been a flagrant breach of Rule 151.'

Got a bite, Danny thought; *result*.

'Mr O'Bourne, have you anything to add?'

'No, sir. I think Mr Daly has said enough.'

'Would you all mind waiting outside while we consider the facts of the case,' he said. 'It shouldn't take long.'

Danny left the room, along with O'Bourne and Sayers. The three dispersed to find a quiet corner within the building before being beckoned back in. After no more than ten minutes, the steward's secretary once again emerged and called them for judgement.

'Frederick Daly,' the senior Steward said with the solemnity of a judge about to deliver a life sentence. 'We've a copy of your jockey's license from the Jockey Club and, despite your impeccable record riding in,' the Steward took his glasses off and held them over the sheet in hand, 'Argentina, we have to take into account the seriousness of your offences. We appreciate your honesty in response to these accusations. However, we also feel it is a serious enough breach of Rule 151 – the deliberate interference of another horse with the intention of altering the result of a race - under the conduct code set down by the British Jockey Club, that we consider it merits a six-month ban from racing in this country.'

221

'You have a right to an appeal,' the stipendiary Steward added.

'I will,' Danny said instantly.

There was a pause as the stewards talked quietly. The stipendiary Steward said, 'An appeal hearing at Headquarters in Portman Square will be arranged and you will be told by post. We will, however, be recommending to our colleagues at the Jockey Club that this punishment should be adhered to. That is all.'

The stewards closed files on their table and keyed something into the laptops resting on the cloth before standing. The Senior steward gestured to the jockeys to exit stage left.

Danny bowed his head. Not from guilt or regret, but from a sense of relief more than anything. He'd be allowed to present the whole case in front of the Jockey Club's elite. *Everything was falling into place.* The humble, sorrowful pretence was also sending the message to both O'Bourne and Sayers that he was getting the punishment he deserved, helping to cool a situation that was threatening to boil into something Danny couldn't afford happening - a fight. Last thing he wanted was the police being called in.

The three jockeys filed out of the room. Sayers rushed off to the changing room as he'd been booked for a ride in the Diomed Stakes scheduled in just 20 minutes time, leaving O'Bourne and Danny stood outside of the stewards' room.

O'Bourne appeared to have mellowed, his once-creased face now ironed and his flushed complexion had returned to his normal bleached-white Irish skin. However, seeing the coast was now clear, his mood darkened.

Without warning, he thrust Danny hard against the wall. 'You heard what the man said, if you so much as step on another British racecourse-' He paused and let Danny drop to the ground. The steward's secretary, who'd just sat in on the meeting, emerged from around the corner and walked by. O'Bourne forced a smile at the official, revealing a bridge plus a couple of cracked and misaligned teeth, picked up from a well documented mid-race fall he'd suffered at York's Ebor meeting a few years previously. The secretary passed without any apparent suspicion. They were alone again. Danny thought of running, but felt he ought to hear O'Bourne out; help the champion jockey work this whole debacle out of his system. *A kind of rough therapy*, Danny thought.

'You've robbed me of the one race that's missing from my trophy cabinet and if I so much as catch a glimpse of you again.' His mouth froze open like a fish. It was as if O'Bourne was searching for the words that could best justify the anger simmering inside. 'Let's just say, I know people that can make sure the only thing that you'll be riding is a wheelchair.'

O'Bourne continued to pin him against the wall by his silks. He clenched his fist into a ball and punched Danny with a crushing blow just below his padded body guard. With no fat to soften the impact, Danny bent double gagging for air.

Once recapturing his breath, he looked up, but O'Bourne was gone. Danny also wasted no time getting out of there. He left via a fire exit to the side of the building, escaping the glare of the media circus camped outside for a quote. He felt sure O'Bourne would have enough to say for the both of them. He wasn't concerned about fronting his side of the story to uphold any public image. After all, Frederick Daly had none. He'd done what he'd come here to do.

Behind the cover of three tall wheelie bins, where he'd left his kit bag, he removed his silks, and changed into creased khaki slacks and a bottle green T-shirt, another gift in the sponsor's goody bag. It was dusk by the time he'd arrived back at Ringwall Prison. He returned to his cell without sounding any proverbial alarm bells and, having netted the Governors' betting partnership the best part of £20,000 from laying Hyper Tension to lose the Derby, he felt sure Simmons wouldn't have minded if he was late back just the once.

CHAPTER 29

Danny sat reclined on a swivel chair – a cast-off from Simmons's office - pressing the taut muscles between his shoulder blades against its back. The mere thought of the enquiry kept Danny awake at night and on edge during daylight hours. It was also just a fortnight away from his first prep meeting with his solicitor regarding next month's court case.

He stared at the TV screen showing a minor maiden at Catterick, though he saw nothing; his mind was elsewhere. His reverie was broken by tinny chimes from his mobile lying on his desk.

'Hello,' Danny said, pinching the bridge of his nose.

'It's John,' Tavistock said. 'We need to meet, make our case watertight. There's something else.'

'What?'

'Find out when you get here.'

Early the following morning, Danny travelled direct to Stevenage and was met by Tavistock at the train station. He was driven to Tavistock's now familiar semi-detached house.

Sat in the lounge, Danny was handed an A5 manila envelope. His furtive eyes skated over both sides of the post in hand. 'There's no official logo. Can't be the police.'

'Well are you going to open it?' Tavistock asked brusquely. He'd clearly watched over the letter and a sense of nervous anticipation had come to a head.

'Alright, alright,' Danny huffed. He ripped one corner and slid his finger along the spine of the envelope. He sat forward, perched on the edge of the settee. With trepidation, he removed a single folded sheet of paper and ran his finger over the watermark that read The Jockey Club across the sheet. The paper shook as he unfolded to see the letter heading and address: The Jockey Club, 151 Shaftesbury Avenue, London WC2H 8AL.

He was expecting formal written communication from the rulers of the sport, but he was fully aware that they could have rumbled his true identity and he'd be locked up before he could reveal the cloning scandal.

He read:

Dear Mr. Frederick Daly,

Further to your request for an appeal in response to the sentence of your ban from riding under all recognized horseracing authorities, a hearing with our Disciplinary Panel is set for 9.00am on June 12. It is your responsibility to arrange a personal solicitor if required. Failure to attend will result in the ban being upheld and a financial penalty will be enforced.

Yours Sincerely

Rupert Lacroix

Disciplinary Department Staff.

Danny's eyes lit as he handed the letter to Tavistock. 'Read it.'

Tavistock stood silent as he absorbed its contents. 'Nothing we don't already know.'

'Look again.'

Tavistock's gaze returned to the paper in hand. 'I see nothing.'

'D'ya recognise the name of the signature?'

Tavistock looked down. 'Rupert Lacroix.'

'Does it ring any bells?'

Tavistock shook his head. 'Should it?'

A faraway look glazed Danny's eyes. 'I know it from somewhere, but I can't put my finger on it. I was hoping you would jolt my memory.'

'Well, it looks like you'll have a chance to meet him at the trial.' Tavistock beamed an ironic smile.

Danny took the letter and pushed it deep in his coat pocket. 'You've got the photocopied breeding registry of Hyper Tension.'

'It's under lock and key upstairs. Don't worry, I'll hand it to you when we arrive at the Jockey Club.'

'You'd better, it's the only thing we have to nail Lockhart,' Danny said.

'What will you do if that's not enough?'

225

'I dunno,' Danny said. 'I'll try and wing it somehow, improvise.'

'Because they'll have you locked up for good and you can kiss your preferential treatment goodbye.'

Danny ran his hands through his hair, the seriousness of the impending trial sinking deep.

'Don't think of it as a trial, more of a pitch. Just make sure you drum home the fact that Hyper Tension is a clone, a fraud. The Jockey Club will be forced to investigate.'

Danny asked, 'And you think the police will investigate?'

'Accusations of fraud have to be looked into.'

Danny glanced across at the photos of Dean and Elena on the mantelpiece. 'Let's hope so.'

He left Tavistock's place, affording himself plenty of time to get back within prison grounds before six. Last thing he wanted was to be grounded before his trial.

The night before the trial, Danny stewed over what the following day held in store. He lay back and stared at the wall. But he couldn't settle, no matter what, so he lifted himself from the bed and started to pace the room, taking just four strides before turning. He ran over what he was going to say, rehearsing the opening lines he'd deliver to Rupert Lacroix and co. *This is no good*, he thought.

He turned to face the newspaper cutting of Lockhart lifting the Chester Vase together with stable connections and supporters. He ripped the clipping from the wall. *I'll wipe that smug grin from your fucking face.* He was about to crush the paper into a ball when the tag line at the foot of the grainy black and white photo caught his eye. It read: Owner Simeon Lockhart collects Group 3 prize with Hyper Tension. Also present (left to right): stable lass Rachel Snowdon, business associate Rupert Lacroix. Danny stopped reading.

A rush of adrenalin spiked his veins as his fingers ran across the picture. Third along was the corpulent silver-haired man who'd raised Danny's suspicions when embracing Lockhart. *A business partner*, Danny pondered. He then recalled where he'd

226

seen the Lacroix name before. Did he have a part in the Hyper Tension clone? Being on the board at the Jockey Club would certainly allow easy access to the breeding registry.

Danny rushed to his computer and booted up. He typed a combined search for Rupert Lacroix and Simcorp Enterprises into a search engine. He prayed for a sizable result, but got just 21 matches. Most were related to legit activities within the Jockey Club, previous investigations into fraud and corruption in the sport. *How ironic*, Danny thought, as he scrolled down the page.

He stopped at an article relating to the imminent bankruptcy of the medical research centre called Simcorp Enterprises. *Please let there be a link between the company and Lacroix.* He clicked on the website of *The Guardian* newspaper which contained the piece. His eyes skated over the short article, published in the newspaper six months previously, until discovering what he was after. And there it was: The chairman and silent partner in Simcorp Enterprises, Rupert Lacroix, is known for his workings within the Jockey Club hierarchy. Lacroix, a renowned horseman in his formative years and owner of the private Waterside Stud at his forty-acre estate in Shropshire, is said to have invested much of his personal wealth into the business, holding a majority stake-hold in the company. He was unavailable for comment.'

The link is made, Danny thought. He allowed himself a brief smile. But how could he prove this undoubted connection? He fished for the letter in his jacket, placed it on the desk in front of him and punched Tavistock's number on his mobile.

'It's Danny.'

'It's late,' Tavistock replied brusquely. 'Get some sleep, you'll need it.'

'I need you to scan and email the Hyper Tension's birth certificate to me pronto.'

'What good would that do?'

'I think I might be on to something. You know I couldn't recall where I'd heard of Lacroix. Well, he was name checked on a newspaper clipping of Lockhart that I'd kept, one that was snapped in the prize giving after the Chester Vase.'

'And?'

'Turns out he's a silent partner in Simcorp. With their business going down the pan, both must be involved with the cloning. After all, they've got the facilities and they're desperate. The tempter of a potential billion-pound windfall would drive 'em to do anything, even kill.'

'How are you going to prove this?'

'I dunno, that's why I need the birth certificate of Hyper Tension.'

'I'll get it scanned and emailed straight away.'

The line went dead.

He went about studying Lacroix's signature, handwritten in blue ink on the trial notice letter sent from the Jockey Club, scrutinizing the distinctive looping curl of the R and the unusual arcing stem of the P.

Danny's computer bleeped, an email had dropped. He refreshed the screen and then clicked the email just sent by Tavistock. The scan's quality was good, giving Danny a clear picture of the breeding registry. The form was dissected into several boxes. Within each one, the pedigree and owner details were hand written.

He stretched his neck forward, face just inches from the computer screen. He knew from shining light through the form when he'd paid a visit to the Jockey Club in Newmarket most of the details had been amended. *But by who?* His eyes flitted between the R and the P of Hyper Tension and those same letters in Lacroix's signature. *A perfect match!*

It seemed like Lacroix had amended the breeding registry of another foal that had perhaps been a still born, or died in the early, most critical weeks of weaning. By doing this, it appeared Lockhart and Lacroix had bypassed the necessity to get an official Jockey Club vet to sign the form and make it official. The signature was already there, for a horse whose sire was Burgundy, dam was Let It Be and was now most probably a skeleton buried six foot under.

Danny visited the Racing Post website while he considered his next move. The front page was dominated by an article concerning a fresh appeal by the police to the horseracing community for the safe return of champion broodmare Mary Rose, still missing with no communication and hopes of her recovery were fading. It was dubbed the biggest mystery since the disappearance of Shergar twenty years previous. Danny's eyes widened as a sudden realisation had struck him. He dropped the letter onto the desk and pressed redial on his mobile.

'John, it's me. I need to meet you before first light.'

'Why on earth? You need to be focussed for the hearing.'

'Focussed or not, I need to do this.'

'Whatever it is, the risk is too great,' Tavistock reasoned.

'We need more on Lacroix and Lockhart to nail 'em. Agreed?'

'Yes, but what else is there? All we can hope is – this Lacroix crumbles under pressure.'

'Look,' Danny said, 'who will the other stewards believe: their colleague friends, or someone waiting trial for murder who brought the game into disrepute in the Derby – the big shop window for the sport.'

'You still haven't told me what this about?'

'Trust me, it could be my last chance before spending the rest of my life in here.' Tavistock paused. 'John?'

'I'm still here. Go on, what time?'

'In three hours, do you know where Waterside Stud is in Shropshire?'

'I can find it on my GPS,' Tavistock replied.

'Pick me up at Ludlow train station at four. And bring your digital recorder.' Danny paused. 'We might be pressed for time getting to Shaftesbury Avenue by nine, so bring Hyper Tension's breeding registry with you. See you there.'

'I will, but I'm still not sure about this.'

'What have we got to lose?' The lack of response told its own story. Danny hung up and pulled on his jacket. He picked up the newspaper clipping of Lockhart and Lacroix. He looked around his well-appointed cell. *Might well be the last time I'm in here*, he hoped.

CHAPTER 30

After their early morning exploits in Shropshire, Danny stepped from the train. He weaved the side streets to make 9 A.M. at Shaftesbury Avenue. He occasionally glanced back to see Tavistock lagging behind; he lacked Danny's youth and fitness.

He arrived at the plush entrance of the Jockey Club with just two minutes to spare, took a couple of deep breaths and collected the files and the digital recorder before being led to the interview room.

Standing in the hallway was Lockhart, who appeared taken aback by Danny's sudden appearance. *Come to see Frederick Daly get punished for foiling his master plan*, Danny thought. Lockhart's eyes narrowed as Danny passed, ushered by a Jockey Club official.

The panel comprised three men and a woman sat behind a long maple table to the far side, forcing Danny to make the tense walk deep into the tall, echoing room. He quickly scanned for the silver haired man called Rupert Lacroix in the picture. *There he is! He was seated on the end, to the right.*

The initial questioning followed a similar line to that of the on-course stewards on Derby Day. Once again, he admitted to all of the charges brought before him.

Open and shut case they reckon, Danny thought. But he had only just begun.

The head judge asked, 'If you have agreed to all of the charges, why have you appealed?'

'And wasted all of our time,' Lacroix added.

'Have you anything more to say for yourself before sentencing is passed,' the head judge continued.

'Yes,' Danny said, eyes lingering on Lacroix, who barely contained the smugness of seeing the jockey who'd tried to ruin his dream now being banned. 'I declare this hearing to be null and void; a mistrial.'

'What?' the end secretary said. 'On what grounds?'

'It's a prejudiced panel.'

'The Jockey Club prides itself on giving the fairest of hearings at all time and I guarantee that none of us here have any goal or agenda other than deliver a ruling that serves racing in the best possible way,' the head judge said. 'I repeat, none of us.'

'Except him,' Danny said and pointed towards Lacroix. 'Rupert Lacroix is the business partner of Simeon Lockhart, who owns the horse Hyper Tension.'

The head judge jotted something on a piece of paper, paused before locking eyes with Danny. 'I'm afraid that doesn't constitute a break of any disciplinary rules, as he doesn't own any part of the horse in question. Am I correct in thinking that Rupert?'

'That's perfectly correct,' Lacroix replied, face flushed. 'Please, let's get back to sentencing.'

'But wait a minute,' Danny interjected. 'I haven't finished.' With the authority of an esteemed lawyer, he slowly paced the hardwood floor. 'Simeon Lockhart and Lacroix own the ailing business Simcorp. Stop me if I'm mistaken.'

'I don't see how this is connected to the Derby,' the woman steward in the middle said.

'You will.'

'We've heard enough of this nonsense,' Lacroix snapped. 'Get this joker out of the building.' The security guard stood by the door stepped forward.

'No, I want to hear what he has to say,' the senior steward replied, showing his palm to the guard.

'I am not Frederick Daly and I've never ridden in South America, I've never been to South America.'

'He's an impostor!' Lacroix shouted, voice shaken. 'A charlatan.'

'Be quiet, I want to hear this,' the head judge said.

Danny stopped pacing and turned. He drew a calming breath and continued, 'Lockhart, with the help of the esteemed colleague to your left, has managed to become the first to successfully clone a racehorse.'

There was a stunned silence.

'Even if this outlandish claim were true,' the head judge said, 'which I very much doubt, I still don't see how that is connected to you and this hearing.'

'The horse they cloned was from the blood of the champion racehorse and sire Hyperion.'

Lacroix let out a nervous, wheezy laugh. 'Complete nonsense, I tell you.'

'Continue,' the judge commanded, holding court.

'Are you aware of Dean McCourt, the stable lad murdered last year?'

'Of course,' the steward said, 'it was big news at the time.'

'His grandfather, John Tavistock, was a racehorse vet back in the fifties, some of his work involved the Jockey Club, I might add. However, his most important patient was the legendary Hyperion, who, by that time was nearing the end of his lengthy stud career. Tavistock had the foresight to take a fresh sample of blood from the ailing champ, and stored it in the airtight base of a small antique box, not to damage the DNA.'

'I demand this man is ejected from the premises,' Lacroix shouted.

Danny gave a knowing look, feeding off Lacroix's growing anxiety. He knew he had already hit a nerve even though he was only just warming up.

'Another word and it will be you Rupert that's ejected,' the senior steward snapped. 'Go on.'

'Lockhart got wind of this potential goldmine and, with Lacroix, they'd stop at nothing to get hold of the fresh DNA concealed within the box.'

They were now hooked. The senior steward asked, 'But what has this got to do with the stable lad?'

'Everything,' Danny replied. 'The box was passed down to Dean for safekeeping and, naively, he made no secret of his gift and its value; a mistake that cost him his life. Word soon got around the yard.'

'Wasn't it Michael Raynham he worked for?' the head judge asked.

'Yeah,' Danny confirmed. 'And it wasn't long before the leading owner there, Simeon Lockhart, heard the rumour and, with his business going belly up and the facilities to create a clone lying dormant, he set about getting Hyperion's blood, no matter what.'

Lacroix protested, 'He's as good as admitted to dangerous riding and being a complete fraud. How can you possibly believe any crap he spouts?'

'I haven't lied at any stage, I've never protested my innocence to charges that have brought me here.'

'For Christ's sakes Rupert, let the man continue.'

Danny said, 'You are just as guilty in your part of the crime, and not content with the breeding potential of Hyper Tension, you kidnapped Mary Rose.'

Danny stepped forward and placed the birth certificate of Hyper Tension onto the table, together with Lacroix's distinctive signature on the Jockey Club letter. 'The amendments on Hyper Tension's breeding registry were made by you, Lacroix. Please, all of you, check out the handwriting on both sheets. There's no mistaking, they were both written in the same hand.'

'I had nothing to do with it,' Lacroix panicked. 'It was Lockhart.'

'So you admit that this all took place?' the senior steward asked incredulously.

'Of course not,' Lacroix protested.

'Notice the style of the R and P on both forms,' Danny said. 'They match perfectly.' He stepped back and waited for the comeback.

The head judge turned to face Lacroix. 'Can you explain this?' Lacroix sunk his now reddened face into cupped hands. 'Well?'

'No,' Lacroix said, with a resigned air about him. 'I admit to changing that, alright! But I swear, I had no part in the murders, or the kidnap of the mare.'

At which point, the oak doors flung open and Lockhart charged into the room, like a raging bull.

'What is this?' the senior steward barked. 'This is a private meeting, get him out.'

'I won't stand back and have my name blackened by this fucking crook,' Lockhart growled, barging past Danny. He'd clearly eavesdropped on the investigation from hallway after realising Danny's involvement. 'What have you told them?' Lockhart asked Lacroix.

'Nothing!'

'My friend is not in a fit state to be in this meeting. I can assure you, there is not a grain of truth in whatever he has said.'

'I recognize you from somewhere,' the senior steward said.

'My name's Simeon Lockhart. I apologize for my rude entrance,' he said, biting his lip. 'But I feel you need to know this . . . man . . . has been serving time for two murders and shouldn't even be allowed to be here.'

'I'm innocence until proven guilty.'

'And furthermore, what hard evidence have you to back these fantasy claims of yours?' Lockhart asked, resting his weight on the maple table, arms crossed. Danny had barely been given the time to open his mouth when Lockhart continued, 'Just as I thought, nothing. I cannot believe such experienced officials like your good selves,' he paused as if to let the panel absorb the hollow compliment, 'could ever conceive that Mr Lacroix, an esteemed businessman and longstanding colleague of yours, and I, a man of honour and outstanding reputation, could carry out such acts of evil.'

Unfazed, Danny calmly plugged the digital camera into the LCD screen to his side. 'Hard evidence? Perhaps these will jog your memory.'

'What is this?' the senior steward asked.

'The kidnapped champion broodmare Mary Rose is held captive at a Waterside Stud on an estate owned by Rupert Lacroix in Shropshire. The reason? They were laying the groundwork for a money-spinning breeding program. The plan was for Hyper Tension, the exact replica of Hyperion, to win the Derby and thereby, ensure the very best breeding rights in Europe, if not the world. However, they wanted more. They wanted to create the perfect racehorse for themselves, by mating the most prolific and successful sire and broodmare of the last century. The progeny genes to die for, literally.'

Lacroix protested, 'Simeon planted her there, this is all nonsense.'

Lockhart turned and instinct made him lunge forward and reel Lacroix in by the blazer. He paused before suddenly letting go of his partner in crime, seemingly now aware of the company present. He emptied his lungs, as if trying to exhale some of the stress building within, and turned back to Danny, who continued, 'I managed to prevent 'em gaining the Classic success they craved and stall their plan, but I fear, if they were prepared to kill for the cause, including my brother, they wouldn't let a small matter of losing a race put them off. They had to be exposed and fast.'

'This is complete bullshit,' Lockhart barked. 'I don't know what he's on about.'

'Methinks he does protest too much,' Danny said.

The judges looked at the slideshow from the footage Danny and Tavistock had taken of Mary Rose together with a close up of the embossed brass name tag on her tack.

The last of the seven shots was displayed. The senior steward voiced to the security guard, 'Get the police on the line.'

'Wait, we can cover this up,' Lacroix pleaded. 'Don, we go way back. This can all be sorted out behind closed doors. I have a reputation to keep.'

'Rupert, shut the fuck up,' Lockhart growled. 'That was no admission of guilt.'

'Reputation is the least of your worries,' Danny remarked. 'And there's no need to call the police, they're already on their way to the stud. It's over.'

Having stood, prepared for flight, a badly shaken Lacroix was unsteady on his legs and slumped back on his seat, resigned. 'I told you not to go so far, but you were desperate, crazed.'

Enraged, Lockhart stepped forward and locked his arm around Lacroix's neck and, lifting him from the seat, he slammed him against the back wall.

'I can't. . .breathe.'

'Put him down,' shouted the senior steward. 'Security!'

A security guard entered and rushed forward.

Lockhart turned and let Lacroix drop to the ground in a dishevelled mess.

'He was obsessed with that damned box and its rewards,' Lacroix said. Having seen the real monster that was Lockhart, he appeared only too willing to land his colleague in it. 'I swear the first I heard of the lad's death was on the news.'

The head judge asked, 'Then why didn't you go straight to the police?'

'For fear of being accused as an accessory.'

Danny interjected, 'Admit it, you were as obsessed as he was to clear the company's debts and make the fortunes that the wonder drug Definca had initially promised.'

'Call Scotland Yard!' the senior steward ordered the security guard. 'Rest assured, we will carry out a full investigation into the events that brought us all here today.'

The secretary said, 'But our primary concerns lie with the wellbeing of Mary Rose.'

'I've already called the police, when this man broke through security,' the guard said, eyes fixed on Lockhart.

Danny noticed Lockhart edge imperceptibly away from the rear wall, his eyes wide and alert. *Was he readying to make a break for it?*

'And the deaths of Elena and Dean McCourt and my brother?' Danny chipped in, still tracking Lockhart's movements.

'That's also a matter for the police,' the head judge replied. 'Out of our hands.' He then turned to Danny and said, 'We need you to stick around and wait for police questioning and I'm sure the Jockey Club will also need your assistance in our enquiries in due course.'

'No problem,' Danny said, but he was distracted by Lockhart's sudden lunge forward, passed the table and towards the oak doors opened invitingly.

Danny was the only person stood in Lockhart's way as he fled for freedom. Fitter and stronger than he'd been for many

236

years, Danny moved forward and wrestled Lockhart to the ground.

He reached into Lockhart's coat pocket and quickly removed what felt like a gun, sliding it across the parquet floor towards the judges' table.

The growing police sirens, for once, sounded like music to Danny's ears as he sat perfectly still, weight anchoring Lockhart to the floor. He held his assailant in an arm lock, pushing his hand further up his back until the floored man groaned in agony. 'Not nearly as much pain as my brother suffered,' Danny whispered in Lockhart's ear.

'I regret nothing,' Lockhart said.

'Tell that to the police,' Danny replied.

The police flooded the room and took hold of Lockhart.

Outside the hearing room, Tavistock stopped pacing the marble-floored corridor and his pensive gaze homed in on Danny, whose attentions were stolen by the woman sat upright on one of three wooden chairs in the foyer area.

'Sara!' he cried. 'You made it.'

Her eyes glistened and bottom lip began to quiver. 'What am I going to do with you, Danny?'

'Whatever you like.'

'What do you mean?' Tavistock asked.

'Lacroix's admitted there were killings, blaming 'em on Lockhart. There are witnesses to his admissions.'

'What about proving their guilt?'

'I'll let the police sort that out,' Danny said, holding Sara close. 'Most importantly, I'm out of the picture for the murders.'

Sara prised herself away from Danny. 'You're free to go?'

'Not exactly, I'll have to go to Scotland Yard. Run them through the chain of events and explain my day releases from prison. Not sure what will come of that, but it probably doesn't look good for Governor Simmons.'

'Serves him right,' Tavistock said. 'Looks like he'll be wearing a different uniform to prison from now on, that's greed for you.'

'I'll put in a good word for him. Wouldn't be here today without him,' Danny said, voice weak, drained of all emotion.

'And what about your brother?' Sara asked.

'I'm guessing they'll question Lockhart and his faithful employees. Doubt they'll be as faithful now they've got the boot. I'm hoping the forensics are gonna find some evidence that my brother had been there.' A sad mist descended over Danny's eyes as the realisation struck home that he would never see his brother again.

Sara once again wrapped her arms around his slight frame and whispered in his ear. 'Yes, I do feel the same way.'

'What?' Danny said, though he'd heard perfectly well.

'I was still awake that night, heard every word,' Sara said. 'And the answer is yes, to your question.'

'Are you saying what I think you're saying,' Danny said, eyes widened.

'Ask me again,' she said, 'and you'll find out.'

She stepped back and let Danny drop his weight to rest on one knee against the cold marble floor. 'Sara Monk,' he said, barely disguising the tremor in his voice. 'Would you do me the honour of being my wife?'

'On one condition,' she smiled.

Danny looked up at her. 'Name it, anything.'

'That you don't make Gash the best man.'

'I think I can manage that.' Danny stood and beamed a smile before gripping her tight again.

Two weeks later, Danny lay on the sofa with Sara alongside watching the nine o'clock news. 'It always takes a scandal for racing to make the lead story,' he said.

The news reporter revealed, 'In light of new evidence and an extensive police enquiry into the deaths of Elena and Dean McCourt, Simeon Lockhart has been charged with three counts of murder and also kidnap, while business associate Rupert Lacroix has been charged with accessory to murder and deception to fraud. Furthermore, DNA samples taken from the human remains found at a chemical waste disposal plant were confirmed to be that of the missing Richard Rawlings, brother of Daniel Rawlings, who was wrongly accused of the McCourt murders, a case that has now been dropped. Mr Rawlings' name has been cleared of all wrongdoing and was unavailable for questioning.'

'Just be glad it's those two on the screen and not you,' Sara replied.

Danny wrapped his hands around her body and gently squeezed and smiled. 'D'ya fancy going to the races tomorrow?'

'Not really, Danny.'

Printed in Great Britain
by Amazon